THE PE[

FOUNDER EDITO[

Editor: Betty Radice

HERMANN PÁLSSON studied Icelandic at the University of Iceland and Celtic at University College, Dublin. He is now Reader in Icelandic at the University of Edinburgh, where he has been teaching since 1950. He is the General Editor of the *New Saga Library* and the author of several books on the history and literature of medieval Iceland; his most recent publications include *Legendary Fiction in Medieval Iceland* (with Paul Edwards) and *Art and Ethics in Hrafnkel's Saga*. Hermann Pálsson has also translated *Hrafnkel's Saga,* and collaborated with Magnus Magnusson in translating *Laxdæla Saga, The Vinland Sagas* and *Njal's Saga* for the Penguin Classics.

PAUL EDWARDS read English at Durham University, Celtic and Icelandic at Cambridge, and then worked in West Africa for nine years. He is now Reader in English Literature at Edinburgh University. As well as several books on Icelandic studies written with Hermann Pálsson, he has published books and articles on African history and literature, and on English literature, mainly nineteenth century poetry.

EGIL'S SAGA

*

TRANSLATED WITH AN INTRODUCTION BY

HERMANN PÁLSSON

AND

PAUL EDWARDS

PENGUIN BOOKS

Penguin Books Ltd, Harmondsworth, Middlesex, England
Penguin Books, 625 Madison Avenue, New York, New York 10022, U.S.A.
Penguin Books Australia Ltd, Ringwood, Victoria, Australia
Penguin Books Canada Ltd, 41 Steelcase Road West, Markham, Ontario, Canada
Penguin Books (N.Z.) Ltd, 182–192 Wairau Road, Auckland 10, New Zealand

—

This translation first published 1976

—

Copyright © Hermann Pálsson and Paul Edwards, 1976

—

Made and printed in Great Britain by
Hazell Watson & Viney Ltd, Aylesbury, Bucks
Set in Monotype Garamond

Contents

Introduction

OF the many memorable characters to be found in the literature of medieval Iceland, none is quite like the title hero of this
tale, Egil Skallagrimsson. From his first appearance as an ugly,
recalcitrant child, greedy for gifts and singing his own praises,
to his last as an old man pushed around the kitchen by serving
women, but still a killer and poet, everything he does and says
bears the stamp of an individual, achieved by the very multi-
plicity of the roles he plays. The ruthless viking is also the poet
of his own grief; he is a sorcerer, yet his mastery of runes can
cure sickness; he is an ingenious lawyer and a raging drunk,
a wanderer on the face of the earth and a settled farmer, an
enemy of kings over family honour and a miser, a Machiavelli
and a puppet. He is inflated far beyond the type of viking hero,
yet he also falls short of it, and while he is often on the edge of
the tragic he eludes definition. He can be vicious, absurd,
infantile, pathetic, but he is never dull, and though we may not
like some of the things he does we are never allowed to settle
into a fixed attitude towards him.

Egil's Saga is one of five major sagas dealing with native
Icelandic figures on a scale akin to the epic novel.[1] It was
probably written about 1230, and though like most sagas it is
anonymous there are good reasons for thinking that it was
composed by Snorri Sturluson (1179–1241), the author of
Heimskringla and the *Prose Edda*. Snorri lived for a while at
Borg, where Egil farmed, and spent most of his adult life in
the district of Borgarfjord. *Egil's Saga* shares with *Heimskringla*
a vision of early Scandinavian and English history, an under-
standing and subtle illustration of human motives, and a
narrative design offering a panoramic view of the viking world

1. The other four are *Njal's Saga* (Penguin Classics, 1960), *Laxdæla Saga*
(Penguin Classics, 1969), *Eyrbyggja Saga* (Southside, 1973) and *Grettir's
Saga* (Toronto University Press, 1974).

from the middle of the ninth century to the end of the tenth. The scene changes constantly in *Egil's Saga*, from the opening chapters set in Norway, to Sweden, Finland and Lapland, south to the Low Countries and west to Britain and Iceland. The Saga starts with King Harald Fine-Hair's establishment of Norwegian unity at the cost of tyranny and war, and the killing or expulsion of many of Norway's greatest chieftains and their followers; it closes in Iceland with the slow growth of unity by common agreement within the law, honouring the achievements of the founding fathers of the Icelandic nation whilst acknowledging the stresses out of which this stability came and the persistence of the impulse towards arbitrary action and crude personal violence. The narrative ranges through several generations from Egil's grandfather Kveldulf, introduced in the opening chapter, to his grandson Skuli mentioned in the last sentence – both of them vikings, for all the changes that have taken place in the years between.

However, Egil's grandson is seen at the end fighting against Olaf Tryggvason, the proselytizing Christian King of Norway, whereas his grandfather Kveldulf belongs to a world that was remote and unfamiliar even at the time of the Saga's composition. The opening pages establish a paradigm for the family to which Egil belongs, with its demonic roots and enigmatic character. Kveldulf marries the daughter of his viking friend Berle-Kari, of whom we are told casually 'he was a berserk'. Kveldulf himself is even more sinister, for his name means 'Evening Wolf' and we learn that 'there was talk of his being a shape-changer'. Yet when their viking days are over, these two killers settle down comfortably on their farms.

A suggestion of the ambiguous poet-viking that Egil is to become appears in the second chapter where Egil's great-uncle, Olvir Hnufa, a famous viking, falls in love with a girl called Solveig the Fair. 'Many were the love-songs that Olvir composed for Solveig,' but her brothers refuse his proposal and Olvir gives up the viking life to join King Harald Fine-Hair as one of his court poets. Members of the family fall into contrasting categories, a light side and a dark. Thus Kveldulf

INTRODUCTION

has two sons, one of them, Thorolf, 'very handsome . . .
cheerful and generous, ambitious in all that he did and full of
life. Everybody liked him.' His brother Grim, Egil's father, is
on the other hand 'dark and ugly, the image of [Kveldulf] in
looks and temper'. In the next generation the same contrast is
found. Grim (or Skallagrim, 'Bald Grim', as he is nicknamed)
has two sons, the one called Thorolf after his uncle being fair
and popular, the other Egil, black, ugly and demonic. The two
Thorolfs are large-hearted men and make friends with the
Norwegian royal family, though this friendship turns sour:
but Skallagrim and Egil are resolutely anti-royal. Both Thorolfs
die violent deaths in their prime, but Skallagrim and Egil are
survivors; they hang on to life in their old age; the last act of
the son echoes that of the father and both are carried out in a
spirit of rage, miserliness and spite. Even so, these contrasts of
character in no way work mechanically towards easily defined
personalities or predictable action and even the demonic
elements often have a more-than-odd look about them: for
example, Egil's first fit of temper is the result of Skallagrim's
refusal to take him to a feast: at three years old, Egil gets too
rowdy when he is drunk (chapter 31). Again, when Egil and a
friend are wrestling with Skallagrim, the demonic element of
old Kveldulf takes over in his son, and as the day darkens
towards evening Skallagrim's power grows. He kills the other
man, then in an insane fit tries to kill his own son (chapter 40).
Egil himself is not characterized just by the 'dark' side of the
family, but by the peculiar interpenetration of apparently
contradictory features. The last chapter sums the matter up on
a note of continuing perplexity: 'It was a very mixed family, in
that some were the most handsome people ever to be born in
Iceland . . . but most of the Men of Myrar were outstandingly
ugly.'

So, as we have said, the hero of the Saga is killer, drunkard,
miser, poet, wanderer, farmer, and can be any of these at any
moment, from his first killing at the age of six because another
boy wins a ball-game, to his last in his senility. We see him
change from the viking his mother predicts after his first killing

(chapter 40), the enemy of kings and berserks, the man of cunning, the sorcerer and destroyer of sorcery, to the settled farmer at Borg where his father established his farm in Iceland, to the ingenious lawyer aiding his son Thorstein, and finally to the senile, blind and deaf old man warming himself by the fire, mocked by the serving-women, apparently helpless, but proving himself still a troublemaker, still a poet, and still a killer. The perplexing nature of this man can be seen even after his death when people find his skull under the altar of a church erected by his niece's husband. One might expect that the new age of Christianity would use this as a *memento mori* to expatiate upon the vanity of the old pagan's life, but what happens is characteristically ambiguous:

Skapti Thorarinsson the Priest, a man of great intelligence, was there at the time. He picked up Egil's skull and placed it on the fence of the churchyard. The skull was an exceptionally large one and its weight was even more remarkable. It was ridged all over like a scallop shell, and Skapti wanted to find out just how thick it was, so he picked up a heavy axe, swung it in one hand and struck as hard as he was able with the reverse side of the axe, trying to break the skull. But the skull neither broke nor dented on impact, it simply turned white, and from that anybody could guess that the skull wouldn't easily be cracked by small fry while it still had skin and flesh on it. Egil's bones were re-interred on the edge of the graveyard at Mosfell (chapter 86).

The old hero won't budge even in death, and his ancient bones, relics of the pagan foundations of Iceland, remain a monument to his strange survival, to be buried in soil that is Christian, but only just.

Egil the man is mortal, and the life of violence he leads points as clearly to the brittleness of the world as do his poems of triumph, of suffering and loss, and of old age. But as the hero of what is in an important sense his own tale, he survives: his poems are at the core of the narrative and tell us not simply what he does, but how he feels about what he does, even what he looks like, from his own lips. The drunken vainglorious lout writes out in verse his own pride and its vanity. The vicious nature of his uncontrollable battle-fury, his narrow meanness and his spite is also manifest in the apparently contradictory articulacy of feeling in his poetry. We have said that the Saga traces by implication the demonic nature of Egil back to his grandfather and great-grandfather, Kveldulf and Berle-Kari, but at a deeper level its source can be found in Egil's own god, the many-faced Odin, the shape-changer and rune-master, lord of drink, wanderer, god of poetry and of the slain.[1]

In Egil's greatest poem, 'Lament for My Sons' ('Sona-torrek') (pp. 204–9) he speaks of the double-face of his god. As rune-master and lord of poetry, Odin has given Egil the power of words; as lord of the dead, Odin has taken away his two sons. Yet it is the gift of poetry which makes the loss bearable, giving Egil the power to cope with his suffering by expressing it. This point is made clear not only by the poem itself, but by the episode which precedes its composition, when Egil's daughter, Thorgerd, manipulates her father back to the acceptance of life and persuades him of his duty to honour his dead sons in verse:

As the poem progressed, Egil began to get back his spirits and when it was completed he tried out the poem before Asgerd, Thorgerd and the household. Then he got up out of bed and took his place on the high-seat (chapter 78).

1. For a similar figure to Egil, the reader might turn to Starkad in *Gautrek's Saga*, whose foster-father, Grani Horse-Hair, turns out to be Odin in disguise. He takes Starkad to a grove where all the gods are seated and grants him gifts – long life, wealth, the finest weapons, invincibility in battle, honour amongst great men, and the power of poetry. But each gift is countered by a hate-gift from Thor, and though Starkad lives out his life as a great warrior, he is hated and self-hating. His last years are a time of misery, mockery and abuse, though he is able to sustain himself by means of his poetry and confirm both his triumphs and his sufferings in verse. (*Gautrek's Saga and Other Medieval Tales*, University of London Press, 1968, pp. 38–42, 53–55.)

Another hero who bears all the marks of the type, though like Starkad and unlike Egil, not traceably historical, is Örvar-Odd (*Arrow-Odd: A Medieval Novel*, New York University Press, 1970). Like Egil, Odd is related to Ketil Trout of Hrafnista.

None of the sagas is richer in poetry than this one, and its translation has set us problems; we are conscious of the limitations of the versions we offer. We have tried to approximate as closely as we can to the form as well as the meaning of the original, but the elaborately metaphoric nature of Icelandic verse makes literal translation virtually incomprehensible. Of the three major poems in the saga, the 'Lament' is the most deeply motivated, by Egil's grief and his feeling of helplessness in face of the power and indifference of the sea which has taken his son. But as the poet discovers in his god Odin the killer behind the killer, his sense of helplessness is moderated by the consolation of the poem: the god has given something and taken something. There is a similar motive in the other two poems though they are different in spirit. The first of these, the 'Head-Ransom' (pp. 158–63), is in an unusual verse form, not simply alliterative but end-rhymed as well. Egil composes it in a single night to save his own neck when he falls into the hands of his old enemies King Eirik Bloodaxe and Queen Gunnhild. Its purpose is plainly to keep Egil alive, and to save himself he cheerfully piles lie upon lie. The King and Queen know this perfectly well but the poem is too good for Eirik not to purchase it, and so with the poem Egil cancels the debt, as he tells us, of his ugly head. How seriously the poem is meant to be taken is to be judged from Egil's subsequent poetic utterances on the royal couple. The third long poem, 'In Praise of Arinbjorn' (pp. 210–15), honours a blood-brother who has presented him with rich gifts, compensated him lavishly with money, granted him hospitality in peace and given him unswerving devotion in times of danger even at the risk of his own life. These are debts which, again, the poet can repay.

So far we have been principally concerned with the central figure, Egil himself. But we have also seen how, in the course of the tale, Egil's personality is explored and elucidated not only in terms of his own actions and poetry, but in the actions and characters of his ancestors. So we might turn now to these members of Egil's family and examine their conduct in such terms as freedom and authority, loyalty and bad faith, generosity and greed, in the tangle of personal and political relationships through which Egil and his forbears move. We have already noted the dialectical nature of the Saga – the light and dark sons, the viking turned farmer – which brings out the complexity both of individual character and of society. Another central duality stems from the issue of personal freedom: when Kveldulf advises his son Thorolf, about to go to Harald's court, 'Never try to compete with men greater than yourself, but never give way to them either,' he is giving expression to another such characteristic tension. As we have said, the Saga moves from the authoritarian order of King Harald Fine-Hair to the very different order of Iceland, where many of the great Norwegian chieftains sailed to avoid Harald's rule and live as settler-farmers. In this Saga, domestic and court issues are inextricably linked and create such strained loyalties as those of Arinbjorn and Olvir Hnufa. Arinbjorn is Egil's cousin by marriage and blood-brother, but also faithful retainer of Egil's old enemy, King Eirik Bloodaxe; Olvir Hnufa is King Harald Fine-Hair's court poet, compelled by the King to stay on at court after Harald has killed Olvir's nephew, the elder Thorolf (chapters 22, 25). At the root of the first half of the Saga are two family conflicts which extend far beyond the domestic issues which give rise to them, and lead ultimately to enmities with the royal household of Norway.

These cases both begin with a man of wealth and power who marries twice, one of the two marriages being in some way of doubtful legality, and illustrate the effect upon the family of the two conflicting lines of descent. Each is of such complexity that genealogies are necessary to explicate the issue, and to reveal how, from the point of view of Kveldulf's descendants, there is a crucial difference between the two cases: in the first, they are in the legitimate line, in the second, the questionable one.

Bjorgolf's first marriage is legal, and his son Brynjolf and grandson Bard are descended from this marriage. But after his first wife's death, Bjorgolf takes a second wife, Hildirid, in a

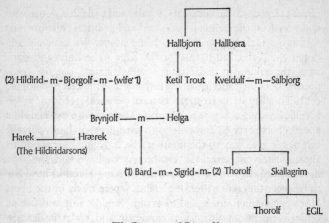

The Property of Bjorgolf

highly suspect way (chapter 7). Hildirid has two sons, called the Hildiridarsons since their father dies while they are still young. On his death, they are cast out with their mother and, though they claim their share of the property as they grow older, first Brynjolf, then his son Bard, refuse to consider this and call them illegitimate. The line of Kveldulf becomes involved through Thorolf Kveldulfsson, who becomes Bard's blood-brother. When Bard dies in the service of King Harald, he bequeaths his property, wife and all, with the King as witness, to Thorolf. With the additional wealth thus gained, Thorolf becomes a man of such power that the King himself grows jealous. The Hildiridarsons work upon this, Harald kills Thorolf and the family feud with the crown of Norway begins, leading directly to the settlement of the farm at Borg in Iceland. After Thorolf's death, Kveldulf and his other son, Skallagrim, sail to Iceland; Kveldulf dies in sight of land, but characteristically even in death he claims his portion of earth – his coffin drifts ashore and Skallagrim builds a cairn over it on a near-by headland.

Bjorn abducts (apparently with her connivance) Thora, the

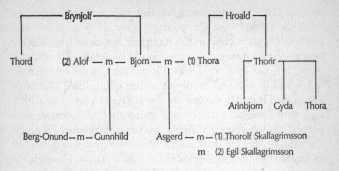

The Property of Bjorn

daughter of Chieftain Thorir Hroaldsson, an old friend of
Skallagrim. Bjorn and Thora go to Iceland and stay with
Skallagrim over winter, claiming to be properly married, but
in the spring rumours of the truth come from Norway and
Skallagrim is furious. But by this time Bjorn and Thorolf
Skallagrimsson are close friends, and Thora is pregnant. The
family make the best of things by sending Thorolf with terms
of reconciliation to Thorir, and these are accepted, so the
marriage is confirmed. Asgerd, the daughter of Bjorn and
Thora, is, however, brought up by Skallagrim as if she were
his own daughter, and in due course marries Thorolf, the much
older brother. After Thorolf's death she marries Egil, nearer
to her in age, but the relationship is a curiously tight-knit one
domestically, almost incestuous, for she is simultaneously his
sister by adoption, his sister-in-law and his wife.

But Bjorn has married again and his second wife, Alof, also
has a daughter, Gunnhild, who in turn marries a man called
Berg-Onund. Thus the grounds for future dispute are laid, and
since Asgerd was born before her parents' marriage con-
tract was sealed, it is now the Skallagrimssons who have
claims to property by way of a suspect line of inheritance.

Further complications are introduced by relationships
between the two groups and the royal family. It will be remem-

bered that the elder Thorolf, Skallagrim's brother, was killed by King Harald: but the younger Thorolf (the 'light' son) has become reconciled to the King and is a close friend of the heir to the Norwegian throne, Eirik Bloodaxe. He also becomes a friend of Eirik's wife, Gunnhild, but the relationship is left ambiguous and in any case they quarrel and Gunnhild becomes Thorolf's enemy, as she is later to become Egil's. Egil now enters the scene as a young man, and proceeds to reopen old wounds by killing a favourite retainer of Eirik and Gunnhild, who are now on the throne. Former enmities are re-established. Some members of Egil's family through the line of Thorir, Asgerd's grandfather, are also the King's men, notably Arinbjorn, Thorir's son and Egil's blood-brother.

Turning to the second of Bjorn's marriages, his daughter Gunnhild is married to Berg-Onund, and since this line is unquestionably legitimate they take over Bjorn's property on his death, with the approval of King Eirik, and we learn that Berg-Onund has replaced Thorolf in the Queen's favour, for not only is he Eirik's close friend, he is 'even closer to Gunnhild'. So once more the private world of domestic disagreement has become entangled with the public life of the court. Another feud follows, over the distribution of Bjorn's wealth, leading to the killings of Berg-Onund and his brothers by Egil and the consequent flaring up of the old quarrel with the throne of Norway. It is after this that Egil saves his life at York with his praise-poem, the 'Head-Ransom', delivered before King Eirik and Queen Gunnhild.

Clearly the creator of the Saga is putting flesh on historic bones here and elsewhere. The close relationship between historical fact and the author's own creative purposes can be seen in connection with Skallagrim's land-claim in Iceland. When we first hear of this claim, we are given what appears rather arid and unexciting information about who were the settlers, the friends and the servants of Skallagrim, to whom he granted land on arrival in Iceland, and in this the Saga agrees with the *Book of Settlements*.[1] But as the Saga progresses, the significance of this information emerges when Thorstein, the son of Egil, has a quarrel with Steinar, the son of an old friend of Skallagrim's, over land boundaries. In the latter stages of the Saga we see how the old warrior can use the law and history of the new country Iceland to ensure his son's rights, as he turns to the evidence of the land claims and proves his son's case. Egil has become the settled farmer and apparently the man of peace. But he rides up to the assembly with eighty armed men, and, as we learn from the last pages of the tale, his killing days are not over, and his actions continue to invite speculation after his death. He disappears one night with his money-chests and two slaves. Next morning the blind Egil is found stumbling about alone near the farm:

They went to Egil and brought him home, but neither the slaves nor the two coffers were ever seen again, and there have been plenty of guesses about where Egil hid his money. East of the fence at Mosfell there is a ravine that plunges down from the top of the hill. People have thought it significant that following a sudden thaw with heavy flooding, English silver coins have been found in the ravine after the water has subsided, and some of them have speculated that Egil may have hidden his money there. But below the homefield at Mosfell there are widespread bogs with deep pits in them, and other people think Egil must have thrown his money into these pits. There are deep pits south of the river where the hot springs are, and since fires have often been seen coming from the burial-mounds there, it has been suggested that this may be where Egil hid his money. Egil admitted that he had killed Grim's slaves and also that he had hidden the money, but he never told anyone where (chapter 85).

Here, as elsewhere in the saga, gossip is seen merging with legend, historical fact with invention, as the author weaves his tale about the shade of this ambiguous hero.

1. The *Book of Settlements*, or *Landnámabók*, was evidently compiled by Ari the Learned and Kolskegg the Learned in the early twelfth century. See the translation published by the University of Manitoba Press in 1972.

Note on the Translation

THE present translation is based on Sigurður Nordal's edition of *Egils saga Skalla-Grímssonar* in the *Íslenzk fornrit* series, vol. 2, (Reykjavik, 1933), whose text is taken from the so-called *Möðruvallabók*, a vellum codex written some time between 1320 and 1350. In addition to this there is another medieval manuscript of the Saga, a defective one, and several fragments, the earliest of which dates from about the middle of the thirteenth century. There are also a good many paper manuscripts.

Egil's Saga has been translated into English three times before, by W. C. Green (London 1893), E. R. Eddison (Cambridge University Press, 1930) and Gwyn Jones (Cambridge University Press, New York, 1960). Since this translation was completed, a fourth, by Christine Fell, has been published in the Everyman Library.

As in previous sagas translated for Penguin Classics, the spelling of proper names has been anglicized. The chapter divisions are original, but we have added our own chapter titles. Our thanks must go to Mrs Betty Radice and Mr C. Chippindale for their careful and helpful reading of the typescript, and to Mrs Sheila Coppock for reading the proofs.

H. PÁLSSON

Edinburgh   P. EDWARDS

EGIL'S SAGA

1. Kveldulf

THERE was a man called Ulf Bjalfason. His mother was
Hallbera, daughter of Ulf the Fearless, and she was the sister
of Hallbjorn Half-Troll of Hrafnista, father of Ketil Trout.
Ulf was so big and powerful that there was no one to match
him. As a young man he used to go off on viking trips looking
for plunder, and his partner in these was a man of good family
called Berle-Kari, strong and full of courage. He was a berserk.
The two of them were close friends and whenever it came to a
question of money they shared the same purse. When their
viking days were over, Kari went back a wealthy man to his
farm on Berle Island.

Kari had three children, two sons called Eyvind Lambi and
Olvir Hnufa, and a daughter, Salbjorg. She was a good-looking
girl and full of spirit. Ulf married her and settled down to live
on his farm, rich in both goods and land. So, like his ancestors
before him, Ulf became a land-holder and soon grew to be a
figure of great authority. People say that he was an exceptionally able farmer. He made a habit of rising early to supervise the
work of his labourers and skilled craftsmen, and to take a look
at his cattle and cornfields. From time to time he would sit and
talk with people who came to ask for his advice, for he was a
shrewd man and never at a loss for the answer to any problem.
But every day, as it drew towards evening, he would grow so
ill-tempered that no one could speak to him, and it wasn't long
before he would go to bed. There was talk about his being a
shape-changer, and people called him Kveld-Ulf.[1]

Kveldulf and his wife had two sons, the elder one called
Thorolf and the younger Grim. They both grew up to be tall,
strong men, just like their father. Thorolf was a man of great
promise and very handsome, taking after his mother's side
of the family. He was cheerful and generous, ambitious in all

1. *Kveld-Ulf*: literally 'Evening Wolf'.

that he did and full of life. Everybody liked him. Grim, on the other hand, was dark and ugly, the image of his father in looks and temper, and a very hard worker. He was a talented blacksmith and carpenter and turned out to be a great craftsman. In winter he used to sail out with nets on fishing trips after herring, along with a good many of his household servants.

When Thorolf was about twenty he made up his mind to go on a viking expedition, so Kveldulf gave him a longship. Kari's sons, Eyvind and Olvir, joined him with another longship and a good number of men, and they spent the summer plundering. There was plenty of loot, so each of them had a good share. That's how things stood for a number of years: every summer they'd go out on viking expeditions and then spend winter at home with their fathers. Thorolf brought his parents back a lot of valuable things. In those days there was ample opportunity for a man to grow rich and famous, and though Kveldulf was getting on in years by this time, his sons were in their prime.

2. Olvir Hnufa

THE king ruling over Fjord Province was called Audbjorn. One of his earls, Hroald, had a son called Thorir. Another earl, Atli the Slender, had his home at Gaular. Atli's children were sons called Hallstein, Holmstein and Herstein, and a daughter called Solveig the Fair.

One autumn a great number of people came to Gaular for the sacrificial feast there. That was when Olvir Hnufa saw Solveig and fell in love with her. Later, he asked for her hand in marriage but the Earl thought Olvir wasn't good enough for her and refused him. Many were the love songs that Olvir composed for Solveig, and he was so taken with her that he gave up his career as a viking, though Thorolf and Eyvind carried on with the viking life.

3. Harald the Shaggy

By this time Halfdan the Black's son, Harald, had come into his inheritance to the east in Oslofjord, and had sworn a solemn oath never to cut or comb his hair until he'd made himself sole ruler of Norway. That was why people called him Harald the Shaggy. First of all he fought and put down the kings nearest to him, and there are long stories about that campaign. After that he conquered the Uplands and travelled north from there to Trondheim, though he had to fight many a battle before he was able to get control of all Trondheim Province. His next decision was to make a move north against two brothers called Herlaug and Hrollaug who ruled over Namdalen; but when the brothers heard of this move, Herlaug went into a grave mound that had taken three years to build, along with eleven other men, and after that the mound was sealed up. Hrollaug, on the other hand, surrendered his kingdom and took the title of earl. He went to see King Harald, handed over all his authority to the King, and that is how Harald won Namdalen Province and Halogaland.

Harald put his own men in charge there, then set out from Trondheim with his whole fleet, sailing south to More where he fought and won a battle against King Hunthjof. Hunthjof was killed there. Harald conquered North More and Romsdalen, but Hunthjof's son, Solvi Splitter, got away and went to South More to ask King Arnvid for help. 'We may be in trouble now,' said Solvi, 'but it won't be long before the same happens to you. Take my word for it, Harald will be turning up here at any moment, just as soon as he's got all the people of North More and Romsdale where he wants them and made slaves of them. You're going to have the same choice on your hands as we had. Either you'll have to defend your freedom and your goods with every man you can muster – and I'll help you fight this tyranny and injustice with all the forces I have –

or else you can choose to place yourselves under Harald's yoke and become slaves, like the men of Namdalen. My father preferred to die with honour like the King he was, not to spend his old age as another King's hired-man, and I think you'll be minded to do the same as anyone who still has some pride and ambition.'

This was argument enough for King Arnvid. He made up his mind to gather his forces and defend his kingdom. He and Solvi entered into an alliance and sent word to King Audbjorn of Fjord Province urging him to come and join them. When the messengers brought him this proposal Audbjorn talked it over with his friends, and every one of them gave him the same advice – to get an army together and join the men of More as he'd been asked. So King Audbjorn mustered his forces, sending the war-arrow right through his kingdom with special messengers to every man of note, asking him to come and join his army.

The messengers came to Kveldulf and told him why they were there; the King, they said, needed him with all his men. This was the answer he gave: 'If Fjord Province is attacked,' he said, 'I suppose the King will consider it my duty to join him in defending his kingdom. But I don't see that it's any of my business to go fighting up north just to defend More. When you see your King you'd better tell him from me that Kveldulf is taking no notice of his call-up, and plans to stay at home. I'm not gathering any forces and setting off on any campaigns against Shaggy Harald. The way I see it, Harald has all the luck he's ever likely to need, while our King hasn't even a fistful.'

The messengers went back to tell the King how things had turned out. As for Kveldulf, he stayed at home on his farm.

4. Victory for Harald

KING Audbjorn gathered all the men he could and set out north to More. There he joined up with King Arnvid and Solvi Splitter, and between them they had a sizeable army. King Harald had already brought his forces down from the north, and the two armies met to the east of Solskel Island. The battle was hard-fought and there were heavy losses on both sides. Two of Harald's earls, Asgaut and Asbjorn, died there, as did Grjotgard and Herlaug, the sons of Earl Hakon of Lade, and a good many other great men too. As for the More army, both of the kings, Arnvid and Audbjorn, were killed but Solvi Splitter managed to get away again and afterwards became a great viking. He got the nickname Solvi Splitter because of all the damage he did in Harald's kingdom.

Afterwards King Harald took control of South More, but King Audbjorn's brother Vemund held on to his power in Fjord Province and became king there. This was late in the autumn, and as the days were getting shorter people advised Harald not to travel south beyond Stad. So Harald put Earl Rognvald in charge of the two Mores and Romsdale Province, and went himself with a big army back north to Trondheim.

That same autumn the sons of Atli had launched an attack on Olvir Hnufa, hoping to kill him. Atli had so many troops that Olvir hadn't a hope of keeping them off and had to run for his life. He made his way north to More, where he fell in with King Harald and took an oath to be his man. In the autumn he went north with the King to Trondheim, and they grew to be close friends. Olvir stayed with him for a long time and became the King's poet.

That winter Earl Rognvald travelled overland across Eid and south to Fjord Province, where he kept a sharp eye on King Vemund's movements. Then when Vemund was attending a feast at a place called Naustdale, Rognvald went there by night, surrounded the house, and burned the King inside along with ninety other men. After that Berle-Kari joined Rognvald with a fully manned longship and went back north with him to More. Rognvald seized every single ship that Vemund had owned as well as all the goods he could lay hands on. Berle-Kari travelled further north to King Harald at Trondheim and became the King's man. In the spring Harald sailed south along the coast with a large fleet. He took control of Fjord and Fjalir Provinces and put his own men in charge of them, appointing Hroald earl over Fjord Province.

Once he'd gained full control of the provinces that had just come into his hands, Harald kept a sharp eye on the landed men and rich farmers, and anyone else he might expect trouble from. He gave them a choice of three things. They could swear loyalty or they could leave the country, but if they chose the third, they could resign themselves to the most savage terms, perhaps even death. There were cases where Harald had people's arms and legs hacked off. In every province, Harald took over both farming land and estates, whether they were inhabited or not, even the sea and the lakes. Every farmer and every forester had to become his tenant, every salt-maker and every hunter on land or sea had to pay taxes to him. Many a man went on the run from this tyranny and many a wilderness became inhabited, both east in Jamtaland and Halsingland and west, in the Hebrides, as well as the parts around Dublin in Ireland, Normandy in France, Caithness in Scotland, Orkney, Shetland and the Faroes. And that's when Iceland was discovered.

5. Kveldulf defies the King

KING Harald stayed on in Fjord Province with his troops and continued to send out messengers to all those men in the Province who had not joined him. He had unfinished business in mind. When the King's men came to Kveldulf he gave them a friendly welcome. They told him why they were there and how the King wanted Kveldulf to pay him a visit.

'He's heard all about your reputation and your famous ancestors,' they said, 'so you can expect him to treat you with great honour. He's very keen to have anyone with him who has a reputation for strength and courage.'

Kveldulf said he was getting on in years, so life aboard fighting ships wasn't for him any more. 'I'm planning to stay at home, not wait on kings,' he told them.

'Why not send your son to the King, then?' said one of the messengers. 'He's a big man and looks like a brave one. If he's ready to serve, the King's sure to make him a land-holder.'

'I'm not becoming any land-holder while my father's alive,' said Grim. 'Until he dies, he's the only master for me.'

The messengers went back to the King and told him everything that Kveldulf had said. The King flew into a rage and had a few things to say himself about the arrogance of these people. What could be in their minds, he asked.

Olvir Hnufa was near by, and asked the King not to be angry. 'I'll go and have a word with Kveldulf,' he said. 'He'll come and see you once he knows how important it is to you.'

After that Olvir went to Kveldulf and told him how angry the King was. The only choice Kveldulf had, he said, was either to go to the King himself, or else to send his son. The King would show them great honour, if only they would submit, he added. Olvir went on at some length, saying that he was only telling the honest truth, and that the King was generous to his own men with both money and promotion.

Kveldulf told Olvir how he felt about it. 'I'll not get much in the way of luck from this King,' he said, 'and neither will my sons so I'm not going to see him. But if Thorolf comes home in the summer it won't be hard to persuade him to take this step and make himself the King's man. You can tell the King this, that I'll be loyal to him and urge all those who value my words to show him friendship. And just as I've always done for his predecessors, I'll govern on his behalf, if that's what he wishes. We'll see in time how the King and I get on.'

Olvir went back to the King and told him Kveldulf was going to send one of his sons, though the son best suited to serve was away from home: and there the King let the matter rest. In the summer he travelled over to Sogn, but got ready in the autumn to go north to Trondheim.

6. Thorolf decides to join King Harald

IN the autumn Thorolf Kveldulfsson and Eyvind Lambi came back from a viking expedition and Thorolf went home to his father. They began talking, and Thorolf asked Kveldulf what business the messengers from the King had had with him. Kveldulf said Harald's message was that either he himself or one of his sons must become the King's man.

'What did you say to that?' asked Thorolf.

'I spoke my mind. I told him I'd never become King Harald's man, and neither would you or Grim if I had my way but I'm afraid that as things are going, this King will be the death of us all.'

'That's not the way I see it,' said Thorolf. 'I think I'll gain a great deal of honour from him. I've made up my mind to go and see the King and become his man. I know for a fact that all his retainers are men of unequalled reputation, and as long as they're willing to have me in their ranks I couldn't wish for anything better than to go and join them. There isn't a man in the land more privileged than they are and I've heard all about how open-handed he is to his men, particularly when it comes to a question of giving power and promotion to those he thinks deserve it. And here's another thing I've been told. Not a soul who turns against him and spurns his friendship ever makes good. Some of them he chases out of the country, and others finish up no better than hired men. It seems very odd to me, father. Here's a shrewd man like you, full of ambition, yet without a sign of gratitude for the great honour the King has shown you. Do you think you can see into the future, with your talk about how we'll come to grief because of the King and how he wants to be our enemy? In that case, why didn't you join the king you used to serve and fight Harald in battle? It's just not right, you don't seem willing to be either his friend or his enemy.'

'I had my reasons,' said Kveldulf. 'The way I saw things the people who went to fight Shaggy Harald north in More weren't likely to come off best. But the truth of the matter is still clear – King Harald is going to cause my kin a deal of suffering. Do as you see fit, Thorolf. I've no doubt that if you join Harald's men, you'll prove yourself a match for them all, and as good a man as the bravest of them in every danger. Just take care not to be too ambitious. Never try to compete with men greater than yourself, but never give way to them either.'

When Thorolf was ready to be on his way, Kveldulf went with him down to his ship. He took his son in his arms and wished him well till their next meeting.

7. The Hildiridarsons

IN Halogaland there was a man called Bjorgolf, farming on Torg Island. He was a land-holder, rich and powerful, though he was a hill-giant on one side of his family, as you could tell from his size and strength. He had a son called Brynjolf, very much like his father. By this time Bjorgolf was getting on in years and his wife was dead. He had given over everything into his son's hands, and found a wife for him, Helga, the daughter of Ketil Trout of Hrafnista. They had a son called Bard who matured early into a tall, handsome man, outstanding in every way.

One autumn they held a feast there, which a great number of people attended, Bjorgolf and his son being the most important. As was the custom, lots were cast every evening to decide which pairs were to sit at the same drinking horn. One of the guests was a man called Hogni who farmed on Leka

Island, rich, handsome and shrewd, but a self-made man of humble origins. He had a beautiful daughter called Hildirid, and the lots decided that she should sit next to Bjorgolf. They had plenty to talk about all evening and he thought her a fine-looking girl. A little later the feast came to an end.

That same autumn, old Bjorgolf set out from home in a skiff he owned, with a crew of thirty. They came to Leka Island and twenty of them walked up to the farm while the other ten guarded the boat. When they reached the house Hogni came out to meet Bjorgolf, giving him a friendly welcome and inviting him to stay on there with his men. Bjorgolf accepted the invitation and they all went into the hall. As soon as they had taken off their top-coats and put on their tunics, Hogni had ale-vats brought into the hall and his daughter Hildirid started serving ale to the guests. Bjorgolf called Hogni over to join him, and said: 'I'll tell you what brings me here. I'm taking your daughter back home with me and mean to tie a loose marriage-knot here and now.'

Hogni realized there was nothing he could do but let Bjorgolf have his way. Bjorgolf bought the girl for an ounce of gold and off they went to bed. Then Bjorgolf took Hildirid back to Torg Island. Brynjolf wasn't at all pleased.

Bjorgolf and Hildirid had two sons, one called Harek and the other Hrærek, but then Bjorgolf died. No sooner had he been carried to the grave, than Brynjolf told Hildirid to take her sons and clear out, so she went back to her father on Leka Island, where her sons grew up. They were short men but very intelligent, taking much after their mother's kinsfolk. People called them the Hildiridarsons. Brynjolf had a low opinion of them and gave them none of their inheritance, but as Hildirid was Hogni's sole heir she and her sons got everything he left. They started farming on Leka Island and were very well-off. The Hildiridarsons were just about the same age as Bard Brynjolfsson.

Bjorgolf and his son Brynjolf had been in charge of trade with the Lapps for some considerable time, as well as looking after the Lapp tribute.

North in Halogaland lies Vefsensfjord, where there's a fine large island, Alsten, with a farm on it called Sandness. The farmer there, Sigurd, was the richest man in the north, a landholder and a man with a powerful mind. He had a daughter called Sigrid, and people thought her the finest match in the whole of Halogaland. As she was an only child, she stood to inherit everything from her father. Bard Brynjolfsson set out from home by ship with thirty men. He sailed north to Alsten Island and went to visit Sigurd at Sandness, where he made a proposal of marriage and asked for Sigrid's hand. He got a favourable answer, and in the end promises were sealed. The wedding was to take place the following summer, and Bard was to go up north to fetch his bride.

8. Thorolf comes to King Harald

THAT summer, Harald had sent word to the leading men of Halogaland, summoning those who had not yet been to see him. Brynjolf was ordered to carry out the mission, and his son Bard was to go with him. So in the autumn they travelled south to meet the King, who welcomed them warmly and appointed Brynjolf one of his land-holders. The King granted him valuable stewardships in addition to those he held already, gave him permission to travel to Finnmark for trade with the Lapps, and appointed him steward over the mountain regions. After that Brynjolf set off home, back to his estates, but Bard stayed behind and became the King's man.

Of all his retainers, the King thought most of his court poets, who were placed on the lower high-seat. Audun the Fake-Poet sat closest to the King as he was the senior and had been court poet to Halfdan the Black, Harald's father. Next to him sat Thorbjorn Hornklofi, then Olvir Hnufa. Bard was given a seat next to Olvir, and people nicknamed him Bard the White or Bard the Strong. Everyone liked him, and he and Olvir grew to be close friends.

That same autumn, Thorolf Kveldulfsson and Eyvind Lambi, son of Berle-Kari, came to the King and were well received by him. They sailed with a fine crew in a longship of twenty oars, the one they had used on their viking expeditions, and were given a place in the visitor's hall along with their men.

After a while they decided it was time to see the King, and Berle-Kari and Olvir Hnufa went along with them. They paid their respects, and then Olvir Hnufa announced that Kveldulf's son had arrived. 'I told you in the summer that Kveldulf would send him to you,' said Olvir. 'Kveldulf won't break any of the promises he makes you, and now that he's sent his son here to serve you it's proof that he wants to be your true friend. You can see for yourself what a brave-looking man Thorolf is. Now, what Kveldulf wants – and that goes for us all – is for you to receive Thorolf with honour and make him one of your chief men.'

The King answered in a friendly way that he planned to do just that, 'as long as Thorolf proves himself the fighting man he looks to be'. So Thorolf became the King's loyal subject and joined Harald's court, but Berle-Kari and his son Eyvind Lambi went south back home to their estates aboard the ship Thorolf had brought there. Thorolf stayed on with the King and was given a seat between Olvir Hnufa and Bard. All three men became close friends and everyone agreed that Thorolf and Bard were much alike in their stature, strength and skills, and in their good looks. Thorolf was well liked by the King, and so was Bard.

After winter had passed and it was summer again, Bard asked the King's permission to fetch the bride he had been promised the previous summer. When the King saw how eager Bard was to be about his business, he gave him leave to travel home. As soon as the King had given his permission, Bard asked Thorolf to come with him, mentioning that Thorolf would be able to visit a number of his relations whom he had never met – maybe never even heard of. Thorolf found this very tempting, and they got the King's consent. They made themselves ready for the voyage, with a fine ship and a good crew, and off they sailed. When they reached Torg Island they sent messengers to tell Sigurd that Bard had come to clinch the agreement of the previous summer. Sigurd said he meant to keep his part of the bargain, so it was agreed that Bard was to come north to Sandness for the wedding, and the date was fixed there and then. Brynjolf and Bard set off at the appointed time with a large company of important people including their kinsmen and in-laws, and just as Bard had said, there Thorolf met many of his own kinsmen he'd never even heard of before. On they travelled to Sandness, where there was a grand feast, after which Bard went back home with his wife. He spent the summer there and Thorolf stayed with him, but in the autumn they went south to join the King and passed the following winter with Harald.

That winter Brynjolf died. As soon as Bard got news of his inheritance he asked for leave to go home, which the King granted. Before they parted, Bard was appointed a land-holder, just as his father had been, and awarded all the privileges that Brynjolf himself had enjoyed. Bard went back home to his estates and soon became a great chieftain, but the Hildiridarsons got no more of their inheritance than they'd had in the past.

Bard had a son by his wife, and he was called Grim. Thorolf stayed on with the King and was treated with great honour.

9. Bard dies and Thorolf marries his widow

KING Harald assembled a war-fleet, along with a massive army, gathering troops from all over the country. After that he travelled from Trondheim to the south. He had been told that a great army had been mustered from Agder, Rogaland and Hordaland, and many other parts of the country, both Oslofjord and the inland districts. Many men of rank had assembled there, all of them determined to defend their territories against King Harald.

In command of a great ship manned by his own retainers, King Harald moved south with his troops. Thorolf Kveldulfsson, Bard the White, Olvir Hnufa and Eyvind Lambi, the sons of Berle-Kari, were all in the prow of the King's ship. Amidships were the King's twelve berserks. The battle fought south in Rogaland, at Hafursfjord, was fiercer than anything Harald had ever experienced, with heavy losses on both sides. The King sailed ahead of his fleet in the thick of battle, and when it was all over, Harald had won the day. King Thorir Long-Chin was killed there, and Kjotvi the Wealthy made off along with those of his men who had survived but had not surrendered to Harald after the battle. The roll-call of Harald's troops showed many dead, and many more who had been badly wounded. Thorolf's injuries were among the gravest there, but Bard's were even worse, and there wasn't a man unhurt before the mast of the King's ship apart from the berserks, who were men that iron could never bite. The King had the wounded seen to, and thanked his troops for what they had done. He offered gifts and words of praise to those he thought best deserved them, and promised even greater honours. In particular he singled out his captains, and after them his forecastlemen and all who had been fighting in the prow.

This was the last battle that King Harald ever fought on his own territory. After that there was no one to offer him any resistance, and he conquered the entire country. If any man seemed to have a chance of recovering, the King had his wounds treated, and the dead were buried according to the custom of the time.

Thorolf and Bard were both laid up with their wounds, but while Thorolf's began to heal, Bard's grew more and more serious, and in the end he asked the King to come and see him.

'If I should die of these wounds,' he said, 'I'd like you to take charge of my legacies.' The King said he would do that, and Bard went on: 'I want my friend and kinsman Thorolf to inherit everything, money, land and wife, and it's Thorolf I want to bring up my son, for I trust him as I trust no other man.'

After Bard had made these arrangements in accordance with the law and with the King's approval, he died and his body was made ready for burial. His death was a great sorrow to everyone, but Thorolf made a complete recovery and was in the King's company that summer, his reputation greater than ever.

In the autumn the King travelled north to Trondheim. Then Thorolf asked for leave to go further north to Halogaland and take charge of what his kinsman Bard had left him that summer. The King gave his permission, along with messages and tokens guaranteeing Thorolf's right to all that Bard had given him. The King let it be known that the bequest had been made with his approval, and that he wanted Thorolf to receive it. Then he made Thorolf a land-holder, granting him all the stewardships Bard had once held, as well as the rights Bard formerly had to the Lappish trade. He gave Thorolf a fully equipped longship and did everything in his power to help prepare for the voyage.

Thorolf parted from the King on the friendliest terms and went on his way north to Torg Island, where he was given a warm welcome. He told them Bard was dead and had left everything to him, his land, his money, even his wife, as the King's messages and tokens proved. The news of her husband's death came as a heavy blow to Sigrid. All the same, Thorolf was no stranger to her, and she knew well enough what a great man he was and how good a husband he would be. And since this was what the King wished, she and her friends agreed that, given the approval of her father, it would be a good thing for her to marry Thorolf. So Thorolf took charge of everything there, including the King's stewardship.

As soon as he was ready, Thorolf put out to sea and sailed north by the coast in a longship with a crew of sixty, arriving one evening at Sandness on Alost. They put into harbour, set up their awnings and made themselves comfortable. Then Thorolf went up to the farm with twenty men. Sigurd made him very welcome and invited him to stay. He and Thorolf had got to know each other well ever since Bard had married his daughter. Thorolf and his men went with him into the hall and settled in for the night. Sigurd took a seat next to Thorolf and asked him the news. Thorolf told him about the battle that had been fought in the south that summer, and about the deaths of many men, some of them well known to Sigurd. He told Sigurd that his son-in-law Bard was one of those who had died of wounds received in the battle, and they agreed that his death was a great loss to them both. Then Thorolf told Sigurd about the private agreement Bard had made with him before he died, and delivered the King's message that all these arrangements were to stand, showing the tokens to prove it. Then Thorolf made Sigurd a proposition and asked for the hand of his daughter Sigrid. Sigurd took it well, saying that there were plenty of reasons why he should give his approval – firstly the King wanted it; next, Bard had asked for it; and lastly, he knew Thorolf and thought his daughter would do well to marry him. In fact, it wasn't hard to get Sigurd's approval for the marriage. The betrothal was settled there and then, and it was agreed that the wedding should be celebrated on Torg Island in the autumn.

Thorolf and his men went back home to his estate. He began making preparations for a grand feast and sent out a great many invitations. Sigurd set off in a longship and sailed south with a massive following. Never had there been such a crowded feast as that one.

It quickly became apparent how open and generous a man Thorolf was. He had a large household, and needed plenty of supplies, so he was soon burdened with heavy expenses, but the season was good, and it wasn't hard to get everything that he required. That winter, Sigurd of Sandness died and Thorolf inherited all that he possessed, which was a very great deal.

The Hildiridarsons went to see Thorolf and asked for their share of the money that had once belonged to their father, Bjorgolf. 'I knew Brynjolf well,' said Thorolf, 'and Bard even better. Men like these would surely have given you a share of Bjorgolf's property had they thought you had any real claim to it. I was there the time you made the same demand of Bard, and when he called you a pair of bastards I didn't get the feeling that he thought you had much in the way of rights.'

Harek said they could produce witnesses that their mother had been paid a marriage fee. 'Still, it's true,' he said, 'we never took up our claim with our brother Brynjolf even though he was so near a kinsman. We trusted Bard to do the right thing, but he didn't have much time for us, and now those who've got their hands on the inheritance aren't even related to us. So we don't intend to keep our mouths shut any longer about what we've lost, even though things will most likely turn out much as before and we'll not be strong enough to win our rights from you, especially if you won't even listen to the evidence of our witnesses that we're men of respectable birth.'

'I don't see that you've any right to the inheritance,' said Thorolf angrily. 'The way I heard it, your mother was taken by force and carried off like a captive.' And with that their conversation came to an end.

10. Thorolf in Finnmark

THAT winter Thorolf set out with a large following, at least ninety men, and travelled north to the mountains. The custom had been for stewards to take only thirty men with them, sometimes even fewer. Thorolf had plenty of goods to sell and it wasn't long before he had arranged a meeting with the Lapps to collect tribute and to do business with them. His dealings with the Lapps passed off in a quiet and friendly enough way, though there was a touch of intimidation about it.

Thorolf journeyed widely throughout Finnmark. When he reached the mountains to the east he learned that the Kylfing tribe had travelled west to trade with the Lapps and pick up some loot on the side. Thorolf appointed several Lapps to keep an eye open for the Kylfings' movements, and set out himself in search of them. At one place he came upon a group of about thirty Kylfings and killed the lot. Not one of them got away. Later he came across more of them in a group of some fifteen or twenty. All in all, he and his men must have killed a hundred of them and taken a fair amount of plunder as well.

In the spring they travelled back south. Thorolf went back home to his farm at Sandness and settled down there for a while. That same spring he built a big dragon-headed longship, fitted out with all the best equipment, and sailed off to the south. He made the most of whatever resources Halogaland offered, sending some of his men after herring while others were busy with the stockfish. There were plenty of seals and eggs to be got as well, and he had it all put in store. He never had less than a hundred free-men on his farm. His nature was open and generous, and he was on excellent terms with all the great people of the district. He grew to be a rich man and was always most particular about the quality of his ships and weapons.

11. King Harald visits Thorolf

IN the summer King Harald travelled to Halogaland and attended a number of feasts there, both on his own estates and at the invitation of land-holders and wealthy farmers. Thorolf prepared a feast for the King and no expense was spared. As soon as it was decided when the King was to come, Thorolf sent out a great number of invitations to all the most important people of his choice. When the King came to the feast with three hundred followers, five hundred of Thorolf's guests were already assembled there. Thorolf had fitted out a huge grain-store on his farm, and set up benches there. Since he had no hall big enough for such an immense crowd of people, that's where the drinking was to take place. A row of shields lined the walls all the way round the barn.

The King sat himself down on the high-seat. Every other seat was occupied, from the top of the hall right down to the lowest part. As the King looked about him his face flushed red, and though he didn't speak a word, people could see that he was in an angry mood. The feast was magnificent and nothing was served but the very best, yet though the King stayed on for three days as had been planned, his sullen temper didn't change.

On the last day, when the King was due to leave, Thorolf came to him and suggested they should take a walk down to the sea. The King agreed. The dragon-ship Thorolf had built was floating near the shore in full rig with its awnings up. This ship Thorolf gave to the King. He asked Harald to make every allowance for good intentions, and said his only reason for inviting so many people was to honour the King, not compete with him. The King took this very well. His mood became friendly and cheerful, and there were plenty of people to put in a good word for Thorolf. They pointed out what no one could deny, that the feast had been magnificent and the parting gifts superb. Such men as Thorolf, they said, were truly the mainstay of the King.

So the two men parted the best of friends. The King travelled further north into Halogaland as he had planned, then turned back late in the summer, continuing to attend all the various feasts that had been prepared for him.

12. Slander

THE Hildiridarsons went to the King and invited him to a three-day feast. The King accepted the invitation, fixed the date and came with his retinue at the appointed time. Not many other people were there but the feast could not have gone better. The King was in such a cheerful mood that Harek decided to have a talk with him, and led the conversation round to the King's travels that summer. Harald answered all of his questions. Everyone, he said, had given him the warmest of welcomes and had done all that could have been expected of them.

'The feasts must have varied quite a lot,' said Harek. 'I

suppose the biggest crowd would have been at Torg Island?'

The King said that he was quite right.

'It's not really surprising,' said Harek. 'After all, that's where they made the biggest preparations. It's a lucky thing for you, sir, that everything turned out so well and there was no threat to your life. But then, it's only to be expected that a man with your sharp wits and good luck should have his doubts, what with all those fighting men gathered together, and feel that things weren't quite above board. I've heard that you had your men carry their weapons and keep their eyes peeled day and night?'

The King gave him a hard look.

'What are you getting at, Harek?' he asked. 'Is there something more you want to tell me?'

'Do you mind if I speak frankly, sir?' asked Harek.

'Speak on,' said the King.

'I'll tell you how I see it, sir,' said Harek. 'You'd soon realize that something is wrong if you could hear how people speak their minds in private and say how much they resent your grip on them. The fact is, sir, that the common people need nothing but courage and a leader to rise up against you. It's no wonder people like Thorolf think themselves so much better than everyone else. He has the power, and the looks for it too, and he surrounds himself with retainers as if he were a king. Even though he had no more than the property that belongs to him, he'd still be enormously rich, but on top of all that he treats other men's money as if it were his own. You may have granted him great stewardships, but don't expect any favours in return. To tell you the honest truth, when it got about that you were travelling north to Halogaland with a mere three hundred men, there was a plot to gather an army and put you yourself and everyone with you to death. Thorolf had been offered the kingship of Halogaland and Namdalen Province, so he was the top man in the conspiracy. He travelled up and down every fjord and visited every island, gathering all the men he could muster and the weapons he could use. It was an open secret that he meant to send his troops against

King Harald in battle. But here's another thing, sir. It wouldn't have made the least bit of difference, no matter how small your force when you faced him, because as soon as the peasants caught sight of your ships they flew into a panic and changed their minds, and decided to give you a friendly welcome after all and invite you to a feast. The idea was that if you happened to get drunk and fall asleep they'd attack you with fire and weapons, and here's the proof – every single building there was chock-full of weapons and armour, but when their trick didn't work they took the only way out and hushed up the whole plot. I can't see many of them admitting their share in it, but once the truth is out, few of them will be able to swear their innocence. Now, sir, I'll tell you what I advise. Take Thorolf with you and keep him with your own men. Let him fight in the prow of your ship and carry your standard, he's better at that sort of thing than anyone else; but if you plan to keep him as your land-holder, give him a stewardship to the south of Fjord Province where all his kinsmen are. You can keep an eye on him there and see that he doesn't get any big ideas. But give the Halogaland stewardships to moderate-minded people with a family background here who'll keep faith with you and have kinsmen who've held this sort of office before. My brother and I are ready and willing to take them on if you'd care to make use of us. Our father held the royal stewardship here for a good many years and made a fine job of it. And visiting these parts as rarely as you do, sir, you won't easily find the right man to take charge. The country is too harsh for you to travel with your army and I can't see you coming here again with such a small force, not with all these people about who can't be trusted.'

The King was in a great rage about what he'd heard but he answered calmly enough, as he always did when he was told about anything of real importance. He asked if Thorolf was at his home on Torg Island, but Harek said he thought it unlikely.

'Thorolf's far too shrewd to risk facing up to your troops, sir,' he said. 'He can hardly expect the secret to be so well kept that it doesn't reach your ears. The moment he heard you were on your way south, he moved up north to Alsten Island.'

The King said very little to anyone else, but went on his way. All the same, people thought he believed what he'd been told. The Hildiridarsons saw him off with fine parting gifts, and he made them a promise of friendship.

The brothers found pretexts to travel east to Namdalen and kept making detours so that from time to time they would meet the King, and whenever they talked to him he was always friendly.

13. Thorgils Gjallandi

THERE was one man in Thorolf's household who was held in particular honour, and that was Thorgils Gjallandi. He had been Thorolf's forecastle man and standard-bearer on viking trips and was a brave and powerful man. At the battle of Hafursfjord he had fought for King Harald and had been commander of Thorolf's viking ship there. After the battle the King had been generous with gifts and promised his friendship.

Whenever Thorolf was away from home, Thorgils managed his estates on Torg Island and used to take charge of everything there. Thorolf was about to set out on a journey, but first he handed over to Thorgils all the Lapp tribute belonging to the King that he had brought from the mountains. Thorolf said that should he not return before the King called in on his way south, Thorgils was to hand it over to the King.

Thorgils rigged out a fine big merchant ship belonging to Thorolf, loaded the tribute aboard and sailed south with a crew of about twenty to find the King. He caught up with him in Namdalen, greeted the King in Thorolf's name and said that he'd brought the Lapp tribute that Thorolf had collected. The King gave him a hard look but said nothing, and people could see how angry he was. Thorgils went away, thinking that he might pick a better time to see the King. He went to have a word with Olvir Hnufa, told him what had happened, and asked if he had any idea of what was going on.

'That I can't say,' answered Olvir, 'but there's one thing I have noticed. Ever since we called at Leka Island, the King goes very quiet whenever anyone mentions Thorolf's name. I think somebody's been spreading tales about him. I know the Hildiridarsons are always having private conversations with the King and you can tell from the way they talk that they're no friends of Thorolf. But I'll go to the King right away and find out how matters stand.' And so Olvir went to see the King.

'Your friend Thorgils Gjallandi is here with that tribute of yours from Lapland,' he said, 'more of it than ever and much better quality too. He's very keen to get on with his affairs, so if you wouldn't mind, sir, do go and take a look. You've never seen such grey furs.'

The King said nothing but he did go down to the ship. Thorgils set to at once and started unloading the furs to show the King. When Harald saw how true it was that the tribute was much bigger and better than ever before he began to look rather more cheerful and permitted Thorgils to have a word with him. As gifts from Thorolf, Thorgils gave the King several beaver pelts and other valuable things that he'd picked up north in the mountains. Now the King looked really pleased. He asked all about the journeys that Thorolf and Thorgils had been making, and Thorgils gave him a detailed account of them.

'It's a sad business when Thorolf won't keep faith with me and wants me dead,' said the King.

A number of people who were near by spoke up and every one of them said the same, that Thorolf was utterly blameless and that whatever the King had been hearing, it was nothing but wicked slander. After a while the King said that he was inclined to believe them, and then his conversation with Thorgils grew quite cheerful, so that they parted on good terms. All the same, when Thorgils got back and joined Thorolf, he told him about everything that had happened between himself and the king.

14. Thorolf's second trip to Finnmark

THAT same winter Thorolf set off north again to Finnmark, taking nearly a hundred men along with him. He went about things just as in the year before, trading with the Lapps and travelling all over Finnmark. He'd penetrated well to the east when some people of the Kven tribe came and told him they'd been sent by King Faravid of Kvenland. They said the Karelians were attacking Faravid's kingdom, and he wanted Thorolf to go there and help him. The message added that Thorolf would get equal share of the plunder with Faravid, and each of Thorolf's men the same as three Kvens. It was a law of the Kvens that their king should get a third of the plunder and his men the rest, though he didn't have to share out the beaver pelts, sables and martens. Thorolf talked the matter over with his men and gave them the choice of whether to go or stay. Most of them chose to take the risk since there was so much money to be had, so they made up their minds to go east with the messengers.

Finnmark is a vast country, with great fjords cutting deep into it right down the western seaboard, as well as to the north and all the way east. To the south lies Norway, but Finnmark stretches southwards through the mountains as much as Halogaland does by the coast. East of Namdalen lies Jamtland, then Helsingland, Kvenland, Finland, and finally Karelia. But Finnmark, lying beyond, is more mountainous than any of these other lands and there are plenty of highland settlements there, some in the valleys and others along the lakes. In Finnmark there are some amazingly big lakes with vast forests between them. A high mountain range called Kjolen stretches right through the country.

As soon as Thorolf joined up with King Faravid to the east in Kvenland they got themselves ready for the campaign, the Kvens with three hundred men and the Norwegians a hundred or so more. They made their way through the highlands of Finnmark until, on a mountain, they found themselves face to face with the Karelians who had been attacking the Kvens. When the Karelians saw the troops, they formed up and turned to meet them, expecting to win the victory as before, but when battle was joined the Norwegians put up a hard fight. They had more reliable shields than the Kvens, so it wasn't long before the Karelians were suffering heavy losses, many being killed and others taking to their heels. King Faravid and Thorolf took a deal of plunder, after which they went back to Kvenland. Later, Thorolf and his men travelled back to Finnmark. He and King Faravid parted, the best of friends.

Thorolf travelled down from the mountains to Vefsensfjord and from there first to his estates at Sandness where he stayed for a while. Then in the spring he went south with his men to Torg Island. When he got there, people told him that the Hildiridarsons had been staying over winter with King Harald at Trondheim, and went on to say that they'd not been sparing in their efforts to slander Thorolf before the King. Thorolf was given plenty of precise details about the slander.

'The King would never believe such a pack of lies,' said Thorolf. 'There's not a scrap of evidence here that I'd betray him. He's been kind enough to give me many things, and never done me a bad turn. It's absurd to think I'd ever harm him even if I wanted to. I'd rather be his land-holder, than have the name of king but under a man who could make a slave of me.'

15. Slander sustained

THE Hildiridarsons had spent that winter with King Harald, and their own retainers and neighbours had been there with them. The brothers kept going time and again to have a word with the King and always carried the same tale about Thorolf and his conduct.

'Were you pleased with the Lapp tribute Thorolf sent you, sir?' asked Harek.

'Indeed I was,' the King answered.

'Then you'd have been really impressed if you'd had all that was due to you,' said Harek, 'but you got a lot less than that. Thorolf took much the bigger share for himself. He made you a gift of three beaver skins, but I know for a fact that he kept thirty more for himself that were rightly yours, and it's my opinion that the same must have happened with other things. Now if you were to hand over the stewardship to my brother, sir, you could be sure we'd bring you better returns.'

And whatever the brothers had to say against Thorolf, it was given full support by their companions. So as things turned out, the King was in a towering rage.

16. Thorolf meets the King

THAT summer Thorolf travelled south to Trondheim to see King Harald along with ninety men, all well equipped, bringing with him the entire tribute and much besides. When he came to the King, he and his men were shown to the guest-hall and offered every hospitality. Later that day Olvir Hnufa came to see his kinsman, and took Thorolf aside for a talk. Olvir told him that he'd been badly slandered and that the

King took these accusations seriously. Thorolf asked Olvir to put his case to the King. 'I'm not wasting my words on the King,' said Thorolf, 'if he'd rather believe the slander of villains than the honest truth he'd get from me.'

Next day Olvir came to see Thorolf and said that he'd talked over his case with the King. 'But I'm none the wiser as to what's in his mind.'

'Then I'll go and see him myself,' said Thorolf, and that is what he did.

As the King sat at table Thorolf went to greet him, and the King returned his greeting. He asked someone to give Thorolf a drink. Thorolf said that he had brought the King's tribute from Finnmark.

'And I've brought more than that, sir, to honour you with,' he added. 'I'm sure I couldn't have done more than I have to show my gratitude.'

The King said he expected nothing but good from Thorolf, adding that this was no less than he deserved.

'All the same,' he said, 'people are giving me conflicting reports about how far you go to please me.'

'If any man says that I've broken faith with you, sir, it's a false accusation,' said Thorolf, 'and it's my opinion that people like that are far worse friends to you than I am, telling you such things. There's one thing that's certain, though, they must be pretty determined enemies of mine. Anyway, if ever they have any dealings with me they can take it that they'll get their moneysworth.'

At that Thorolf left, but the next day he handed over the tribute in the King's own presence. After it had all been presented, Thorolf produced a number of beaver pelts and sables, and said that he was making a gift of these to the King. Many of the people there remarked that this was generous on Thorolf's part, and deserved the King's friendship, but the King said that Thorolf had already taken all the reward due to him. Thorolf answered that he'd done everything in his power to show his loyalty to the King.

'And if he's not satisfied there's nothing I can do about it,' he added. 'The King knows very well how I handled matters when I was in his retinue, and it would strike me as very odd if he thought me a different man now from what I was then.'

'You conducted yourself admirably when you were with me, Thorolf,' said the King, 'and I think it would be best for you to come back as one of my retainers. You can take charge of my banner and lead my other great men. No one can slander you while I'm keeping a watch day and night on your doings.'

Thorolf looked to left and right, where his own men were standing. 'I'm not keen to let these men go,' he said. 'It's up to you, sir, how you hand out your titles and gifts, but even though I have to fall back on my own resources, I'll never let go of my men, not as long as I can last out. But it's my earnest wish, sir, that you accept my invitation to come home with me and listen to the people you trust, and the testimony they'll give about this business. After that you can take whatever steps you think fit.'

The King's answer was that he would never accept another invitation from Thorolf, so Thorolf went off and got ready for the journey home.

As soon as Thorolf was on his way, the King gave into the hands of the Hildiridarsons the charge over Halogaland which Thorolf had held, and also the right to trade with the Lapps. Next the King laid claim to the Torg Island estate along with everything else there that had been the property of Brynjolf, put it all into the hands of the Hildiridarsons, and sent messengers to Thorolf with tokens to confirm the new arrangements he had made. At that Thorolf launched every ship he owned, loaded them with whatever he could carry, got every man aboard both free and enslaved, and sailed north to his farm at Sandness. He had as many men with him as ever, and he lived in just as grand a style.

17. Tribute for the King

THE Hildiridarsons took over the stewardship in Halogaland, and no one said anything against it for fear of the King's authority, though there were plenty of people of a very different mind, particularly the friends and kinsmen of Thorolf. The Hildiridarsons went up to the highlands over winter with thirty men but the Finns had a poorer opinion of these stewards than they'd had of Thorolf, so their tribute was a lot less than usual.

That same winter Thorolf went up to the highlands with a hundred and twenty men, travelling east directly to Kvenland where he met King Faravid. They laid their plans for a joint expedition in the highlands, just as in the previous winter, and made their way down to Karelia over four hundred strong, attacking every settlement they felt they had enough men to deal with. They got a great deal of plunder from these attacks, and then, as winter wore on, they made their way back to Finnmark. In the spring Thorolf went home to his farm. He sent his men fishing to the Vago Islands, some for cod, others for herring, and provisioned his farm from every conceivable source.

Thorolf had a big, ocean-going ship. Great pains had been taken over it. It was richly painted above the sea-line, the rigging was of the highest quality, and it had a blue-and-red striped sail. Thorolf had this ship made ready and manned it with his household servants. He had it loaded with dried fish, hides and furs, amongst which were plenty of squirrel and other pelts that he'd taken in Finnmark. It was all very valuable.

He put Thorgils Gjallandi in charge of the ship and told him to sail it west to England to buy cloth and other commodities that he needed. They sailed the ship south along the coast, then out into the open sea, and landed in England where they did good business. They loaded their ship with flour and honey, wine and cloth, and sailed back home in the autumn. They had a favourable wind and put in at Hordaland.

That same autumn the Hildiridarsons went to the King with the Lapp tribute, and handed it over in the King's own presence.

'Is that everything you took in Finnmark, that you've just handed over?' asked the King.

'It is,' they replied.

'Then I must say,' declared the King, 'it's a lot smaller and much poorer quality too, than when Thorolf used to collect it. You told me he was a bad steward.'

'It's a good thing, sir,' said Harek, 'that you've been thinking about how large the tribute was that used to come from Finnmark. Now you'll realize how much you'd miss, what with Thorolf spending it all for you. There were thirty of us in Finnmark this winter, the same number that the stewards normally took, but then Thorolf turned up a hundred and twenty strong. We've been told that he said he was planning to put us brothers and all our men to death, and he put the blame on us, sir, just because you'd given us the stewardship he thought he ought to have. So we decided our best choice would be to keep out of his way and save ourselves, which explains why we didn't go very far from the settlements into the mountains, what with Thorolf and his men on the move all over Finnmark. He got all the trade, the Finns paid him the tribute, and he made sure that your stewards weren't going to get into Finnmark. He wants to make himself king of the north, of both Finnmark and Halogaland, and it's a strange thing that you should let him get away with whatever he likes. It will be easy enough to prove the truth about this money-grabbing of his in Finnmark. The biggest cargo-ship in the whole of Halogaland was loaded at Sandness in the spring, and Thorolf claimed the entire cargo, nearly a full load of furs it was carrying, I think, with more beaver and sable pelts than Thorolf gave to you. Thorgils Gjallandi was in charge, and I think it was west he sailed, to England. But if you want to find out the truth of it, keep a close eye on Thorgils's movements when he comes back east. I don't believe a ship ever carried a more precious cargo. To tell the honest truth, sir, I think every penny on board was rightly yours.'

Everything Harek said his companion supported, and there was no one to contradict them.

18. Thorgils returns from England

THERE were two brothers, Sigtrygg the Fast-Sailer and Hallvard the Hard-Sailer, staying with King Harald, both from Oslofjord, but belonging to Vestfold on their mother's side and distant relations of King Harald. Their father had kinsmen on either side of the Gota River, and had been a wealthy man with a farm on Hising Island. By this time the brothers had taken over their inheritance after the death of their father. There were four brothers in all, the two younger ones called Thord and Thorgeir looking after the farm back home.

Sigtrygg and Hallvard were in charge of all the King's missions, both in Norway and abroad, and had undertaken many a dangerous journey either to execute people or confiscate the property of those the King had decided to attack. The brothers had a large band of men and weren't very popular with most people, but the King had a high regard for them. They could beat any man both at running and on skis and they were the best of sailors when it came to speed. They were both brave men, and shrewd too, on the whole.

At the time all this was taking place they were staying with the King. That autumn he went to Hordaland to attend some feasts, and one day he had the brothers summoned to a meeting with him. When they came, he told them to take their men and keep a look-out for the ship that Thorgils Gjallandi was in charge of, the one he sailed west with in the summer to England. 'Bring the ship to me,' said the King, 'and everything on board apart from the crew. Let them go their way in peace unless they insist on defending the ship.'

The brothers were ready and willing for this and set out to

look for Thorgils, each in his own longship. They learned that he'd returned from the west and had sailed north along the coast. They set off north after him and caught up with him at Furu Sound. As soon as they recognized the ship, they sailed one of their own ships up to it on the seaward side while other men went ashore and walked aboard up the gang-way. Thorgils and his crew suspected nothing and it took them completely by surprise. The first thing they knew, a swarm of fully-armed men had come aboard. So they were all taken captive and led ashore without arms or anything at all but the clothes they stood up in. Hallvard and his men slid back the gangway, untied the moorings and towed the ship out to sea, after which they turned south and sailed back to the King to present him with the ship and all its cargo. When the cargo had been unloaded the King could see that it was of great value, and that Harek had been telling him no lies.

After Thorgils and his men had got themselves transport, they went to see Kveldulf and his son Grim, and told Kveldulf all about the treatment they'd had. But he gave them a good welcome. He said it would all turn out just as he'd thought and that Thorolf would get no luck from King Harald's friendship.

'I'll not worry so much about Thorolf's loss of property,' he said, 'as long as there's nothing worse to follow. But it's still my guess that Thorolf won't see how hopeless the odds are against him in this business.' Then he asked Thorgils to take a message to Thorolf.

'This is my advice,' he said, 'let him go abroad. He's likely to do better for himself if he joins the King of England or Denmark or Sweden.'

Kveldulf let Thorgils and his men have a rowing skiff, fully rigged, along with tents, provisions and anything else they needed for their trip. After that they set off and sailed without pause until they reached Thorolf in the north. There they told him everything that had happened. Thorolf took his loss well and said he would never go short of money. 'It's good to share something with the King,' he said.

Thorolf bought flour, malt and other things he needed for the upkeep of his household but told them they weren't going to be as well-dressed as he'd hoped. He sold some of his farms and mortgaged others, but still kept up his usual style of living. His men were no fewer than in the previous winter, in fact he had rather more, and paid out more, too, on feasts and invitations to his friends. All that winter he spent at home.

19. Thorolf goes raiding

IN spring when the snow thawed and the ice was breaking up, Thorolf launched a great longship that he owned, had it rigged out, and manned it with over a hundred of his household, a fine well-armed band of men. As soon as the weather was favourable, Thorolf sailed south along the coast and when he reached as far south as Bjoro Island he steered for the open sea, by-passing all the islands. Sometimes he was so far out that the mountains were half-hidden below the horizon. They sailed round the southern tip and made no contact with anyone until they came east into Oslofjord. Then they heard King Harald was staying there and meant to make a journey to the Uplands that summer. The people ashore knew nothing of Thorolf's movements.

Thorolf got a good wind and sailed south to Denmark. From there he went into the Baltic where he looted all summer without getting much in the way of plunder. In the autumn he sailed west back to Denmark just about the time that the merchant fleet was leaving Eyr. It was usual for a large number of Norwegian vessels to go there during the summer. Thorolf let the whole merchant fleet sail on and kept himself out of their way. But one evening he sailed up to Mostrar Sound, where a large cargo vessel was lying just out of Eyr. The captain of this ship, a man called Thorir Tromo, was one of King Harald's stewards and in charge of his estate on Tromo Island, a large farm on which the King used to spend a great deal of time when he was in Oslofjord, so that plenty of provisions were needed for it. The reason Thorir had gone to Eyr was to buy a cargo of honey, malt and flour, and on this he'd spent a lot of the King's money.

Thorolf and his men lay alongside the cargo vessel and offered Thorir the chance to defend himself, but as Thorir did not have enough men to put up any serious resistance to Thorolf's large force, there was nothing for him to do but surrender. Thorolf seized the ship and all its cargo and put Thorir ashore on the island. After that he sailed north along the coast with the two ships.

When they got to the Gota River they dropped anchor and lay there till nightfall. Then, under cover of darkness, they rowed the longship up river till they reached the farm owned by Hallvard and Sigtrygg. They arrived just before dawn, surrounded the house and shouted out their war-cry. The noise woke the men inside, they rushed for their weapons and Thorgeir ran out from the sleeping-hall. There was a high stockade around the farmhouse. Thorgeir made for it, grabbed one of the posts and swung himself out over the wall. Thorgils Gjallandi was standing near by and took a swing with his sword at Thorgeir. The sword caught him on the hand against a stockade-post and severed it. Thorgeir ran off into the wood, but his brother Thorir and twenty other men were killed there.

Then Thorolf and his men looted the place of everything valuable, set fire to the farmhouse, and sailed down the river and out to sea. From there they made north with a fair wind to Oslofjord. There they came across another merchantman belonging to the men of Oslofjord, carrying a cargo of malt and flour. Thorolf and his men made straight for it and as the crew didn't think themselves strong enough to put up any resistance, they surrendered and walked ashore weaponless, while Thorolf and his men took the ship and its cargo and sailed on. So Thorolf had three ships as he sailed west out of the fjord then south by the normal route to Lindesness. They made fast progress even though they kept raiding every headland they came to and plundering the coastline. Sailing north from Lindesness they kept mainly to the deep-sea route, but whenever they came to land they would start looting. When Thorolf got north to Fjord Province, he made a detour and went to see his father Kveldulf, who gave them all a good welcome. Thorolf told his father the news about his expedition that summer. and stayed there for a short while, after which Kveldulf and his son Grim saw Thorolf on his way down to the ship. Before they parted, he and Kveldulf had a talk.

'It's all turned out much as I told you it would, Thorolf, when you first set out to join King Harald's court,' said Kveldulf. 'I said there'd be no luck in it either for you or for your kinsmen. And now you've done the one thing I warned you not to do, you've tried matching fortunes with King Harald. You may have plenty of courage and all the ability but what you don't have is the luck you need to hold your own against the King. That's something nobody in the land has managed to do, no matter how much power and support he had. I have a feeling that this is the last time we shall ever meet. It would have been more natural for you to outlive me, but I'm afraid that's not the way it is to be.'

After that Thorolf boarded his ship and sailed on his way, and there's nothing to tell of his voyage till he got back home to Sandness. He had all the plunder he'd brought home with him carried up to the farm and then he beached his ship. There was no shortage of supplies that winter to feed the household. Thorolf settled down at home, and for the most part he had no fewer men with him than he'd had over the previous winter.

20. Skallagrim marries

THERE was a rich and powerful man called Yngvar who had been a land-holder of the earlier kings, but had settled down on his farm after Harald had come to power, and refused to serve him. Yngvar was a married man. He lived in Fjord Province and had a daughter called Bera, his only child and sole heir. Grim Kveldulfsson asked for her hand, was promised her, and married her the winter after Thorolf's summer visit. Though Grim was only in his mid twenties he was already bald, so he got the nickname Skallagrim.[1] He had charge of everything on his and his father's estate, which included making all provision for the household, though Kveldulf was still a hearty and capable man. They had a large number of free-men with them, some of whom had grown up there on the farm and were much the same age as Skallagrim. Many of them were great fighting men, for Kveldulf and his son picked out the very strongest to join them and trained them up in their own spirit. Skallagrim took after his father not only in strength and stature but in temper and looks as well.

21. Plots against Thorolf

AT the same time as Thorolf was out raiding, King Harald was staying at Oslofjord, but in the autumn he went to the Uplands and from there north to Trondheim where he spent the winter with a large following. Sigtrygg and Hallvard were there with the King. They had heard what Thorolf had done to their farmstead on Hising Island and of the damage he'd caused to both life and property. They kept reminding the king of this, as well as the way Thorolf had robbed

1. *Skallagrim*: literally 'Bald Grim'.

Harald and his subjects and carried war into the realm itself. The brothers asked the King's permission to take their usual band of followers and attack Thorolf at his own home. This was how the King replied.

'Maybe you think you've good reason to kill Thorolf,' he said, 'but as I see it you're short of the luck you'd need for that job. You may think yourselves brave and capable men but you're no match for him.'

The brothers said that could easily be put to the test if the King would give them leave to do so. They added that they had often taken great risks with less cause for revenge and had always won.

In the spring, when people were getting ready for their travels, Hallvard and his brother came to talk about this again with the King, who now said he would give them permission to take Thorolf's life. 'I've no doubt that you'll bring back his head along with other valuables,' said the King, 'though there are people who say that while it may be plain sailing all the way north, you'll be needing your oars on the way back.'

As fast as they could the brothers equipped two ships and a hundred and eighty men. As soon as they were ready they put out into a north-easterly wind, which meant that as they sailed north along the coast the wind was against them.

22. The King kills Thorolf

WHILE Hallvard and his brother were pushing north, King Harald was in residence at Lade. No sooner had they left than he made rapid preparations, boarded his fleet and rowed up the fjord through Skarnasound, then along Beitstadsfjord and over to Namdalseid. There he left the ships and marched north across the isthmus to Namdalen, where he took some longships belonging to the farmers there and boarded them with his forces. He had his personal guard with him and about three hundred men in five or six ships, all of them large ones.

They ran into strong headwinds but kept rowing night and day as hard as they could, for it was light enough to travel by night. They reached Sandness in the evening just after sunset and saw a big longship there with the awnings up, floating off-shore, which they recognized as Thorolf's. He'd had it fitted out and was planning to sail abroad, and the farewell feast had already been prepared. The King told his men to disembark all together and had his standard carried ashore. It was a short walk up to the farm, and as Thorolf's watchmen were sitting inside drinking and had not returned to their posts there was nobody outside the hall. All the other men were inside drinking.

The King had the house surrounded, then his men shouted their war-cry and the signal for attack was blown on the King's trumpet. When Thorolf and his men heard it they ran for their weapons, for every man had his full set of arms hanging over his seat. The King had someone shout into the house that women, children, old people, slaves and bondsmen could go outside. At that the housewife Sigrid walked out, along with the women of the house and all the others allowed to leave. Then Sigrid asked if the sons of Berle-Kari were there, and they both came up to ask what she wanted of them.

'Take me to the King,' she said, and so they did. When she came before him, she asked, 'Is there any point in trying to reconcile you and Thorolf, sir?'

'If Thorolf surrenders and gives himself up to my mercy he'll lose neither life nor limb,' said the King, 'but his men must be punished according to their deserts.'

Then Olvir Hnufa went up to the house and had Thorolf called to speak with him, telling him the terms offered by the King.

'I'm not having any terms dictated to me by the King,' said Thorolf. 'Ask him to let us outside and then we'll have to see how things go.'

Olvir went back to the King and told him what Thorolf had asked for. 'Set fire to the house,' said the King. 'I've no intention of fighting these men and losing my own. I know what kind of slaughter there'd be if we fought him out here. He'll be hard enough to beat inside, even though he has fewer men than we have.'

So they set fire to the house, and it was soon ablaze as the wood was tarred and dry and all of the roofing had been done with bark. Thorolf told his men to break through the partition wall separating the hall from the vestibule, and that was soon done. Once they were able to reach the beams, as many as possible got hold of one of them and kept ramming at one of the corners so hard that the joints gave way and the walls came apart, giving the men plenty of room to get outside. Thorolf was the first out, then Thorgils Gjallandi, then the rest one after another. Fighting broke out at once and for a time Thorolf and his men used the house to shield their backs, but as it blazed up the fire started threatening them and soon many had been killed. Thorolf ran forward towards the King's banner striking out to left and right. It was then that Thorgils Gjallandi was killed. Thorolf came right up to the thick wall of shields and ran the standard-bearer through with his sword.

'I'm just three paces short,' Thorolf said.

He had been pierced with spears and swords, but it was the King who gave him his death-wound and Thorolf dropped down dead at his feet. Then the King called out to his men to stop the killing and they did as they were ordered. The King told them to go back down to the ships, and then spoke to Olvir and his brother, Eyvind Lambi: 'Take your kinsman Thorolf,' he said, 'prepare his body decently for burial and do the same for the others killed here, then bury them. See to it that the wounds are dressed of those who might live. I'll have no looting: everything here is mine.'

After that the King went down to the ships along with most of his troops, and as soon as they were aboard they started dressing their wounds. The King walked up and down the ship looking at the wounds on his men and saw somebody bandaging one which was large but superficial. 'That couldn't have been inflicted by Thorolf,' the King said, 'his weapons had a different kind of bite to them. I can't see many of the wounds he gave being worth dressing. It's a great loss, losing a man like him.'

As soon as morning came the King had the sails hoisted and they made south with all speed. Later in the day the King and his men noticed a good many rowing skiffs in every sound. These were the forces intending to join Thorolf, whose spies had been at work as far south as Namdalen and all over the islands. They had learned that Hallvard and his brother had come from the south with a large number of men to attack Thorolf. However, Hallvard and his men had faced constant headwinds and had been weatherbound in several harbours. But Thorolf's spies, having found out about this, sent word inland, which is why all these troops were assembling.

The King had a fast voyage to Namdalen, and left his ships there. He travelled overland to Trondheim and took over the ships he had left behind, then sailed them over to Lade. The news of what had happened soon spread to Hallvard and his men, who were still lying weatherbound. They made their way back to the King and people thought their expedition a great joke.

Olvir Hnufa and his brother Eyvind Lambi stayed on at Sandness for a while. They had the dead laid out for burial, prepared Thorolf's body according to the custom of those days for the treatment of the bodies of noble men, and raised memorial stones over him. They had the wounded men seen to and helped Sigrid get things organized on the farm. Most of the property was still intact apart from what had been burnt in the fire, such as furnishings, tableware and clothing.

As soon as the brothers were ready they set off south to King Harald, who was then at Trondheim. They stayed with him for a while but they were taciturn and spoke very little to people.

One day the brothers went to see the King, and Olvir said, 'Sir, my brother and I would like you to give us leave to go home to our farms. After what's happened we've no inclination to sit drinking with men who used their weapons on our kinsman Thorolf.'

The King looked at him and his reply was very curt. 'I'm not going to grant you this leave,' he said; 'you'll stay here with me.'

The brothers turned about and went to their seats. Next day, when the King was in his conference room, he had Olvir and his brother called in to him. 'I want you to know what I've decided about your request for leave to go back home,' he said. 'You've been with me quite a while now and conducted yourselves admirably. You've always given me good service and pleased me in every way, so now I want you, Eyvind, to go north to Halogaland, and I'd like you to marry Sigrid of Sandness, Thorolf's widow. I'm going to let you have all the money that used to belong to Thorolf, and as long as you take care you'll have my friendship. But I don't wish to lose an artist of the quality of Olvir, so he's to stay with me.'

The brothers thanked the King for the honour he was showing them and accepted his offer gladly. Eyvind got himself ready for the voyage and sailed in a fine ship, as befitted his rank. The King gave him tokens of possession for everything he was to have. Eyvind's voyage went well and when he reached Sandness on Alsten Island Sigrid gave him and his crew a friendly welcome. Then he produced the tokens from the King and made a proposal of marriage, saying that it was the King's wish that she should be his wife. Sigrid realized that as things stood she had no choice and must let the King have his way, so it ended up with Eyvind marrying her and taking over the farm at Sandness along with everything else Thorolf had owned. Eyvind was a fine man and these were his children by Sigrid: Finn the Squint-Eyed, father of Eyvind the Plagiarist, and Geirlaug who married Sighvat the Red. Finn the Squint-Eyed married Gunnhild, Earl Hakon's daughter, whose mother was Ingibjorg, daughter of King Harald Fine-Hair. For the rest of their lives Eyvind Lambi and the King remained on friendly terms.

23. Ketil Trout

THERE was a man called Ketil Trout, son of Thorkel, Earl of Namdalen and of Hrafnhild, daughter of Ketil Trout of Hrafnista. Ketil was a fine, well-born man and had been a close friend of Thorolf Kveldulfsson, one of his near relations. Ketil had joined the force that mustered, as we have said, in Halogaland for the purpose of helping Thorolf.

When King Harald travelled back south and people realized that Thorolf had been killed, the force disbanded. Ketil Trout had sixty men and made his way over to Torg Island with them, where the Hildiridarsons were staying with only a few men. As soon as Ketil got to the farmstead he made an attack on them and killed the Hildiridarsons and most of their men, after which Ketil and his followers seized everything they could lay their hands on. Then Ketil took the two largest cargo-boats there and loaded them with all the goods the ships could carry, along with his wife, his children, and everyone who had taken part in the attack. Ketil Trout's blood-brother, Baug, a rich man of good family, was in charge of one of Ketil's ships.

When they were ready to leave and the wind was favourable, they put out to sea. Only a few years before, Ingolf and Hjorleif had sailed off to settle in Iceland and their voyage was on everybody's lips. Reports of the quality of the new land were very favourable. Ketil sailed westward out into the open sea in search of Iceland. At last they sighted land and found that they had approached it from the south, but as there was a gale blowing, heavy surf off the coast and no harbour, they sailed west beyond the sandy beaches. When the storm eased and the surf was less fierce they came to a large estuary. They sailed up into it, putting their ships in by the eastern bank. Nowadays this is known as the Thjors River, but it was deeper then and flowed through a narrower channel than it does now. They unloaded the ships and began exploring the land to the east of the river, taking their livestock with them. Ketil spent the first winter west of the Outer Rang River, then in the spring he explored the land to the east and took possession of the region between Thjors River and Markar River, from the mountains right down to the sea, making his home at Hof near the Eastern Rang River. So they passed their first winter, and in spring Ketil's wife Ingunn gave birth to a boy who was given the name Hrafn. After they dismantled the house there, the place got the name of Hrafnstead.

Ketil gave Baug land in Fljotshlid from the Markar River down to the river west of Breidabolstead. Baug made his home at Hlidarend and many people in that district are descended from him. Ketil also gave land to his crew, or sold them land at low prices, and these men too are listed as settlers.

Ketil had a son called Storolf. He owned Hval and Storolfsvoll, and his son was Orm the Strong. Ketil's second son, Herjolf, got land to the west of Baug's own settlement down as far as Hvals Brook. He farmed at Brekkur and his son was Sumarlidi, father of the poet Veturlidi. Ketil had a third son, Helgi, who lived at Vellir and owned land from the Rang River down to the settlement of his brothers. Ketil's fourth son was Vestar, and he owned land east of the Rang River as far as the Thver River, including the lower part of Storolfsvoll. He married Moeid, daughter of Hildir of Hildis Isle, and their daughter, Asny, married Ofeig Grettir. Vestar lived at Moeidarhvoll. Ketil's fifth son, Hrafn, was Iceland's first Lawspeaker, and he farmed at Hof after his father. Hrafn's daughter Thorlaug married Jorund the Priest, and their son was Valgard of Hof. Hrafn was the greatest of Ketil's sons.

24. Kveldulf mourns the death of Thorolf

WHEN Kveldulf heard of his son Thorolf's death it grieved him so deeply that he took to his bed, overcome by sorrow and old age. Skallagrim kept going to him, telling him to keep his spirits up. He said that anything was preferable to making a fool of oneself by lying in bed like an invalid. 'Better for us,' he said, 'to seek our revenge for Thorolf's killing. It may be we'll get our chance with some of those who had a hand in it, but even if that fails there are still others we can reach whose deaths won't please the King.'

Then Kveldulf spoke a verse:

> Now comes word from the northern isle,
> Norns are cruel, too soon
> Odin chose to throw down
> Thorolf and end his day.
> Weary am I and age-worn,
> War-wrestling is not for me.
> Slow is revenge, though sharp the killer's mind,
> Stay my arm, cradling my vengeance.

That summer King Harald travelled to the Uplands. In the autumn he went west to Valdres and from there all the way to Vors. Olvir Hnufa accompanied the King and kept asking him if he was going to pay compensation to Kveldulf and Skallagrim for Thorolf's killing, or do something to satisfy their honour. The King didn't give a blunt refusal, but wanted Kveldulf and Skallagrim to come and see him. So Olvir set off north to Fjord Province, travelling without delay to their house. It was evening when he came and they were glad to see him. He stayed for a while and Kveldulf questioned him on every detail of the events at Sandness when Thorolf was killed. In particular he wanted to know what Thorolf had done to his credit before his death, which men had used their weapons on him, where his worst wounds were, and the circumstances in which he died. Olvir answered all his questions, adding that King Harald gave Thorolf a wound severe enough to kill him and that Thorolf had then fallen face down at the King's feet.

'You've spoken well,' said Kveldulf. 'Old men used to say that anyone who fell face down would be avenged, and that retribution would come as close to the killer as the victim's fall was close to him. But it doesn't seem likely that we'll have enough luck for that.'

Olvir told father and son he hoped they would go and ask the King for compensation, since that would add greatly to their honour, and urged them at some length to take the risk. Kveldulf said he was far too old for travel. 'I'll stay at home,' he said.

'Will you go, Grim?' asked Olvir.

'I can't see that I've any business there,' answered Grim. 'The King won't find me particularly eloquent. I don't imagine myself spending much time on requests for compensation.'

Olvir said he didn't see much need for that. 'We'll do all the talking for you that we can,' he said. And since Olvir pressed the matter, Grim promised to go as soon as he felt the time was ripe. He and Olvir then agreed on when he should pay a call on King Harald and after that Olvir went on his way, back to the King.

25. Skallagrim sees the King

SKALLAGRIM got ready for the journey we've been speaking of and picked out from his household and neighbours all the strongest and most stout-hearted men he could find. Ani, a wealthy farmer, was one of them and Grani another, then there was Grimolf and his brother Grim, members of Skallagrim's household. Next were two brothers, Thorbjorn Krum and Thord Beigaldi, who had been a real coal-eating layabout.

The brothers were known as the Thorarnasons and their mother, who lived not far from Skallagrim, was a witch. The other men were Thorir Troll, his brother Thorgeir Land-Long, Odd the Lone-Dweller, and Gris the Freedman. Altogether there were twelve of them in the party, all the hardest of men, with a touch of the uncanny about a number of them. They made their way south along the coast in a rowing-boat that belonged to Skallagrim and put in at the Ostrarfjords. From there they travelled overland up to Vors till they reached a lake there which they had to cross, so they got a convenient skiff and rowed over. The place where they landed was near to the farm at which the King happened to be holding a feast.

Skallagrim and his men got there shortly after the King had settled down to eat. They had a talk with some men inside the yard and asked what was going on there. When people told them, Skallagrim asked someone to call Olvir Hnufa outside to talk with him. The man went into the hall across to Olvir. 'There are some men outside,' he said, 'twelve of them, that's if you could call them men for they're built and shaped more like trolls than human beings.' Olvir got up at once and went outside, for he'd no doubt about who'd come. He gave his kinsman Skallagrim a warm welcome and asked him to come with him into the hall.

Grim said to his companions, 'The custom here will be for people approaching the King to go unarmed; so let six of us go in, but the other six had better wait outside and keep an eye on our weapons.' Then they went inside. Olvir stood before the King with Skallagrim behind him and began to speak:

'Grim Kveldufsson has just come in, sir,' he said, 'and we'd be grateful if you'd see fit to make his journey worth while, as we're sure you will. You show great honour to plenty of people who are much inferior to him and rarely come anywhere near him in ability. You could do it, sir, and, if it makes any difference, it would certainly please me very much if you would.'

Olvir spoke well and at length, being an eloquent man, and he had plenty of friends to help put his case. The King looked around and behind Olvir he saw someone standing a head taller than all the others, completely bald.

'Is that Skallagrim,' asked the King, 'that big man there?'

Skallagrim said the King had guessed right.

'What I'd like,' said the King, 'if you want compensation for Thorolf, is for you to become one of my men, join my household and serve me. Maybe I'll come to like the way you serve me so much that I'll give you compensation for your brother or honour you in some way, but if I make you as great a man as I made him you'll have to watch your step better than he did.'

'Everyone knows how much greater Thorolf was than me in every way,' replied Skallagrim, 'but serving you didn't bring him much luck, sir, so I'm not going to follow him in that. I won't be your man and my reason is this: I know I haven't the luck to serve you as you deserve, or as I'd wish to. I don't think I'm quite in Thorolf's class.'

The King said nothing but his face flushed a deep red. Right away Olvir turned and asked Skallagrim to come outside, so Skallagrim's men went out and took up their weapons. Olvir told them to get away as fast as they could, then he and a number of others went down to the lake to see them off. Before they parted, Olvir spoke to Skallagrim.

'Your visit to the King hasn't turned out the way I'd hoped, kinsman,' he said. 'It was I who persuaded you to come here and now I have to ask you to get back home as fast as you can, and don't ever try to see Harald again unless the two of you can come to better terms than you're on now. Keep an eye open for the King and his men.'

So Skallagrim's party rowed off across the lake, while Olvir and his men went over to where the boats lay beached and hacked at them so that they were unseaworthy. They'd seen a great crowd of men coming down from the King's farm, all of them fully armed and running fast, sent by King Harald to kill Skallagrim.

The King said nothing till Skallagrim and his men had left the hall, but then he spoke.

'I can see this big bald fellow has a lot of hatred in him,' said the King, 'and if we give him the chance he'll be the death of some men we wouldn't want to lose. Believe me, if this bald-pate thinks he's got a score to settle he'll not spare anyone he can get at, so be after him now and kill him.'

They went down to the lake but couldn't find a seaworthy boat, so they went back to tell King Harald what had happened, and how Skallagrim must have already crossed the lake. Skallagrim and his men made their way home, and there Skallagrim told his father all about their trip. It pleased Kveldulf very much that Skallagrim had not gone to Harald with the idea of putting himself under the King's thumb, but he added that there would be more they'd have to suffer from the King, without any redress. Kveldulf and Skallagrim talked often about their plans, and were in complete agreement that they could no more remain in Norway than any other of the King's enemies. They decided it would be best to emigrate and that Iceland was an attractive place to go, for people had spoken highly of the quality of its land. Their good friend Ingolf Arnarson and his companions had settled and made their homes in Iceland, and people could get land there for nothing and choose their own homesteads. So Kveldulf and Skallagrim made up their minds to give up their Norwegian estates and leave the country.

Thorir Hroaldson had been fostered as a child by Kveldulf and was much the same age as Skallagrim. They were blood-brothers and very attached to one another. By this time Thorir was one of the King's land-holders, but it made no difference to his friendship for Skallagrim.

Kveldulf and his son got their ships ready early in the spring. They owned a fine big fleet and fitted out two large cargo-ships, each with thirty able-bodied men aboard as well as women and children. They took with them all the property they could, but nobody dared buy their land for fear of the King's power. As soon as they were ready they put out and sailed across to the Sulen Islands. There are a good many large islands in this group, with heavily indented coastlines, and it's said that few people know all of the anchorage there.

26. Harald and the sons of Guttorm

GUTTORM, the son of Sigurd Hart, was Harald's uncle and foster-father. He had acted as regent when the King came to the throne as a child. Guttorm had been leader of the King's army during Harald's rise to power, and had taken part in every battle which led to the conquest of Norway. After Harald had made himself sole ruler of the land and settled down in peace, he gave his uncle Guttorm charge over Vestfold, East-Agder and Ringerike, as well as all the land that had belonged to the King's father, Halfdan the Black.

Guttorm had two sons and two daughters, the sons called Sigurd and Ragnar, and the daughters Ragnhild and Aslaug. Then Guttorm fell ill, and when his end drew near he sent messengers to King Harald asking him to take over his authority and look after his children. Shortly after that Guttorm died. The King was staying at Trondheim at the time, and when he heard the news, he had Hallvard the Hardsailing and his brother Sigurd called before him, and ordered them to go on a mission east to Oslofjord. The brothers prepared to travel in style, with a company of hand-picked men and the finest ship they could get, the one that had belonged to Thorolf Kveldulfsson and had been taken from Thorgils Gjallandi. When they were ready to sail, the King explained what was to be done, that they should travel east to Tonsberg where Guttorm had been living. At that time there used to be a big market there.

'Go and bring back Guttorm's sons,' said the King, 'but leave his daughters to be brought up there till I can marry them off. I'll find people to take over from Guttorm and arrange fosterage for the girls.'

The brothers sailed off when they were ready and had a good passage. They got to Oslofjord in the spring and made their way east to Tonsberg where they told people why they'd come. Hallvard and his brother took charge of the sons of Guttorm and much of value, and when everything was done they set off back again. This time they didn't get such good winds, and there's little to tell about their progress until they began to sail north across Sognfjord with better winds, fair weather, and in high spirits.

27. Kveldulf and Skallagrim take revenge

ALL that summer Kveldulf and Skallagrim kept a close watch on the main coastal sea route. Skallagrim was an unusually sharp-sighted man and it was he who spotted Hallvard under way and recognized the ship, having seen it before when Thorgils was master of it. Skallagrim kept a sharp eye on their movements and noted where they put in for the night. Then he went back to the others and told Kveldulf what he'd seen, the ship Hallvard and his brother had taken from Thorgils, once Thorolf's property, with men aboard and well worth the taking. So they got themselves and their two boats ready with twenty men aboard each. Kveldulf commanded one of them and Skallagrim the other. They rowed out looking for the ship, and when they sighted it they made for land. Hallvard and his men had set up the awnings and gone to sleep. When Kveldulf and his men came up, the watchmen sitting by the gangway jumped to their feet and shouted a warning to the men aboard that they were being attacked. Hallvard and his men grabbed their weapons but by this time Kveldulf had reached the stern gangway and Skallagrim the one at the bow. Kveldulf was carrying a halberd.

When he was aboard, Kveldulf told his men to make their way along the gunwale and cut through the pegs holding the awnings. Then he stalked like a madman back to the forecastle, and it's said that he was in a state of frenzy, as were most of his companions. They cut down every man in their path, wherever Kveldulf went on the ship. Skallagrim did the same. Neither father nor son would let up until the decks had been cleared of the enemy. When Kveldulf reached the forecastle he raised the halberd and hewed at Hallvard, slicing through both helmet and head and burying the weapon right up to the shaft. Then he gave it a hard tug towards himself, lifted Hallvard into the air and tossed him overboard. Skallagrim cleared the bow of the ship and killed Sigtrygg. Many of the crew jumped overboard, but Skallagrim's men launched their boat, rowed after them, and killed everyone in the water. Altogether, more than fifty men died there with Hallvard, and Skallagrim seized their ship and everything in it. They took captive two or three of the men who seemed least important and spared their lives in order to get reports from them, asking about the people who'd been aboard, and the purpose of their expedition. When they learned about this they started searching among the dead and realized that there must have been even more who'd jumped into the sea before they died than those who'd been killed in the ship. The sons of Guttorm had jumped overboard and been drowned. One of them had been twelve years old, the other ten, both lads of great promise.

After that Skallagrim set free the men he had spared. He said they should go to King Harald and tell him precisely what had happened and who had been responsible. 'Take this verse to the King,' he said:

> Complete is the valiant man's
> Vengeance on the King:
> Wolves and eagles walk
> Wading through his kin;
> Hacked to bits, Hallvard
> Was heaved into the waves;
> Spiteful, at Sigtrygg's wounds
> Snatches the grey eagle.

Then Skallagrim and his men moved the ship and its contents out to their own, and switched cargoes. They loaded their newly-won ship, clearing out the smaller one of their own, which they filled with stones, then holed and scuttled. After that as soon as they had a favourable wind they sailed out into the open sea.

What people say about shape-changers or those who go into berserk fits is this: that as long as they're in the frenzy they're so strong that nothing is too much for them, but as soon as they're out of it they become much weaker than normal. That's how it was with Kveldulf; as soon as the frenzy left him he felt worn out by the battle he'd been fighting, and grew so weak as a result of it all that he had to take to his bed.

So the good wind carried them out to the open sea, with Kveldulf in charge of the ship they had taken from Hallvard. The wind stayed in their favour and they sailed close together so that each of them always knew where the other was. But the further they went, the sicker grew Kveldulf, and when he drew close to death he called his crew together and told them he thought it likely that their ways would soon part.

'I've never been one for sickness,' he said, 'and if things go as I think they most likely will and I die, make me a coffin and throw me overboard. If I'm never to get to Iceland and take land there, things will be very different from the way I'd hoped they'd be. Greet my son Skallagrim for me when you see him and tell him that if, however unlikely it may seem, I should get to Iceland before him, he's to build his homestead close to the place where I come to land.'

Not long after that Kveldulf died and his crew did as he'd ordered, laid him in a coffin and threw it overboard. Aboard Kveldulf's ship there was a wealthy man of good family called Grim. He was the son of Thorir, Ketil Keel-Farer's son and an old friend of Kveldulf and Skallagrim, having taken part in expeditions both with them and with Thorolf, which is why the King hated him. He took charge of the ship after Kveldulf's death.

They made landfall to the south of Iceland and continued to sail west along the coast as they'd heard that Ingolf had made his home there. When they rounded Reykjaness they saw the bay open up and sailed in with both ships. Then a hard gale started to blow, with heavy rain and mist so that the ships drifted apart. Grim Thorisson sailed up to Borgarfjord beyond all the skerries and lay there at anchor till the wind eased and the weather improved. They waited for high tide, then moved the ship into an estuary there, called Gufa River nowadays, hauled it up-stream as far as they could, and unloaded the cargo, preparing to settle in for their first winter there. They began to explore the land along the coast in both directions, and before they'd gone very far they saw where Kveldulf's coffin had been washed ashore into a creek. They carried it over to a near-by headland, set it down and covered it with stones.

28. Skallagrim's land-claim

SKALLAGRIM put in near a big headland jutting out into the sea and only linked to the mainland by a narrow neck of land. They unloaded the cargo there and called it Knarrarness.[1] Afterwards Skallagrim set out to explore and could see that there were great marshes and woods there, with plenty of land between the mountains and the sea, as well as ample seal-hunting and fishing. Exploring the land southwards to the sea they found a vast fjord. They walked inland to the head of the fjord and nothing stopped their progress until, to their great delight, they found their companions, Grim Thorisson the Halogalander and his crew. Grim's men told Skallagrim that Kveldulf had landed already and that they had buried him. They took Skallagrim to the place, and it seemed to him that close by was an ideal spot for a farmstead. Grim the Halogalander went back with his men and each party settled down for the winter at the place where they'd landed.

After that Skallagrim took possession of everything between the mountains and the sea, all of Myrar to the west as far as Selalon, north up to Borgahrun and south to Hafnarfells, all the land bounded by the rivers right down to the sea.

In the spring he moved his ship south to the fjord and into

1. *Knarrarness*: literally 'Cargo-boat Ness'.

the creek closest to where Kveldulf had come ashore. There he built his farm and called it Borg, and the fjord he called Borgarfjord, but the same name was given by people to the district above the fjord. To Grim the Halogalander he gave land on the south side of Borgarfjord and his farm was called Hvanneyri. Not far from there where a small creek cuts into the coast, they saw a good many ducks, so they called the place Andakil[1] and the river that flows into the sea there they called the Andakils River. Grim's land-claim stretched between that river and the one called the Grims River.

In the spring, when Skallagrim had his livestock driven north along the coast, they came to a small headland where people caught some swans, so they called it Alftaness.[2]

Skallagrim gave land to his crew. Ani got land between Lang River and Hafs Brook and made his home at Anabrekka. He was the father of Onund Sjoni. Grimolf's first farm was at Grimolfsstead, and Grimolfsfit and Grimolfs Brook are named after him. He had a son called Grim who made his home south of the fjord, and his son in turn was Grimar of Grimarsstead, the one who was involved in the quarrel between Thorstein and Tongue-Odd. Grani settled at Granastead on Digraness. And to Thorbjorn Krum Skallagrim gave land along Gufa River, as he did to Thord Beigaldi too. Krum settled at Krumshills and Thord at Beigaldi. To Thorir Thurs Skallagrim gave land above Einkunnir and as far west as Lang River. Thorir Thurs made his home at Thursstead and his daughter was Thordis Stang who lived at Stangarholt afterwards. Thorgeir made his home at Jardlangsstead.

Skallagrim explored the whole district. First he went up into Borgarfjord right to the head of the fjord, then followed the west bank of the river he called the Hvit River[3] because he and his men had never seen a glacial river before and thought it had a strange colour. They travelled up along Hvit River until they came to another river that flowed from the mountains lying to the north, so they called it the Nordur

---

1. *Andakil*: literally 'Duck Channel'.
2. *Alftaness*: literally 'Swans' Ness'.
3. *Hvit River*: literally 'White River'.

River. This they followed until they came to a much smaller river, which they crossed, still following the Nordur River. A little later they saw that the smaller river flowed through some ravines so they called it the Gljufur River.[1] After that they crossed the Nordur River, went back to the Hvit River and up along it, and shortly after found another river that flowed across into it so they called that one the Thver River.[2] They soon realized that every one of the rivers was teeming with fish. Then they made their way back home to Borg.

29. Skallagrim the farmer

SKALLAGRIM was a great man for hard work. He always had a good number of men working for him to get in all available provisions that might be useful for the household, for in the early stages they had little livestock, considering how many of them were there. What livestock they had were left to fend for themselves over winter in the woods.

Skallagrim was also a great shipwright. There was plenty of driftwood to be had west of Myrar, so he built and ran another farm at Alftaness and from there his men went out fishing and seal-hunting, and collecting the eggs of wild fowl, for there was plenty of everything. They also fetched in his driftwood. Whales often got stranded, and you could shoot anything you wanted, for none of the wildlife was used to man and just stood about quietly. His third farm he built by the sea in the west part of Myrar. From there it was even easier to get at the driftwood. He started sowing there and called the place Akrar.[3] There are some islands lying offshore where a whale had been washed up, so they called them the Hvals Isles.[4] Skallagrim also had his men go up the rivers looking for salmon, and settled Odd the Lone-Dweller at the

1. *Gljufur River*: literally 'Ravine River'.
2. *Thver River*: literally 'Cross River'.
3. *Akrar*: literally 'cornfields'.
4. *Hvals Isles*: literally 'Whale's Isles'.

Gljufur River to look after the salmon-fishing. Odd lived at Einbuabrekkur,[1] and Einbuaness[1] takes its name from him. Then Skallagrim gave a place at the Nordur River to a man called Sigmund, and he lived at Sigmundarstead, or Haugar as it's called nowadays. Sigmundarness takes its name after him. Later on Sigmund moved house to Munadarness, which was handier for the salmon-fishing.

As Skallagrim's livestock grew in number the animals started making for the mountains in the summer. He found a big difference in the livestock, which was much better and fatter when grazing up on the moorland, and above all in the sheep that wintered in the mountain valleys instead of being driven down. As a result, Skallagrim had a farm built near the mountains and ran it as a sheep farm. A man called Gris was in charge of it, and Grisartongue is named after him. So the wealth of Skallagrim rested on a good many foundations.

Some time after Skallagrim had come to Iceland a ship from abroad put in at Borgarfjord. It belonged to a man called Oleif Hjalti who brought with him his wife, his children and other kinsfolk, intending as he did to settle in Iceland. Oleif was a rich man of distinguished family, and had an exceptionally good mind. Skallagrim invited Oleif and all his people to live with him, and Oleif accepted, spending his first winter in Iceland with Skallagrim. In the spring, Skallagrim showed him a fine piece of land to the south of the Hvit River and between the Grims River and the Flokadale River. Oleif accepted the offer gladly and moved over there to make his home at the place called Varmabrook. Oleif was a great man. His sons were Ragi of Laugardale and Thorarin, Ragi's brother, who became Lawspeaker of Iceland after Hrafn Hængsson.[2] Thorarin lived at Varmabrook and married Thordis, the daughter of Oleif Feilan and sister to Thord Gellir.

1. *Einbuabrekkur, Einbuaness:* literally 'Lone-Dweller Slopes', 'Lone-Dweller Ness'.
2. *Hængsson:* literally 'Trout's son' – see Ketil Trout, chapter 23.

30. The arrival of Yngvar

KING Harald Fine-Hair took over all the estates that Kveldulf and Skallagrim had left behind in Norway, and anything else of theirs he could lay his hands on. He searched out all of the men who had had dealings with, or had known about, or had done anything to help Skallagrim and his father in any way at all before they had left Norway, and the King's hostility towards father and son grew so fierce that he directed his hatred towards all their kinsmen and in-laws and anyone whom he knew to have been close friends of theirs. Some of them had sentences imposed on them by the King, many had to run for their own safety, a number of them seeking it in Norway itself, while others left the country. One of these was Skallagrim's father-in-law, Yngvar, who decided to invest all he had in movable property. He got himself a ship, hired a crew and made ready to sail to Iceland as he'd heard Skallagrim had settled there and had more than enough good land. When they had everything ready and a fair wind, Yngvar put out to sea. After a good passage he made landfall to the south, sailed west round Reykjaness and into Borgarfjord, then up Lang River as far as the waterfall, where they unloaded the cargo.

As soon as Skallagrim heard of Yngvar's arrival he went to see him and invited him home to stay, with as many men as he liked. Yngvar accepted the offer, had the ship beached and went to Borg with a good number of men. He stayed with Skallagrim through the winter, and in the spring Skallagrim offered him a fine piece of land, his farm at Alftaness and all that lay east and west from Leiru Brook to Straumfjord. Yngvar moved out to the farm and took over, turning out an excellent farmer and a rich one. Then Skallagrim built another farm at Knarrarness which he owned for a good many years.

Skallagrim was a great blacksmith and used in winter to

smelt a lot of bog-iron. He had a smithy built close to the sea
but well away from Borg. It was at a place called Raufarness
where it seemed to him the woods were closer than at Borg,
but he couldn't find a boulder hard and smooth enough to
hammer the iron on, as there are no sizeable stones on the
beach there, only fine sand. One evening when everyone else
had gone to bed, Skallagrim went down to the shore and
launched an eight-oared ship that he had. He rowed it out to
Midfjord Isles and dropped anchor from the bows. Then he
stepped overboard, dived down into the sea and came up
with a boulder which he loaded on to the ship. After that he
climbed back aboard, rowed up to the mainland, carried the
boulder to his smithy, set it down outside the door, and used
it to hammer his iron. The boulder still lies there with a pile
of slag alongside it, and the hammer-marks can be seen on
the top. It has been polished by the waves and there's no other
stone there like it. Four men nowadays couldn't lift it.

Skallagrim was a hard worker in the smithy but his servants
complained about having to get up so early, so he made this
verse:

> Early must the ironsmith
> Arise to forge ore,
> Aided by air blasting
> From the blown-bellows;
> Hard the hammer blows
> Blazing on the hot iron
> I beat, while busily
> Work the wind-bellows

31. Egil's childhood

SKALLAGRIM and Bera had many children but all the older
ones died in infancy. Then they had a son. They sprinkled
him with water and called him Thorolf. He grew up tall and
handsome, so that everybody agreed that he was the very

image of his uncle Thorolf Kveldulfsson after whom he'd been named. He was a lot stronger than all the other boys of his age and by the time he reached manhood he was skilled in everything that talented men of the time chose to do. He had a cheerful personality, and from his early days he was so strong people thought him as capable as any full-grown man. He was popular with everyone and his father and mother loved him very much.

Skallagrim and his wife had two daughters, one called Sæunn and the other Thorunn, both very promising girls. And finally, Skallagrim and his wife had another son whom they sprinkled with water and called Egil. As he grew up it soon became obvious that he was going to be just as black-haired and ugly as his father. By the time he was three years old he was as big and strong as a boy of six or seven years. He soon grew to be a great talker, never at a loss for words, but when it came to playing with the other lads he was a hard one to handle.

That spring, Yngvar came over to Borg with an invitation for Skallagrim to visit him. Yngvar also invited his daughter Bera, her son Thorolf, and anyone else she and Skallagrim cared to bring with them. Skallagrim said he would go, so Yngvar went back home to get everything ready for the feast and brew the ale for it.

When the time came for the visit Skallagrim, Bera and Thorolf prepared themselves for the journey, taking a number of servants so that there were fifteen of them altogether. Egil went to his father and said he wanted to go too. 'The people there are as much my relations as they are Thorolf's,' he said.

'You're not going,' said Skallagrim. 'You don't know how to behave yourself when there's company gathered and a lot of drinking going on. You're difficult enough to cope with when you're sober.'

With that Skallagrim mounted his horse and rode off, leaving Egil behind in a very sour frame of mind. Egil set off from the farm and came across one of his father's cart-horses, so he mounted it and rode after Skallagrim and the others.

He didn't know the route and found it heavy going over the marsh, but he caught sight of them whenever they weren't hidden by the woods or ridges. It's said that he reached Alftaness in the evening when people had settled down to drink, and made his way into the hall. When Yngvar saw Egil he gave him a great welcome and asked why he'd come so late. Egil told him about having had words with Skallagrim, and then Yngvar gave Egil the seat next to himself and opposite Skallagrim and Thorolf. People were entertaining themselves by making up verses while they drank and Egil composed this one:

> Here I am at the hearth
> Of my host, Yngvar
> The Generous, who grants
> Gold to heroic men;
> Free-handed fosterer,
> You'll find no three-year
> Babe among bards
> More brilliant than me.

Yngvar thought highly of this and thanked him, and next day he gave Egil three shells and a duck's egg as a reward for his poem. So later that day after the drinking session, Egil made another poem, this time about the gift:

> The wily weapon-wielder
> Gave Egil the word-spinner
> Three aye-silent sea-snails
> To settle the song-debt.
> He knew how to win me,
> This wave-seasoned warrior,
> With a river-duck's egg,
> The offer of Yngvar.

Egil got plenty of congratulations for his poetic talents, but nothing else worth telling happened on this visit and Egil went back home with Skallagrim.

32. The abduction of Thora

LIVING at Aurland in Sogn there was a great chieftain called Bjorn. When he died his son Brynjolf inherited everything that he had. Brynjolf's sons were called Bjorn and Thord, and at the time we're speaking of they were still young men.

Bjorn Brynjolfsson was a man of outstanding talents and a great seafarer. He divided his time between viking raids and trading voyages. One summer it happened that he was attending a great feast in Fjord Province. There he saw a very pretty girl to whom he took a great fancy, so he asked about her family background: people told him she was the sister of Chieftain Thorir Haraldsson and called Thora Lace-Cuff. Bjorn made a proposal and asked for Thora but Thorir turned him down, and that was how they parted. In the autumn Bjorn gathered some men and sailed with a full crew north to Fjord Province. He got to Thorir's place but Thorir wasn't at home. Bjorn carried Thora off and took her back to Aurland where they spent the winter. He wanted to marry her, but Brynjolf didn't like what Bjorn had done, for he and Thorir were old friends, and he considered Bjorn's conduct outrageous. 'Not only won't I have you marrying Thora against her brother's wishes,' he said, 'it's my intention to look after her as if she were my own daughter and your sister.' And it didn't matter whether or not Bjorn liked it, things had to be done the way Brynjolf wanted, for he was very much the master in his own house.

Brynjolf sent messengers to Thorir offering him both settlement and compensation for Bjorn's escapade; and Thorir asked for the return of Thora, otherwise there was not going to be any settlement. But however much Brynjolf urged him Bjorn would not let her go, and that is how things stood throughout winter.

One day in spring Brynjolf and Bjorn had a talk about

81

what should be done. Brynjolf asked his son what he had in mind and Bjorn said that most likely he'd go abroad. 'The best thing you could do for me would be to give me a ship and crew,' he said, 'so I could go off raiding.'

'That's out of the question,' said Brynjolf. 'I'm not giving you a ship and fighting men just for you to go off and attack the very last people I'd want you to. You've caused enough trouble already. I'm going to get you a merchant-ship and a cargo and then you can go south to Dublin. That's the place everyone's talking about. I'll make sure you've good men with you.'

Bjorn said there was nothing for him to do but accept what Brynjolf wanted. So Brynjolf had a good trading-ship fitted out and hired a crew. Bjorn got ready for the voyage but took his time over it.

When at last he was quite ready and had a favourable wind he boarded a boat along with a dozen men and rowed over to Aurland. They all walked up to the farmstead and into his mother's private room where she was sitting with Thora and a number of other women. Bjorn said that Thora was to come with him and led her off. His mother told her women to keep their counsel in the hall about what had happened, saying that Brynjolf would take a poor view of it if he found out, and there would be bad trouble between him and his son. Thora's clothes and things were all bundled together and Bjorn and his men took everything along with them. That night they went to their ship, hoisted sail and set off down Sognfjord out into the open sea.

The winds were bad and they were tossed and driven about in the waves for a long time, for they were determined to keep as far away from Norway as they could. Then one day when they were sailing up the east coast of Shetland before a strong gale, they damaged the ship as they tried to put in at Mousa. They carried the cargo ashore and into the broch there, then beached the ship and repaired the damage.

33. Bjorn goes to Iceland

JUST before winter a boat from Orkney put in at Shetland, and brought news that a longship from Norway had arrived in Orkney that autumn. Harald's agents had been aboard carrying the message to Earl Sigurd that the King wanted Bjorn dead, no matter where they laid hands on him. The same message had been sent to the Hebrides and even as far as Dublin.

Bjorn heard the news and also that he had been declared an outlaw in Norway. He had celebrated his marriage to Thora shortly after reaching Shetland and they spent the winter at Mousa in the broch. With the coming of spring and a calmer sea, Bjorn launched his ship and fitted it out as fast as possible. When he was ready and the wind was right, he put out to sea. They ran before a strong gale and were only a short while at sea, making landfall in the south of Iceland. The wind was blowing towards land but they were driven west of the land out to sea. Then the wind began to blow fair and they sailed up to the coast. Not one man on board had ever been to Iceland.

They sailed the length of a great fjord and were driven up to the west of it, but the only land they could make out was a harbourless coast and some reefs. They tried following the coast on a westward tack till they came to another fjord, and sailed in beyond the reefs and the breakers, putting in at a certain headland. There they saw an island, and in the deep channel between it and the headland they moored their ship. A creek ran in west of the headland and above it was a large hill shaped like a fort.[1] Bjorn boarded a boat along with some of his followers, but warned them not to say anything about their travels as it might lead to trouble. They rowed up to the

1. '*Shaped like a fort*': the Icelandic word is '*borg*', the name of Skallagrim's farm.

farm where there were men about, so they talked to them. First of all they asked what part of the country they'd come to. People told them it was called Borgarfjord, that the farm was called Borg and the farmer Skallagrim. Immediately Bjorn realized who it was and went to have a word with him. Skallagrim asked who they were and Bjorn introduced himself, mentioning the name of his father. Brynjolf was well known to Skallagrim, who then offered Bjorn all the help he needed, which he accepted gratefully.

Then Skallagrim asked if there was anyone else of importance aboard, and Bjorn told him that Thora Hroald's daughter was there, the sister of the Chieftain Thorir. Skallagrim was delighted to hear it and said that it was a duty and a privilege to offer the sister of his blood-brother Thorir all the hospitality she needed and he had the means to provide. He invited Bjorn and the girl to stay with him, along with the whole crew, and Bjorn accepted gladly. So they unloaded the ship and moved the cargo up to the home-meadow at Borg, where they pitched their tents. The ship was hauled over to the stream.

The place where Bjorn and his men camped is still known as Bjornartodur. Bjorn and his crew all went to stay with Skallagrim, who would never have less than sixty able-bodied men with him.

34. Thorolf goes abroad

IN the autumn when ships had begun to arrive from Norway, the rumour got around that Bjorn had eloped with Thora against her kinsmen's wishes, and as a result the King had made him an outlaw in Norway. When Skallagrim heard this he called Bjorn in for a talk and asked him about his marriage – whether or not he'd had the approval of his wife's family.

'I never expected to hear anything but the truth from the son of Brynjolf,' said Skallagrim.

'What I've told you is the literal truth, Grim,' Bjorn answered, 'and you can't blame me for telling you no more than you asked. Still, I have to admit now that your information is correct: I didn't ask for her brother's approval.'

'What do you mean, bringing her to me?' roared Skallagrim. 'It's sheer impudence! Didn't you know how close a friend of mine Thorir was?'

'I knew you were close friends and blood-brothers,' said Bjorn, 'but once I'd landed here I went to look for you because I knew it would be useless trying to avoid you. So now it's up to you to decide what's going to happen to me, though I'll hope for the best now that I've become one of your household.'

At this point Thorolf Skallagrimsson broke in, and spoke at some length. He asked his father not to hold it against Bjorn now that he'd taken him into his home. There were plenty of others who spoke up for Bjorn, so the outcome was that Grim calmed down and told Thorolf to have his way – 'You can look after Bjorn yourself,' he said, 'and treat him as generously as you like.'

35. Reconciliation

In the summer Thora gave birth to a girl, who was sprinkled with water and given the name Asgerd. Bera engaged a woman to look after the child.

Bjorn and all his crew spent the winter with Skallagrim, and Thorolf grew very attached to Bjorn, following him around everywhere. One day in spring Thorolf went to have a word with his father. He asked what he planned to do for Bjorn, his winter-guest, and what kind of help he meant to offer him. Skallagrim asked Thorolf if he had anything in mind.

'I think what Bjorn wants most of all is to go back to Norway, if only he could be safe there,' said Thorolf, 'so what

I suggest, father, is that you send messengers to Norway and offer a settlement on Bjorn's behalf. Thorir's bound to take notice of whatever you say.'

Thorolf argued away until Skallagrim had been talked into sending people to Norway that summer. They went to Thorir Hroaldsson with messages and tokens of goodwill, and tried to arrange a reconciliation between him and Bjorn. As soon as Brynjolf heard of this he set his mind wholly on getting a settlement for Bjorn, and eventually Thorir agreed to the settlement since, as matters stood, he saw that nothing he could do would trouble Bjorn. Brynjolf accepted the settlement on Bjorn's behalf and Skallagrim's messengers stayed over winter with Thorir, while Bjorn wintered with Skallagrim.

Next summer Skallagrim's messengers set out for home, arriving in the autumn to announce the news that Bjorn's reconciliation had been agreed to in Norway. Bjorn spent the third winter with Skallagrim, then in the spring he got ready to sail with the same crew that had come with him. When Bjorn was ready to leave, Bera told him she wanted her foster-daughter Asgerd to stay behind. Bjorn and his wife agreed, and the girl grew up with Skallagrim and Bera.

Thorolf Skallagrimsson decided to go with Bjorn and Skallagrim provided him with all he needed for the journey. He went abroad with Bjorn that summer, and after a good passage they put in at Sognfjord. Bjorn sailed up into the fjord to his father's home taking Thorolf with him, and Brynjolf welcomed them gladly. Then word was sent to Thorir Hroaldsson, and he and Brynjolf arranged a meeting. Bjorn came too, and there they confirmed their settlement. After that Thorir paid out Thora's share of the estate, then Thorir and Bjorn sealed their relationship with friendly ties. Bjorn stayed at home in Aurland with Brynjolf and Thorolf stayed there too, enjoying high favours from them both.

36. Eirik Bloodaxe

KING Harald was usually in residence in Hordaland or Rogaland, at the great estates he owned at Utsten, Avaldsness, Fitjar, Aarstad, Lygra and Seim. However, he spent the winter we've just been speaking of in the north.

When Bjorn and Thorolf had wintered in Norway and spring had come, they got their ship ready, gathered together a crew, and then set off on a viking expedition to the Baltic. They came back in the autumn with a great deal of plunder. When they got home they heard that King Harald was in Rogaland and meant to stay there over winter.

By this time King Harald was getting very old, while most of his sons were grown men. His son Eirik, nicknamed Bloodaxe, was still quite young and was being fostered by the Chieftain Thorir Hroaldsson. Harald loved him best of all his sons and Thorir was on the friendliest of terms with the King.

When they returned, Bjorn and Thorolf went home to Aurland at first, but set off north to visit Chieftain Thorir in Fjord Province. They had a fast ship with twelve or thirteen oars a side and a crew of about thirty men. They had taken the ship that summer. It was richly painted above the sea-line and magnificently decorated. When they came to Thorir's place were given a great welcome, and there they stayed for a while, with the ship anchored not far from the farmstead, its awnings up.

One day when Thorolf and Bjorn went down to the ship they saw that Eirik, the King's son, was there. He kept stepping aboard the ship, then back ashore, and then he stood there gazing at it.

'The King's son seems to have taken a great fancy to the ship,' said Bjorn to Thorolf. 'Ask him to take it from you as a gift. It would help us a lot in dealing with the King if we had Eirik as our spokesman. I've heard it said that the King bears you a grudge because of your father.'

Thorolf said that was good advice, and so they walked down to the ship.

'You're taking a good close look at the ship, prince,' said Thorolf. 'How do you like it?'

'Very much,' he said, 'it's a beauty.'

'Then I'll give it you,' said Thorolf, 'if you'll take it.'

'I'll take it,' said Eirik. 'You won't think it much compensation if I pledge you my friendship, but that stands to rise in value if I live long.'

Thorolf said he thought the compensation worth more than the ship, and with that they parted. Afterwards Eirik was very cheerful in Thorolf's company.

Bjorn and Thorolf asked Thorir's opinion, whether or not it was true that the King bore Thorolf a grudge. Thorir couldn't deny that he had heard it said.

'Then what I'd like,' said Bjorn, 'is for you to go to the King and plead Thorolf's case for him. Thorolf and I must share the same destiny. That's how he treated me when we were in Iceland.'

So Thorir promised to go to the King, and asked them to find out whether Eirik was willing to come with him. Thorolf and Bjorn took the matter up with Eirik and he agreed to use his influence with his father.

After that Thorolf and Bjorn went on their way to Sogn, while Thorir and Eirik got the newly-given ship ready for sea and went off south to the King, finding him in Hordaland and getting a good welcome. They stayed there for a while, waiting for the right moment to approach the King, when he was in a cheerful mood. Then they took the matter up with him, saying that a man called Thorolf, son of Skallagrim, had come to Norway.

'What we're asking you to bear in mind, sir,' they said, 'is all that his kinsmen have done for you: don't hold against him what his father did to avenge his own brother.'

Thorir had plenty to say about this, but the King gave a

curt reply, that Kveldulf and his sons had been the cause of a great deal of trouble, and added that Thorolf probably had much the same disposition as his kinsmen. 'They're arrogant, every one of them,' he said. 'They've no sense of proportion and don't care who they're dealing with.'

Then Eirik put a word in, saying how friendly Thorolf had been to him and how he had given him a magnificent gift, the ship that they had with them. 'I've sworn him my lasting friendship,' he said, 'and it's not likely that many men will ever have my friendship if this man can't. Father, you must not let this happen to the first man who ever gave me a gift of such value.'

So eventually the King promised to leave Thorolf in peace. 'I don't want anything to do with him,' said the King, 'though you're welcome to make as close a friend as you like of him, or of any of his kinsmen. But it will go one way or the other: either they'll listen to you more carefully than they did to me, or you'll live to regret this request of yours, particularly if you let them stay with you for long.'

After that, Eirik Bloodaxe and Thorir went back to Fjord Province and sent a messenger to Thorir so that he would know how their mission to the King had turned out.

Thorolf and Bjorn stayed that winter with Brynjolf. They went out on viking expeditions together for a number of summers but spent the winter alternately with Brynjolf and Thorir.

37. Eirik marries Gunnhild

THEN Eirik Bloodaxe came to the throne and ruled over Hordaland and Fjord Province, gathering his retainers around him. One spring he made preparations for an expedition to Permia, taking every care to fit things out properly. Thorolf went with Eirik as his forecastleman and standard-bearer. Like his father, Thorolf was exceptionally big and strong.

Plenty happened on this voyage. Eirik fought a great battle in Permia on the River Dvina, and won the victory as poems about him tell. On this trip he married Gunnhild, daughter of Ozur Toti, and took her home with him. Gunnhild was the best-looking and shrewdest of women and a very clever sorceress. A close friendship grew up between her and Thorolf who was now spending every winter with Eirik and going on viking expeditions in summer.

The next thing to happen was that Thora, Bjorn's wife, fell sick and died. A little later Bjorn married his second wife, Alof, daughter of Erling the Wealthy of Oster Isle, and they had a daughter called Gunnhild.

There was a man called Thorgeir Thorn-Foot who farmed on Ask Island in Hordaland at a place called Ask. He had three sons, the first called Hadd, the second Berg-Onund and the third Atli the Short. Berg-Onund was exceptionally big and strong, a greedy man and hard to deal with. Atli the Short was a stockily built man, not very tall but physically powerful. Thorgeir was very wealthy and a great man for sacrifices and sorcery. Hadd used to go on viking expeditions and was seldom at home.

38. King Eirik's gift

ONE summer Thorolf Skallagrimsson got ready for a trading voyage. His plan, which he later completed, was to go to Iceland and see his father. Thorolf had been abroad for a long time, and had unlimited money to spend as well as a number of very valuable things. When he was ready to sail he went to see King Eirik, and as they parted the King handed him an axe which he said he wanted given to Skallagrim. The blade was huge and crescent-shaped, inlaid with gold, as the shaft was with silver; it was a really fine weapon.

As soon as he was ready Thorolf set out and had a fair passage. He put in at Borgarfjord and went at once to his father's house, where each was delighted to see the other. Later, Skallagrim went down to join Thorolf at the ship and had it hauled ashore, after which Thorolf went home to Borg with eleven men.

Then Thorolf gave Skallagrim the greetings of King Eirik and the axe the King had sent him. Skallagrim took the axe, held it up and looked at it for a while, but said nothing and hung it up beside his bed.

One autumn day at Borg, Skallagrim sent for a number of oxen to be slaughtered. He had two of them led up to a wall and tethered with their heads crossing. He took a great slab of stone, set it under their necks, then went up and hacked at the oxen with so hard a stroke of the axe, the King's Gift, that both their heads flew off. The axe struck the stone slab, breaking the steel edge and shattering the tempered part of the blade. Skallagrim looked at the edge but said nothing. Then he went into the hall, climbed onto a bench and stowed the axe on the rafters above the door, and there it lay over winter.

In the spring Thorolf made it known that he meant to go abroad that summer. Skallagrim tried to dissuade him and said it was a good thing to be safely back home. 'Your travels have earned you a great reputation,' he said, 'but there's a saying, "when travels are many, experiences are mixed". Take as much of the property here as you think you need to be a great man.'

Thorolf said that he wanted to make one more trip. 'I've necessary business to do,' he said. 'When I come back next time I'll settle down here. Your foster-daughter Asgerd must come abroad with me to visit her father. Before I left Norway he asked me to see to it.'

Skallagrim said that Thorolf must have his own way – 'but my heart tells me that if we part now we'll never meet again.'

At that, Thorolf went to his ship and got it ready. When everything was in order they took the ship over to Digraness and waited for a favourable wind. Asgerd went to the ship with Thorolf.

Before Thorolf left Borg, Skallagrim took down the axe,

the King's Gift, from the rafters above the door and carried
it outside. The shaft was black with soot and the blade had
gone rusty. Shallagrim looked at the edge of the axe, then
handed it to Thorolf and made this verse:

> Many flaws in the edge
> Of this fearsome fighter;
> It's blunt, this big warrior,
> Weak in the blade.
> Let's send the curved coward,
> The sooty shaft, back:
> No good reason to regale me
> With this royal gift.

39. Geir marries Thorunn

ONE summer while Thorolf was abroad and Skallagrim farming at Borg, it happened that a trading vessel from Norway
put in at Borgarfjord. In those days people used to berth their
ships at various places, in rivers, estuaries or creeks. The man
who owned the ship was called Ketil and had the nickname
Ketil Blund. He was a Norwegian, rich and from a good
family, and had his grown-up son Geir aboard with him.
Ketil hoped to find a farm for himself in Iceland. It was late
in the summer when he came.

Skallagrim knew a good deal about him and invited Ketil
and all his company to stay with him. Ketil accepted the offer
and spent the winter with Skallagrim. That winter Geir
Ketilsson asked for the hand of Skallagrim's daughter,
Thorunn. His proposal was accepted and he and Thorunn
were married.

In the spring Skallagrim recommended Ketil to take land
up above Oleif's land-claim along the Hvit River, between
the estuaries of the Flokadale River and the Reykjadale River,
including the whole tongue of land as far up as Raudsgill and
all Flokadale above the slopes.

Ketil farmed at Thrandarholt. Geir farmed at Geirstead, but he had another farm in Reykjadale, at Upper Reykir, and people called him Geir the Wealthy. His sons were Blund-Ketil and Thorgeir Blund, and a third son, Thorodd Hrisa-Blund, was the first man to farm at Hrisar.

40. Egil at the ball-game

SKALLAGRIM took great pleasure in trials of strength and competitive sports, and always enjoyed talking about them. Ball-games were a common sport in those days and there were plenty of strong men about, though none more powerful than Skallagrim. But he was beginning to grow old.

Grani of Granastead had a son called Thord, a very promising lad and devoted to Egil Skallagrimsson. Egil often took part in the wrestling. He was impetuous and quick tempered, so everyone took care that their sons knew when to give in to him.

Early in the winter a ball-game was arranged at Hvitarvellir. People came to it from all over the district, so it was well attended. A good many of Skallagrim's men went to the games, with Thord Granason principally in charge. Egil, who was six years old at the time, asked Thord to take him along. Thord let him come, and sat Egil behind him in the saddle.

When they came to the gathering the players were divided into groups. A good many youngsters were there and they were divided too, for their own separate games. Egil was to play against a boy called Grim, son of Hegg of Heggstead, ten or eleven years old and strong for his age. The game began and Egil proved to be the weaker, while Grim made the most of his strength. Then Egil got so angry that he lifted the bat and struck at Grim with it, but Grim took hold of him, hurled him to the ground and gave him some very rough treatment. He said that if Egil wouldn't behave himself, he'd do him some real damage. Egil scrambled back onto his feet and left the field with the youngsters jeering at him.

Egil went to look for Thord Granason and told him what had happened.

'I'll come with you,' said Thord. 'The two of us will pay him back.'

Thord gave Egil a thick-bladed axe he was carrying, common enough at that time, and they went to the field where the boys were playing. Grim had just caught the ball and was racing along with the other boys after him. Egil ran up to him and drove the axe into his head right through to the brain.

After that Egil and Thord went off and joined their own people. The men of Myrar and those on the other side both took up their weapons. Olaf Hjalti raced over to join the people of Borg, so they had the larger number of men, but it was a parting that led to strife between Oleif and Hegg. A battle was fought at Laxfit on Grims River. Seven men were killed, Hegg receiving a fatal wound and his brother Kvig losing his life.

When Egil came home, Skallagrim made it clear that he was far from pleased, but Bera said that Egil had the makings of a real viking and it was obvious that as soon as he was old enough he ought to be given fighting-ships. Egil made this verse:

> *My mother wants a price paid*
> *To purchase my proud-oared ship;*
> *Standing high in the stern*
> *I'll scour for plunder,*
> *The stout viking-steersman*
> *Of this shining vessel:*
> *Then home to harbour*
> *After hewing down a man or two*

When Egil was twelve he was bigger and stronger than most fully grown men, and there were few of them who could beat him at games. That winter, his twelfth, he played a great deal. Thord Granason was about twenty by then, and a powerful man.

Late in the winter it often happened that these two, Egil and Thord, had to compete against Skallagrim. On one occasion a ball-game was held at Sandvik, south of Borg, and Egil and Thord were playing Skallagrim. They found the game easier than he did, and were wearing him down. Then the evening came, and once the sun had set Egil and Thord found it much harder going. Skallagrim grew so powerful that he picked Thord up bodily and dashed him down so hard that every bone in his body was broken and he died on the spot. Then Skallagrim grabbed Egil.

Skallagrim had a slave-woman called Thorgerd Brak, who had fostered Egil when he was a child. She was a big woman, as strong as a man and a great sorceress.

'That's your own son you're going for, Skallagrim,' she said.

Skallagrim let go of Egil and made a grab for her, but she broke free and started to run for it with Skallagrim after her. When they got to the tip of Digraness she jumped down from the cliff and began swimming away. Skallagrim hurled a great piece of rock after her that caught her between the shoulder-blades, and neither she nor the rock ever came to the surface again. Nowadays the place is called Brakar Sound.

When they came home to Borg that night Egil was in a fury. Skallagrim and the rest of the household sat down at table but Egil didn't take his seat. He went across to the hall and up to the man who was in charge of the farm hands and managed Skallagrim's estate. This was a man Skallagrim particularly liked. Egil struck him dead and after that went to his seat. Skallagrim said nothing and that was the end of the matter, but for the rest of the winter father and son spoke not a single word to each other, for good or ill.

The following summer Thorolf came to Iceland, as we said earlier, and after spending the winter there he got his ship ready in the spring at Brakar Sound.

Just as Thorolf was ready to sail, Egil went to have a word with his father to ask for travelling expenses. 'I want to go abroad with Thorolf,' he said. Skallagrim asked whether Egil had talked things over with Thorolf, and Egil said that he hadn't. Skallagrim told him he must do that first. But when Egil raised the matter, Thorolf said it was out of the question.

'I'm not taking you abroad,' he said. 'If your father doesn't think he can control you in his own home, there's not much chance of my doing it overseas. People over there won't let you go on the way you do here.'

'In that case,' said Egil, 'maybe neither of us will be going.'

The weather that night was rough with a south-westerly gale blowing, and at high tide, under cover of darkness, Egil made his way to the ship and climbed aboard outside the awnings. He cut the anchor ropes on the seaward side, then ran down the gangway, pushed it into the sea, cut the ropes that held the ship on the landward side and let it float out into the fjord. When Thorolf and his men realized that the ship was adrift they ran to their boats, but the wind was too fierce for them to do anything about it. The ship drifted across to Andakil and ran aground on a beach. Egil went home to Borg.

When people realized the prank that Egil had played, most of them took a poor view of it. Egil answered that unless Thorolf agreed to take him there would be still more trouble and damage to come, but people stepped in and as things turned out, Thorolf let Egil sail with him that summer.

Thorolf had the axe that Skallagrim had handed over to him. When he got to the ship he threw the axe overboard into the deep sea, and it never came up again. Thorolf put to sea that summer and had a good crossing, making landfall at Hordaland, then going north directly to Sogn.

It so happened that the previous winter Brynjolf had died in his bed, and his sons had divided their inheritance, Thord getting Aurland, the estate their father had farmed. He became the King's retainer and one of his land-holders. Thord had a daughter called Rannveig whose sons were Thord and Helgi. This Thord was the father of Rannveig, the mother of Ingirid who married St Olaf. Helgi was the father of Brynjolf, the father of Serck of Sogn and Svein.

41. In Norway

BJORN got himself another fine, impressive farm, and did not become the King's retainer, which was why people called him Bjorn the Yeoman. He had grown to be a man of considerable wealth and power.

Thorolf wasted no time but went to Bjorn as soon as he landed, taking Bjorn's daughter Asgerd with him. It was a happy reunion. Asgerd was a fine-looking girl, intelligent, very talented, and a woman to be reckoned with.

Thorolf went to see King Eirik and when they met he gave the King greetings from Skallagrim, saying that he had been pleased to accept the King's gift. Then he showed the King a splendid longship-sail that he said was Skallagrim's gift to Eirik. King Eirik accepted the gift cheerfully and invited Thorolf to stay with him over winter. Thorolf thanked him for the offer, but added, 'First I must go back to see Thorir: I've some urgent business with him.'

So Thorolf went to Thorir as he had said he would and was given a hearty welcome. Thorir invited him to stay and Thorolf accepted the offer.

'But I've someone with me who must stay in the same place as myself,' he added. 'It's my brother. He's never been away from home and needs me to keep an eye on him.'

Thorir said Thorolf was welcome to bring him, and more if he wanted. 'As we see it,' he said, 'your brother will be a great asset to us if he's anything like you.'

So Thorolf went down to his ship and had it hauled ashore and seen to, then he and Egil joined Chieftain Thorir.

Thorir had a son called Arinbjorn who was a little older than Egil. Even at an early age Arinbjorn was an impressive looking man and a great athlete. Egil grew very attached to him and followed him everywhere, but didn't get on too well with his own brother.

42. Thorolf wins Asgerd

THOROLF Skallagrimsson made a marriage offer and asked
Thorir how he would react if he were to propose marriage to
Thorir's niece Asgerd. Thorir gave a favourable answer,
saying that he would support the proposal. Then Thorolf
travelled with a fine retinue north to Sogn. When he arrived
Bjorn gave him a friendly welcome and invited him to stay
as long as he liked. Thorolf soon brought up the reason for
his visit and asked for the hand of Bjorn's daughter. Bjorn
was in favour and created no obstacles, so they were betrothed
and the wedding date agreed for the autumn, with a feast to
be held at Bjorn's place. When Thorolf went back and gave
Thorir an account of what had happened, he was delighted
at the news of the marriage. So the time to go to the wedding
feast drew nearer for Thorolf and he began to invite people,
a great company of select men, with Thorir, Arinbjorn and
their followers at the head, along with other important
farmers. But just as Thorolf and his men were about to set
off at the appointed time, Egil took sick and had to stay behind. Thorolf and his men had a big, fully-manned longship,
and went on their way according to plan.

43. Bard's hospitality

THERE was a man called Olvir in Thorir's household, an
overseer who managed the estate, collected debts and also
acted as treasurer. Olvir was getting on in years but still very
active. It so happened that he had to travel some distance in
order to collect the rents outstanding since spring from
Thorir's tenants. His skiff was manned by twelve of Thorir's
men.

By now, Egil was feeling better so he got up. He found things rather dull at home with most people away, and had a word with Olvir, saying that he wanted to go along with him. As Olvir saw it, a good man wouldn't be in the way since there was room enough in the boat, so Egil joined the party. The weapons he took with him were a sword, spear and buckler, and as soon as everyone was ready, off they went. They ran into continuous storms and fierce contrary winds, but by rowing and tacking they made good progress.

As it turned out, they reached Atley Island in the late afternoon and put in at a place not far away from a large estate belonging to King Eirik. The man in charge was called Atley-Isle Bard, a meticulous and hardworking man of common origins, though the King and Gunnhild were very fond of him. Olvir and his men hauled their boat above the tide-mark and walked up to the farm. Outside they met Bard, told him their mission and asked if he would put them up for the night. Bard saw that they were soaked to the skin and took them to an out-house away from the main building, where there was a fire-place. There he had a big fire made for them to dry out their clothes.

When they had their clothes on again, Bard came back. 'I'll have the table laid for you here,' he said. 'I expect you're tired out after your ordeal and you'll be wanting to sleep.' This pleased Olvir very much indeed. Then the table was laid with food, bread and butter, and large bowls of sour curds. 'I'm sorry there's no ale here,' said Bard, 'and I can't give you the welcome I'd wish, but make the most of what there is.'

Olvir and his men were terribly thirsty and swilled down the sour curds. Then Bard had them served with sour whey and they drank that too. 'I'd be glad to give you something better to drink,' said Bard, 'if only I had it.' There was no shortage of straw in the house, and Bard told them to lie down and sleep on that.

44. Egil kills Bard

THE same evening, King Eirik and Gunnhild came to Atley Isle, and Bard had prepared a feast for the King, as sacrifices were to be held there to the Fates. Nothing but the best was provided, with plenty to drink in the main hall. The King asked where Bard was. 'I can't see him anywhere,' he said. Someone answered, 'He's outside looking after his guests.' 'What guests are they that occupy him more than to be here with us?' asked the King.

The man told him that some people from Chieftain Thorir's household had arrived, and the King said 'Go at once and tell them to come in here.' So they were told that the King wanted to see them. They came, and the King gave Olvir a friendly welcome, inviting him to sit on the high-seat opposite with his companions ranged below. They did as the King suggested and Egil sat next to Olvir. Then ale was served to them, and plenty of toasts were drunk with a full horn to each of them. As the evening wore on it happened that a number of Olvir's companions became quite incapable, some of them spewing right there in the hall, others managing to get outside the door. Bard came along and urged that more drink be given them. Then Egil took the horn that had been given to Olvir and drank it down. Bard made the remark that Egil must be very thirsty, poured him another horn-full and told him to drink it. Egil took the horn and made this verse:

> To this enemy of ogres
> You spoke of an ale-drought,
> While you stood at the sacrifice,
> You shifty grave-breaker;
> Your guests little guessed
> They'd be greeted with lies;
> Behold the truth-blaster,
> Black-hearted Bard.

Bard told him to drink up and stop making slanderous verses. Egil drank every toast that came his way, and Olvir's share too. Then Bard went to the Queen and said that there was a man who kept mocking them by claiming to be thirsty no matter how much he was given to drink. The Queen and Bard added poison to the drink and brought it into the hall, where Bard made a sign over it and passed it to the serving-girl. She carried it over to Egil and asked him to take a drink. Egil drew out his knife and stabbed the palm of his hand, then took the horn, carved runes on it and rubbed it with blood. After that he made this verse:

> *Carve runes on the horn,*
> *Rub them with red blood,*
> *With these words I bewitch*
> *The horn of the wild ox;*
> *Let's swallow and sup*
> *This slave-girl's brew,*
> *With the blessing of Bard*
> *This beer should do much for us.*

Then the horn split apart and the drink poured onto the straw. Olvir was just about to pass out so Egil got up and helped him to the door. Egil had his sword in his hand. As they got to the door, Bard came after them and asked Olvir to drink his parting toast. Egil took the horn and made this verse:

> *I'm drunk, and Olvir*
> *Is ashen-faced with ale,*
> *This brew from the beast's horn*
> *Bubbled through my lips;*
> *Your feet won't follow*
> *Instructions, old fellow,*
> *Though my poetry patters*
> *And pours like rain on you.*

Egil threw away the horn and gripped his sword. The doorway was dark. He thrust the sword into Bard waist-high, so that the point was driven right through the back, and Bard slumped down with blood spurting from the wound. Olvir collapsed, spewing out vomit, and Egil rushed out of the house. As he raced off the night was pitch dark.

In the vestibule people could see that both Bard and Olvir had fallen. The King came up and had a light brought, and then people realized what had happened: Olvir was lying there in a drunken stupor and Bard was dead, the whole floor awash with his blood. The King asked where that big man had gone, the one who had drunk more than anyone else that evening, and people told him the man had gone outside.

'Search for him and bring him to me,' said the King.

They searched for him all over the farmstead but he was not to be found. When they came to the out-house with the fire, they found most of Olvir's men lying there and asked if Egil had been in. The men told them he had come to pick up his weapons – 'right after that he went off,' they said. When the King was told, he ordered his men to hurry and seize all the boats on the island.

'Tomorrow when it's daylight, we'll scour the whole island and kill him,' he said.

45. Egil escapes

DURING the night Egil went to see if there were any boats, but wherever he came down to the beach he found men waiting for him, so he spent the night wandering about without finding one. At dawn he found himself on some headland, from where he could see an island far away on the other side of a broad channel. What he decided to do was this: he took his helmet, spear and sword, but broke the shaft off his spear and threw it into the sea. He wrapped the weapons in his top coat, bundled them up and tied them to his back. Then he jumped into the water and didn't stop swimming till he reached the island, which was called Saud Isle, a small place overgrown with brushwood. Some animals were kept there, cattle and sheep, and it belonged to Atley Island. When he got to the isle he wrung out his clothes. The sun had just risen and it was daylight.

As soon as it was light, King Eirik had Atley Island searched but it was a slow business since the island is a big one. Egil was not to be found so they took a boat and started searching for him on the other islands. In the evening twelve of them rowed over to look for him on Saud Isle, though there were many islands lying much closer. Egil saw the boat approach the island and nine men go ashore, then split up to look for him. He had lain down to hide in the brushwood before the boat had landed.

There were three men in each search party, with the remaining three staying to look after the boat. When the searchers had vanished behind a hill, Egil got to his feet and walked down to the boat. Before the men who were keeping an eye on the boat had any idea of what was happening, Egil was right on top of them. One he struck dead on the spot, and another started to run. He was trying to climb a slope but Egil hewed at him, slicing his leg off. A third man ran for the boat and started pushing it out with a pole, but Egil heaved at the mooring rope, then jumped into the boat, and there weren't many blows exchanged before Egil had killed him and thrown him overboard. Then he took the oars and rowed off, travelling all night and the whole of the following day without pause until he came to Chieftain Thorir. In spite of all that had happened, the King let Olvir and his companions go in peace.

The men stranded on Saud Isle had to spend a good many nights there. They killed something for meat, made a fire and dug a cooking pit, then built a pyre big enough to be seen back home, set fire to it and made a beacon. When people saw it they rowed out and rescued them. The King was away by then, off to another feast.

Olvir and his men got home before Egil, just after Thorir and Thorolf had returned from the wedding feast. Olvir reported the news about the killing of Bard and all the other things that had happened, but he couldn't tell what had become of Egil. Both Thorolf and Arinbjorn were very worried for it seemed to them unlikely that Egil would ever come back. Then next day Egil came home. As soon as Thorolf learned of this he went to see Egil, to ask how he had escaped and what had happened to him on his travels. Then Egil spoke this verse:

> *I made a mockery of*
> *Their Majesties' mastery,*
> *I don't deceive myself*
> *As to what I dare;*
> *A trio of true*
> *And trusty royal servants,*
> *Have I hacked and hurled*
> *Down to Hell eternal.*

Arinbjorn was impressed by Egil's performance and said it was his father's duty to arrange a reconciliation between Egil and the King.

'Folk will agree that Bard only got what he deserved,' said Thorir, 'but Egil takes after his family, he's far too reckless about making the King angry and there aren't many who can get away with that. Still, I'll get you your reconciliation.'

Thorir went to see the King, but Arinbjorn stayed at home, declaring that the fate of one should be the fate of all. When Thorir met the King he made a plea on Egil's behalf, offered himself as surety and submitted the case to the King's judgement. King Eirik was in such a rage, it was very difficult to come to terms with him. He said that his father's prediction would turn out to be true and that this was a family that it would be hard to trust. He asked Thorir to make sure that 'even if I agree to a settlement, Egil won't be long in my kingdom.'

'But for your sake, Thorir,' he said, 'I'll accept compensation for the men killed.'

The King awarded himself the sum he thought appropriate and Thorir paid it in full. Then he went back home.

46. A viking trip to the Baltic

THOROLF and Egil were treated to good entertainment by Thorir, but in the spring they started getting a big longship ready. Once it was manned they went plundering that summer in the Baltic, won a great deal of loot and fought a good number of battles. They sailed all the way to Courland and lay there at anchor for two weeks of peaceful trading. Then they started plundering again and made attacks on several places.

One day they put in near a large estuary that lay beneath a vast area of forest. They decided to go ashore and divide into groups, each of them twelve strong. They went into the forest and it wasn't long before they came to the settlements, where they started pillaging and killing. Some people made a run for it and got away, but there was no resistance. Late in the day Thorolf had the horn sounded to call his men down to the ship, so wherever they were, back they turned into the forest since there would be no chance of a roll-call till they got to the coast. When Thorolf got back Egil had not shown up and as night was falling and it was growing dark they knew it would be useless to search for him.

Egil had walked through the forest with his twelve men, and come to a large open plain with settlements. Not far away was a farmstead so they made for it, and on reaching it they charged into the buildings. They found no one there, but they grabbed everything they could lay their hands on. There were a good many houses there so this couldn't be done quickly, and by the time they were back in the open and on their way a force of men had gathered between them and the forest, and started to attack them.

Between Egil's men and the forest there was also a high stockade, and Egil told them to follow him close so that they could not be attacked from all sides. Egil was in the lead, then the rest one after another, walking so close together that no one could get between them. The Courlanders went for them hard with thrust and shot but avoided hand-to-hand fighting. As Egil and his men went along the foot of the stockade, they suddenly found themselves facing another wall so that they could go no further. The Courlanders had them penned in and went after them, some from the outside by thrusting their spears between the stockade-posts, others by throwing clothes onto their weapons. Egil and his men were wounded and bound captive, and then led back to the settlement.

The owner of the estate was a wealthy man with a grown-up son, and on the question of what was to be done with the prisoners, the farmer recommended killing them one by one. His son said that since night had fallen, it was too dark to get much fun out of torturing them, and it would be best to wait till morning. So people threw them into a building and bound them firmly, Egil with his hands and feet attached to a pole. After that the place was securely locked, and the Courlanders went into the hall to eat, drink and enjoy themselves.

Egil twisted and tugged at the pole till it jerked up out of the floor and fell down. Then he was able to free himself. After that he untied the ropes on his hands with his teeth, and once his hands were free he was able to loose the bonds on his feet. Then he freed his companions.

When they were all free, they started looking for the best way to get out of the building. The walls were made of big logs, with a smooth timber partition at one end. This they rammed and broke through, to find themselves in another room, also surrounded by log walls. Then they heard voices from beneath their feet and after looking around they discovered a trap-door in the floor. They opened it to find a deep pit, from which the voices they heard were coming. Egil asked who was there and a man answered, saying that his name was Aki. Egil asked if he wanted to come up out of the pit and Aki answered that he would like nothing better. So Egil lowered the rope they had been tied with into the pit, and pulled out three men. Aki said the other two were his sons, and that they were Danes who had been captured the previous summer.

'I was well treated over winter,' he said, 'and I had a big job to do as farm steward, but the boys didn't take to being slaves, so in spring we planned an escape. They caught us, though, and put us in this pit.'

'You'll know the lay-out of the buildings here, then,' said Egil. 'What's the best way out?'

Aki said there was another timber partition. 'Break through that and you come to a grain store,' he said, 'and that's easy to get out of.'

So that was what Egil and his men did; they smashed through the timber wall into the barn and made their way out from there. The night was black as pitch, and Egil's men said it would be best to make for the wood as fast as possible.

'If you know your way round the buildings here,' said Egil to Aki, 'you ought to be able to put us in the way of some loot.' Aki said there was plenty of money. 'There's a big loft where the farmer sleeps, and he's not short of weapons either.'

So Egil said they ought to go to this loft. When they got up to the balcony they could see that the loft was open, with lights inside and servants making the beds. Egil told some of his people to wait outside and make sure that nobody got away. Then he rushed into the bedroom, grabbed some weapons, of which there were plenty to be had, and killed all the people in there. His men fitted themselves out with arms, then Aki led the way to a trap-door in the floor, pulled it open, and told them to climb down into the room below. They took a light, and when they got down they found themselves in the place where the farmer kept all his valuables, his treasures and silver. Each man gathered his own load and carried it out. Egil picked up a big jewel-case, and with that under his arm he went with his men towards the wood.

They were inside the wood when Egil stopped in his tracks. 'This is a poor sort of expedition,' he said, 'it's not warrior-like. We've stolen the farmer's property and he doesn't know it. We mustn't let a shameful thing like that happen. We'll go back to the farmstead and tell people what's been going on.'

Everyone protested, saying that they wanted to get back

to the ship, but Egil put down the jewel-case and started racing towards the farmstead. When he got there he saw servants carrying trays with platters from the kitchen to the hall, and a fire blazing in the kitchen with cauldrons hung over it. Egil went into the kitchen. Great logs had been carried in to build the fires, and in the usual way only one end of the log had been set on fire so that it would burn right through. Egil grabbed the log, carried it to the hall and pushed the burning end up under the eaves to the roof, where the faggots soon began to blaze.

The people drinking inside had no idea what was happening till they saw flames pouring from the ceiling. They made a rush for the door but it wasn't easy going, partly because of the blazing timbers, partly because Egil was at the door barring the way. He cut men down both in and outside the doorway. In no time at all the hall was burned to the ground, and of all those inside not one survived.

Egil went back to the forest and joined his companions, and they made their way down to the ship. Egil said he wanted the jewel-case for himself, quite apart from the loot they were to share, and it turned out to be full of silver. Thorolf and his men were glad to see Egil back again and they put out to sea as soon as it was daylight. Aki and his sons joined Egil's party. Late in the summer they sailed for Denmark, to lie in wait for trading vessels and plunder wherever they could.

47. Attack on Lund

IN Denmark, Harald Gormsson had come to power on the death of his father, Gorm. The country was in a state of war, and the seas around it swarming with vikings. Aki knew his way about Denmark by sea and land, and Egil was always asking him where they could find likely spots for looting. When they came to Ore Sound, Aki told him that there was a big market town inland called Lund, where there was a good chance of getting some money, though the townspeople were likely to fight back. They put it to the rest of the crew, asking whether or not they should make a landing, and got a mixed reception. Some were all for it, others raised objections, so the matter was referred to the leaders. Thorolf favoured going ashore, and when Egil was asked for his opinion he made this verse:

> *Warrior, the wolf's fangs*
> *You've crimsoned, the worm-season*
> *Of the hero comes, hold*
> *High the flashing blades;*
> *Let's race to Lund*
> *And launch the rites*
> *Of the battle song*
> *Ere the sun sets.*

Then they got everything ready for the landing, and made their way up to the market town. When the townspeople got to know about the enemy they gathered forces against them. The town was protected by a wooden stockade and that was where battle was joined. Egil was the first to get into the town, and the people soon ran, with heavy loss of life. The raiders rifled the town and set fire to it. Then they went back to their ships.

48. Back to Norway

THOROLF and his men sailed north along the coast of Halland and when the weather grew rough they brought their ship into harbour, but did no looting. There was an earl called Arnvid living a few miles inland and when he heard that vikings had landed he sent people to find out what they wanted, war or sanctuary. When they had given Thorolf the message, he answered that there was no plan to raid there and no point in harrying and plundering where the land was so poor. The messengers went back to the earl to report how their mission had turned out, and once the earl realized that he had no need to gather an army he rode out alone to meet the vikings, and got on well with them when they met. He invited Thorolf to a feast, along with as many of his men as he wished, and Thorolf promised to come.

On the appointed day, the earl sent horses over for them, and both Thorolf and Egil decided to go, along with thirty of their men. The earl gave them a hearty welcome when they arrived and showed them into a hall where there was ale ready on the table. They were served with drink and sat there till evening. Before the tables were cleared, the earl said that seating arrangements must be decided by lot, and that each of the men should have a woman as his drinking partner, as long as there were enough women. After that, the rest of the men were to drink on their own. Each man threw his lot into a folded piece of cloth and then the earl gathered them all up. The earl had a very pretty daughter of just the right age, and Egil drew the earl's daughter for the rest of the evening. She strolled up and down enjoying herself, but Egil got up and went to the seat she had been sitting in during the day. When people went back to their seats, she walked up to her own place and said:

> *Why linger, little lad,*
> *I'd like to sit alone,*
> *What wolves did you feed*
> *Ever on warm flesh?*
> *Did you revel with the raven,*
> *Red-beaked in autumn-gore?*
> *You're keen to shun the slice*
> *Of the sharp cutting-edge.*

Egil picked her up, set her beside him and spoke these words:

> *I've borne the bloodstained sword*
> *And bitter spear-shaft,*
> *The raven at my right hand*
> *As we raiders strode forward.*

Burning for battle
We made their barns blaze,
Gory at their gates
Groaned those fast sleepers.

For the rest of the evening they sat drinking together and enjoyed themselves. It was a great feast and the one next day was just as good. After that the vikings went back to their ships, exchanging gifts with the earl and parting good friends.

Thorolf and his men made next for the Brenn Islands, very much a viking haunt in those days, since merchant ships in large numbers had to sail the sea-route between them. Aki went back home with his sons to his estates, a rich man and owner of many a farmstead in Jutland. Egil and Thorolf sealed their friendship with Aki and parted from him on the best of terms.

In the autumn, Thorolf and his men sailed north along the coast of Norway till they reached Fjord Province, where Chieftain Thorir gave them a great welcome and his son Arinbjorn an even better one. Arinbjorn invited Egil to stay there over winter and Egil accepted the offer gratefully, but when Thorir heard about the invitation he said he thought it a bit rash.

'I don't know how King Eirik is going to take it,' he said. 'After Bard was killed, Eirik declared that he wouldn't have Egil in the country.'

'You can use your influence with the King, father,' said Arinbjorn, 'so that he doesn't raise objections to Egil's being here. You'll be inviting your nephew Thorolf to stay and Egil and I can share our winter-quarters.'

Thorir could tell from this that Arinbjorn wanted his own way in the matter, so he and his son invited Thorolf for the winter, an invitation that he accepted. Thorolf and Egil spent the winter there with twelve men.

There were two brothers, Thorvald the Overbearing and Thorfinn the Strong, who were closely related to Bjorn and had been brought up by him. They were tall and strong, men of ambition and enterprise. They had been on viking expeditions with Bjorn, and after he settled down they had been on expeditions with Thorolf. They used to be on the forecastle of his ship, so when Egil got command of one he made Thorfinn his forecastleman. The brothers were always following Thorolf around and he thought more of them than of anyone else in his crew. The brothers were in his company that winter and sat next to him and Egil. Thorolf was in the high-seat with Thorir as his drinking-companion, while Egil drank with Arinbjorn. As every toast was drunk, people were supposed to step on to the floor.

In the autumn Chieftain Thorir went to visit King Eirik, who gave him a generous welcome. When they got talking together, Thorir asked the King not to blame him for letting Egil stay with him over winter, and the King gave a friendly reply, saying that Thorir was welcome to any favour he wanted.

'Though it would have been another matter,' he added, 'if any man but you had taken Egil in.'

But when Gunnhild overheard their conversation, she had something to say.

'It seems to me, Eirik,' she said, 'that you're just as credulous as ever, and you've got a short memory for an insult. You'll go on helping the sons of Skallagrim until they've murdered some of your nearest kinsfolk. But even if you don't care about the killing of Bard, I do.'

'More than any other person, Gunnhild, you try to goad me into behaving like a savage,' said the King, 'but there was a time when you felt a lot warmer towards Thorolf than you do now. I'm not breaking my word to the brothers.'

'Thorolf was doing fine here till Egil came and spoiled everything,' she answered, 'but now the one's no different from the other.'

Thorir returned home as soon as he was ready and told the brothers what the King and Queen had said.

49. A viking expedition

GUNNHILD had two brothers called Eyvind Shabby and Alf Askman, the sons of Ozur Toti. They were big, powerful, enterprising men, and highly thought of by King Eirik and Gunnhild though few other people were very fond of them. They were quite young at the time, but full-grown men.

A great sacrificial feast was to be held in the spring at Gaular, where the most renowned high-temple stood. There was a large gathering of people, most of them important men, from Fjord, Fjalir and Sogn Provinces, and King Eirik was there too. Then Gunnhild had a word with her brothers.

'Now that all these people have gathered here,' she said, 'there's something I want done. Kill one of Skallagrim's sons, or better still, kill them both.' The brothers said they'd do it.

Chieftain Thorir got himself ready for the journey, and called Arinbjorn over for a talk.

'I'm going off to the sacrifice now,' he said, 'but I don't want Egil to go. I know what Gunnhild's been saying, and what with Egil's recklessness and the King's great authority, it's not going to be easy to keep an eye on everything. Nothing will keep Egil away unless you stay behind too, but Thorolf and the rest are to come with me, since he has sacrifices to carry out for his own good luck and his brother's.'

So Arinbjorn told Egil that he was staying behind – 'both of us together,' he said – and Egil agreed. Thorir and the rest went to the sacrifice, where there were a lot of people and plenty to drink: but wherever Thorolf went, Thorir was close by and never left his side both day and night. Eyvind told Gunnhild that they didn't have a chance with Thorolf, so she told him to kill any one of his men instead. 'Better that, than let him off scot-free,' she said.

One evening the King had gone to bed. So had Thorir and Thorolf, but Thorfinn and Thorvald stayed up and the brothers Eyvind and Alf joined them. They sat down together in the best of spirits and at first all drank from the same horn, but then they started drinking one horn to a pair, each man to drink half. Eyvind and Thorvald had one horn, Alf and Thorfinn the other. As the evening wore on, they began to cheat over their drinks, then they started squabbling and finally there was a slanging-match. Suddenly Eyvind jumped up, pulled out his short-sword and made such a thrust with it that he gave Thorvald a gaping death-wound. Both sides leapt to their feet, the King's men and Thorir's, but everyone was unarmed as the presence of the temple made it a sacred place, so people were able to intervene and separate the more impetuous ones, and nothing else happened that night.

Since Eyvind had committed a killing in a sacred place he was declared an outlaw and had to leave at once. The King offered to pay compensation, but Thorolf and Thorfinn said that they had never taken money in compensation for a killing and didn't mean to start doing so now. That was how things stood when they parted, and Thorir and his men made their way back home.

Since Eyvind could not stay in Norway because of the laws of the land, King Eirik and Gunnhild sent him south to King Harald Gormsson in Denmark, where he and his companions got a good welcome. Eyvind brought a great longship with him to Denmark and the King put him in charge of the country's defences against the vikings. Eyvind was the best of fighting men.

When the winter was over and spring had come, Thorolf and Egil got ready once more for a viking expedition, and when everything was prepared they sailed east for the Baltic. But once they reached Oslofjord they sailed south by Jutland plundering there, then made for Friesland, where they spent most of the summer before turning back to Denmark. When they reached the border between Denmark and Friesland they put in, and one evening when the people aboard were getting ready for sleep two men came to Egil's ship. They said they had business with him so he met them. They told him that Aki the Wealthy had sent them with a message.

'Eyvind Shabby is lying in wait off the coast of Jutland for you to come back from the south,' they said. 'You won't have a chance with the great force that he's gathered. As for himself, he's at sea in a pair of skiffs and not far off.'

When Egil heard the news he had the awnings taken down and told people to be quiet, so that's what they did. They came on Eyvind just about dawn, where he was lying at anchor, and went for him right away with stones and weapons. Eyvind's men were slaughtered in large numbers, but he managed to jump overboard and swim ashore along with all those men of his who got away. Egil and his men took the ships, along with the crews' weapons and clothing, and later in the day came back to their own ships. When they met Thorolf, he asked Egil where he had been and where he had got the ships. Egil told him the ships had belonged to Eyvind Shabby but they'd taken them from him. Then Egil made this verse:

> It was just off Jutland
> That we jumped him:
> The defender of Denmark
> Was brave and dashing;
> But ingenious Eyvind
> Had to vault from his ocean-steed
> And swim for life shorewards
> To sandy safety.

'After what you've just done,' said Thorolf, 'it wouldn't be wise for us to go back to Norway this autumn.' Egil agreed that it would be sensible to look elsewhere.

50. In Athelstan's England

ALFRED the Great reigned in England, the first of his kinsmen to be sole ruler there. That was in the time of King Harald Fine-Hair of Norway. Alfred was succeeded by his son Edward, father of Athelstan the Victorious, who fostered Hakon the Good.

It was about the time we're speaking of that Athelstan came to the throne of England on his father's death. There were several more brothers, the sons of Edward.

After Athelstan took over the kingdom a number of chieftains who had lost their authority to his forebears started to make war against him, thinking it easy to get back what they had lost now that a young king ruled. These chieftains were Welsh, Scots and Irish. So King Athelstan began to gather his forces, promising rewards to all who joined and were looking for money, whether they came from home or abroad.

Thorolf and his brother Egil sailed southwards to Saxony and Flanders where they learned that the King of England needed troops and the rewards were likely to be high. So they made up their minds to go, and travelled over autumn till they reached King Athelstan. He gave them a good welcome and it seemed to him their support would be a great asset to his army. They hadn't been talking to him long before he made them an offer to guard his frontiers, whereupon terms were agreed and they became Athelstan's men.

England was a Christian country, and had been so for a long time when these events were taking place. King Athelstan was a staunch Christian, and people called him Athelstan the Faithful. He asked Thorolf and his brother to accept preliminary baptism as was the custom in those days both for merchants and mercenaries serving Christian rulers, since people who had been given this form of baptism could mix equally with Christian and heathen and were free to hold any belief that suited them. So Thorolf and Egil did what the King wanted and received preliminary baptism. They had three hundred and sixty men under them, all on the King's pay-roll.

51. King Athelstan's enemies

THE King of Scotland, Olaf the Red, was a Scot on his father's side and Danish on his mother's, being descended from Ragnar Hairy-Breeks. He was a powerful king, for the power of Scotland is said to be a third of that of England.

Northumberland is reckoned one-fifth of England, being the northernmost part of it down the east side, south of Scotland. It used to be ruled by the kings of Denmark in the old days, and its main town is York. This land belonged to King Athelstan and he had put earls in charge of it, one called Alfgeir and the other Godrek, to defend it against the attacks of the Scots, Danes, and Norwegians who kept raiding and making claim to it. The reason given for this was that all the important people in Northumberland were of Danish descent, either on their father's side or their mother's, and in many cases on both.

Ruling Wales were two brothers, Hring and Adils, who were tributary to King Athelstan and duty-bound to fight in the forefront of his troops under his banner. The brothers were the best of fighting men but getting on in years.

Alfred the Great had deprived all his tributary kings of titles as well as power, so that men who used to be kings and princes were now called earls, and this continued throughout his own reign and his son Edward's. Since Athelstan was young when he came to power people stood in less fear of him and there were many who had been eager to serve him, but could no longer be relied on.

52. Preparations for battle

KING Olaf of Scotland gathered a great army and led it south into England, plundering everywhere as soon as he came to Northumberland. When the earls in charge there got word of this, they mustered their force and went out to face the King. King Olaf won a fierce battle when they clashed, Earl Godrek was killed and Alfgeir had to make a run for it with most of the troops who had survived. Since Alfgeir could offer no resistance, King Olaf was able to take the whole of Northumberland.

Alfgeir went to King Athelstan and told him how badly things had gone. When Athelstan heard the size of the army that had invaded his land he sent out his own men to gather forces, with messages to his earls and his other leaders, and without wasting any time set out with all the men he could muster to face the Scots.

As soon as people heard that King Olaf of Scotland had won a victory and was in control of a large part of England with a greater army than Athelstan's under his command, a good many important men joined forces with him. The news had reached Hring and Adils, and they went over to the side of King Olaf with the large army they had assembled, so that the combined force was immense.

Athelstan heard about this and met with his chief men and counsellors to decide what course he should take, explaining in detail to everyone all that he had learned about the King of the Scots' activities and those of his great army. There was general agreement that Earl Alfgeir had come out of it badly and that it would be right for him to lose his title. However, the decision was that King Athelstan should retreat to the south of England, then build up an army northwards, for people thought it would be a slow mustering, in view of the numbers needed, unless the King himself were to lead the army.

The troops that had already gathered there were placed by the King under the command of Thorolf and Egil. They were to lead the force that had come with the vikings, but Alfgeir was still in charge of his own men. After that the King appointed captains as he saw fit. When Egil came back to his own people from the meeting, they asked what news he had of the King of Scots, and he answered them with this verse:

> One earl fled from Olaf,
> Life ended for the other;
> The lusty war-leader
> Was lavish in blood-gifts.
> England's enemy conquered
> Half Alfgeir's earldom,
> While the great Godrek
> Rambled on the gore-plain.

After that messengers were sent to Olaf from Athelstan challenging him to a pitched battle, with Vin Moor near Vin Forest as the battlefield. Athelstan added that he wanted no plundering of the kingdom and that whoever won should rule England. The battle was to be fought in a week's time, and whoever arrived first should wait up to one week for the other. It was the custom in those days that once a field of battle had been declared for a king, he could not honourably wage war until that battle had been fought. King Olaf abided by this. He took his troops in hand, permitted no looting and waited for the appointed day. Then he moved his army over to Vin Moor.

King Olaf settled in a town to the north of the moor, along with most of his troops. There were large inhabited areas near by and he thought it better placed for provisioning the army. Some of his men he sent up to the moor where the battle was to be fought, to choose camping sites and make things ready for the main body of troops. When they came to the place selected for the battle, the hazel-rods to fix the boundaries were already set up and the battlefield itself fully marked out. The choice of ground had to be made with great care, for it had to be level, and big enough to line up a great army. That is what had been done in this case: the battlefield was a flat moor with a river flowing on one side and a large wood on the other. But the shortest distance between the river and the wood was still a very long way, and that was where King Athelstan's men had made camp, their tents taking up the whole space between river and wood. But the camp had been arranged so that every third tent was empty, and there were few men in the others.

When King Olaf's men turned up, the English had ranged themselves in front of all the tents in full force and there was no way the others could get into the camp. Athelstan's men said that their tents were so crowded there was not enough room for all their troops. The tents stood on high ground so that it was impossible to see their tops and so work out how many deep they were, but Olaf's men assumed that there must be a great army. They pitched their own tents north of the hazel poles, on a gentle slope. Day after day Athelstan's men would say that their King was just about to arrive, or else that he had just reached the town south of the moor, and day and night new forces came to join them.

On the appointed day Athelstan's men sent messengers to King Olaf announcing that King Athelstan, with a massive army, was ready for battle but didn't want these troops to have on their hands the slaughter which now seemed likely. Their message was that it would be better for Olaf to go back to Scotland, and that as a gesture of friendship Athelstan would give him a silver shilling for every plough in his kingdom, and in that way seal their relationship.

As the messengers came, King Olaf had his army form up and get ready to ride away, but once the message had been delivered he put things off for the day and settled down for discussions with the leaders of his army. Opinions were sharply divided. Some urged him to accept the terms since the campaign had been highly successful and now they could go back home with the load of tribute Athelstan was ready to hand over; but others were against it, arguing that if they were to reject this offer of Athelstan's, he would have to make a bigger one next time, and this was what they agreed on.

So the messengers asked King Olaf for time to go back to King Athelstan and see if he was ready to pay more in order to keep the peace. They asked for one day to ride home, one for discussion, and one to ride back, and to this King Olaf agreed. Off went the messengers and three days later back they came as agreed, to tell Olaf that over and above the offer made before, Athelstan would pay a shilling to every free-born man in Olaf's army, a silver mark to every captain in charge of twelve or more men, a gold mark to every head man and five marks in gold to every earl.

King Olaf put the terms to his men, but just as before, some were against it and others in favour. As matters turned out, the King said that he would take the offer as long as Athelstan would let him have Northumberland as well, along with all its dues and tributes.

Again the messengers asked for a delay of three days and added a further request, that Olaf send his own messengers to hear King Athelstan's decision whether or not to accept the terms. It seemed unlikely, they said, that Athelstan would let anything stand in the way of a peace settlement. King Olaf agreed to send his own envoys to Athelstan, and all the messengers rode together to meet him at the town just south of the moor. Olaf's envoys announced their mission and the peace terms they had brought. But when Athelstan's men told about the offer they had carried to King Olaf, they added that it was done on the advice of wise men, in order to delay the battle until King Athelstan could be there. Wasting no time, Athelstan gave his decision to Olaf's envoys like this:

'Carry this message to King Olaf,' he said, 'that I give him leave to go back with all his men to Scotland, but that he must give up everything that he has plundered here in the land. After that we can declare a peace between our kingdoms, and neither shall attack the other. But it follows from this that Olaf must become my liegeman and govern Scotland on my behalf as tributary king. Now go back and tell him how things stand.'

That same evening the envoys started back for King Olaf's

camp and reached there about midnight. They woke the King and without delay they told him Athelstan's message. Olaf had the earls and other leading men summoned to him, and then ordered the envoys to tell about the outcome of their mission and repeat King Athelstan's words. When the men learned about this, they all agreed that there was nothing to be done but to get ready for battle. The envoys added that Athelstan had a massive army, and had arrived at the town on the same day as themselves.

Then Earl Adils spoke up. 'It's happening, sir,' he said, 'just as I told you it would: you'll find the English tricky people to deal with. While we've been sitting around here all this time, they've been gathering their whole army: their King must have been nowhere near when we arrived, and since then they've got a great force of men together. Now this is my advice, sir. Let me and my brother ride out at once with our men this very night, for it could be that they're not on their guard now that they've learned their King and his army are so near. In that case we'll attack them, and if they're routed they'll suffer such heavy losses that they won't be so keen to attack us.'

This seemed a good idea to the King. 'We'll get our own troops ready as soon as it's light and come to join you,' he said. That was the plan they agreed upon, and so the meeting ended.

53. The battle begins

EARL Hring and his brother Adils got their men together and set off that same night south across the moor. At daybreak Thorolf's guard saw them approaching, so the war-horn was sounded, and the men armed themselves, forming up in two columns. Earl Alfgeir was in command of one and had a banner carried before him. His column was made up of the troops he himself had led, and the extra forces gathered from the neighbouring districts. It was much larger than the one commanded by Thorolf.

Here is how Thorolf was equipped: he had a broad, thick shield, a tough helmet on his head, and a sword called Long about his waist, a big, fine weapon. The thrusting-spear he carried had a blade two ells long with four edges tapering to a point at one end, broad at the other. The socket was long and wide, the shaft no taller than might be grasped at the socket by the hand, but wonderfully thick. An iron spike was in the socket and the whole of the shaft was bound with iron. It was the kind of spear that is called a halberd.

Egil had the same kind of outfit. At his waist was a sword called Adder, taken in Courland, the very finest of weapons. Neither of the brothers wore a coat of mail.

They raised their banner, borne by Thorfinn the Strong. Every man had a Norwegian shield and other Norwegian gear. All the Norwegians in the army were gathered together in this column, and every man in it was Norwegian. Thorolf and his men formed up close to the wood, and Alfgeir's went by the river.

Earl Adils and his brother saw that they could not take Thorolf's men by surprise so they began to form up in two columns under two separate banners, Adils raising his against Earl Alfgeir and Hring against the vikings. Then the battle started, with both sides going forward bravely. Earl Adils pressed ahead so determinedly that Alfgeir had to fall back. At this, Adils's men fought twice as hard, and it was not long before Alfgeir was routed. It's said of him that he rode south over the moor with a small party of men, and kept on riding till he came close to the town where the King was staying. Then the Earl spoke.

'I don't think we'll go into the town,' he said. 'I had hard words from the King last time we met after losing to King Olaf, and I don't think my chances will have been improved by this venture. There's no point in expecting any honour from him now.'

After that he rode southwards through the land, and it's

said of his travels that he rode day and night till he reached the west at Jarlsness, and from there got a boat to take him south over the sea to France, where one branch of his family lived. He never came back to England.

Adils first went after the flying enemy but not for long. Soon he came back to the battlefield and went on fighting. Thorolf turned to meet the Earl when he saw that, and gave orders for the banner to be carried there, telling his men to give one another all the support they could and stay close together. 'Edge towards the forest,' he said, 'so that it protects us from the rear, and they can't all get at us.'

So that's what they did. They kept to the edge of the wood but as the fighting grew fiercer, Egil moved forward against Adils and it went hard between them; but for all the heavy odds against Egil it was Adils who had the worst casualties. Thorolf grew so mad that he swung his shield onto his back, took hold of his spear with both hands and charged forward. He laid about him on either hand and a good many men were killed, and so he cleared a path right through to the banner of Earl Hring. There was no stopping him. He killed the man carrying it, then cut down the banner-pole. After that he lunged his spear at the Earl's breast, piercing his mail-coat and trunk so that the point stuck out betweeen the shoulder-blades. Next he lifted the halberd up above his head and plunged the base of the shaft into the earth, and the Earl died on the spear point before everyone's eyes, before his own men as well as his enemies. Thorolf drew his sword, striking out with it to right and left with his men close behind him, so that many of the Scots and the Welsh began to fall, and others turned and ran.

When Earl Adils saw that his brother was dead, and many of his men, and that others were running away, he knew his cause was lost. He turned and ran himself towards the woods, and fled into them with a small band of men. After that his whole army took to its heels, suffering heavy losses, and scattering all over the moor. Earl Adils had lowered his banner so that no one knew where he or the men with him had gone.

Night was falling and it was just beginning to grow dark as Thorolf and Egil turned back to their camp-site. Just then King Athelstan came up with his army, pitched his tents and settled in. A little later King Olaf arrived with his troops, and they too pitched their tents and settled down where their own men had camped earlier. People told King Olaf that both his earls, Hring and Adils, were dead along with many more of his men.

54. The death of Thorolf

KING Athelstan had spent the previous night in the town we spoke of. When he heard about the battle on the moor, he set out at once to cross it with his whole army, and got a full account of how the battle had gone. When the brothers Thorolf and Egil came before him he thanked them generously for the courage they had shown and the victory they had won, and promised them his constant friendship. That night they all stayed together.

Early in the morning King Athelstan roused his troops and called together his leaders, explaining how he wanted his army deployed. He put his own column to the fore, spear-headed by the best fighting men he had, and ordered Egil to take charge of it. 'But Thorolf is to lead his own men,' he said, 'and any other troops I decide on. The column he leads is to be our second one. The Scots columns are very mobile, they're always on the move and may come in from any direction. They can do a lot of damage unless our men keep their wits about them, and they're quick to move once they meet with any resistance.'

'I don't want myself and Thorolf separated in battle,' said Egil to the King, 'and it seems best to me that we should be put where the need's greatest and the opposition toughest.'

'We must let the King decide where he wants us to be,' said Thorolf, 'and we'll give him all the support he needs. But I'll take the place you've been given if you like.'

'Have it your own way,' said Egil, 'but it's a decision I'll live long to regret.'

Then the troops deployed themselves in columns according to the King's orders and the banners were raised. The King's column stood on open country near the river and Thorolf's on higher ground close to the forest.

As soon as King Olaf saw that Athelstan had formed up his troops he began to do the same with his own. He also had two columns, and in front of the one he led against King Athelstan he had his banner carried. There were so many men on either side that numbers didn't matter. King Olaf's second column stayed close to the forest and marched against the troops commanded by Thorolf. It was a big column, made up mostly of Scotsmen and led by several Scottish earls.

The columns met and soon a fierce battle was raging. Thorolf pressed forward and had his banner carried along the edge of the wood so that he could position himself for an attack on the King's flank. His men held their shields in front of them, letting the trees protect them to the right. Thorolf made so much ground that hardly any of his men were ahead of him, but then when he least expected it, Earl Adils and his troops swept out of the forest lunging at him with a mass of halberds, and there he fell, just at the edge of the forest. Thorfinn was carrying the banner and had to withdraw to where their troops were thicker: but Adils kept up the attack, and the fighting was fierce, with the Scots raising the victory cry for having killed the leader of the enemy.

When Egil heard the shouting and saw Thorolf's banner on the retreat, he knew that Thorolf wasn't going to be able to follow it, so he raced over from his own column to the other and as soon as he got to his people he saw how things were. He marched ahead of them, urging them forward, and brandishing the sword Adder, striding in front and hewing men down left and right. With Thorfinn and the banner at his heels he led the men into the thick of battle, pressing forward until he was face to face with Earl Adils. Not many strokes were exchanged before Adils and many of the men about him had fallen dead, and once he had been killed his whole army started to run. Egil and his troops raced after them killing everyone within reach, so there wasn't much point in asking for mercy. Once they saw their countrymen on the run, the Scottish earls didn't put up much resistance and took to their heels.

Then Egil and his troops moved over against King Olaf's column and caused utter havoc by attacking his unguarded flank. The whole column gave way and began to disintegrate, and as King Olaf's men fled, it was the vikings' turn to raise the cry of victory. When King Athelstan realized that Olaf's column was breaking up he shouted encouragement to his troops and had his banner carried forward in the fierce on-slaught, routing Olaf's men and cutting them down in large numbers. King Olaf was killed along with most of his army, for everyone caught running away was put to death. So King Athelstan won a great victory there.

55. Compensation for Thorolf's death

WHILE his troops chased after the routed enemy, King Athel-stan left the battlefield and rode without pausing overnight back to the town. Egil was among the pursuers, keeping up a long chase and killing everyone he could get at. Then he came back with his men to the battlefield and found his dead brother. He took up the body, washed it and prepared it for burial according to custom. They dug a grave there and placed Thorolf in it with all his weapons and clothing. Before they parted, Egil clasped a gold bracelet around each of Thorolf's arms, then they carried stones to the grave and heaped earth upon it. Egil made this verse:

> The earl's killer,
> Who cringed to no man,
> Fell, the fierce Thorolf
> Fighting like a warrior.

Beneath Vina's green bank
Lie my brother's bones,
Sore is my sorrow
Though I show no grief.

Then he made another:

West over water
I wallowed in the slain-stack,
Angry, my Adder struck
Adils in the battle-storm.
Olaf played the steel-game,
The English his enemies;
Hring sought the raging blades,
No ravens went hungry.

After that he went at once with his men to Athelstan's table where the King was enjoying himself drinking. As soon as the King saw Egil had arrived he had the opposite benches cleared for him and his men and invited Egil to take the seat of honour facing him. There Egil sat, his shield at his feet and his helmet on his head. He had his sword across his knees and kept pulling it part of the way out of the scabbard, then thrusting it back. He sat bolt upright but his head was bent low.

Egil was a man who caught the eye. He had a wide forehead, bushy eyebrows and a nose, not long, but impressively large. A great broad beard grew on a chin as massive as his jaws; his neck was stout and his shoulders heavy, far heavier than those of other men. When he grew angry there was a hard, cruel look on his face. He was far above normal height but well-proportioned and though he once had a head of thick wolf-grey hair, he had grown bald early in life.

There he sat, just as we describe him, with one eyebrow sunk down right to the cheek and the other lifting up to the roots of the hair. His eyes were black and his eyebrows joined in the middle. He refused to touch a drink even though people were serving him, and did nothing but pull his eyebrows up and down, now this one, now the other.

King Athelstan was sitting in the high-seat. He, too, had laid his sword across his knees and so the two men sat for some time. Then the King drew his sword from its scabbard, took a fine big bracelet from his arm, and hung it on the sword-point; he stood up, stepped down to the floor and stretched over the fire with it towards Egil. Egil got to his feet, drew his sword and stepped down himself to the floor. He put his own sword-point inside the arc of the bracelet, lifted it towards him and went back to his place. Then the King sat down on the high-seat.

As soon as Egil was seated he put the bracelet on his arm and his eyebrows went back to normal. He laid down the sword beside him along with the helmet, picked up the horn that had been offered him and drank it down. Then he made a verse:

> The King in his coat
> Of steel sets this gold coil,
> This ring, on my right arm
> Where falcons have rested:
> The gift hangs glowing,
> My arm its gallows:
> Honour was earned
> By the feaster of eagles.

After that, Egil took his full share of drink and talked to the others.

Then the King had two chests carried into the hall, each borne by two men. Both chests were full of silver.

'These chests are for you, Egil,' said the King. 'When you get back to Iceland I want you to give them to your father from me, in compensation for his son's life, though some of the money is to be shared between the kinsmen of you and Thorolf, the ones you think the greatest men. As compensation for yourself I want you to take either land or movables, whichever suits you best, and if you choose to stay long with me, I offer you a place of honour and worth. You only have to say what you want.'

Egil took the money and thanked the King for his gifts

and good words. His mood grew more cheerful and he made
this verse:

> *In bitterness my brows*
> *Beetled over my eyes;*
> *Now my forehead has found one*
> *To smooth its furrows:*
> *The King has conquered*
> *My louring cliff-face,*
> *The granter of gifts,*
> *The gold-flinger.*

After that the wounded were seen to, all those fit enough
to survive. Along with those of his and his brother's men
who had not been killed, Egil spent the winter following
Thorolf's death with King Athelstan, who had a high opinion
of him. Egil composed a poem in Athelstan's honour and here
is one of the verses:

> *The royal warrior rises*
> *Above his realm,*
> *The pride of three princes*
> *Ælla's stem overpowers;*
> *Countries are conquered*
> *By Athelstan the King,*
> *All kneel to the noble*
> *And generous knight.*

The poem has this refrain:

> *Now the Highlands, deer-haunted,*
> *Lie humbled by Athelstan.*

Again Athelstan made Egil a gift, this time rewarding him
for his poem with two gold bracelets each half a mark in
weight and a valuable cloak that had been worn by the King
himself.

When spring came, Egil told the King he planned to go
off to Norway in the summer to find out how Asgerd was
getting on.

'That's the woman who was married to my brother
Thorolf,' he said. 'There's a good deal of money involved

and I don't know if any of their children are alive. If they are, it's my duty to look after them, but if he's died childless I'm his sole heir.'

'It's for you to decide whether you go or stay, Egil,' said the King, 'if you think you've urgent matters to deal with. But I'd like it best if you were to settle down here, and choose whatever position you want.'

Egil thanked the King for his words. 'I must leave now,' he said, 'my duty demands it, but I'm likely to come back and take up your offer when I get the chance.' The King told him to do just that.

Then Egil got ready to leave with his troops, though a good many of them decided to stay on with the King. He had a big longship manned with a crew of over a hundred and twenty. When he was ready to leave and the wind was favourable, he put out to sea. Egil and King Athelstan parted the best of friends and the King asked him to come back as soon as he could. Egil said that he would.

He sailed to Norway, and as soon as he made land he hurried north to Fjord Province, where he heard the news that Chieftain Thorir was dead and that Arinbjorn had taken up his inheritance and become a land-holder. Egil got a warm welcome from Arinbjorn and accepted his invitation to stay. He had his ship hauled ashore and found billets for his crew. Arinbjorn took in Egil and eleven of his men, and Egil stayed with him through the winter.

56. Egil marries Asgerd

BY this time Berg-Onund, the son of Thorgeir Thorn-Foot, had married Gunnhild, the daughter of Bjorn the Yeoman, and she had moved over to Berg-Onund's farm at Ask, but Asgerd, Thorolf's widow, was staying with her cousin Arinbjorn, along with Thordis, her young daughter by Thorolf. Egil told Asgerd that Thorolf was dead and offered to look after her. She grieved sorely at the news, but though she had little to say about Egil's offer her response was a friendly one.

As autumn wore on, Egil grew extremely miserable and spent a great deal of time with his head buried under his cloak. One day Arinbjorn came and asked him why he was in such low spirits.

'Even though you suffered a great loss when your brother died,' he said, 'you have to bear it like a man. People have to go on living. What are you composing these days? Let me hear something.'

Egil said he had just made this verse:

> Beauty must bear with
> My boorish manner:
> Braver in boyhood
> I lifted my brow;
> Now my cloak must cover
> The craggy cliff-face,
> When wife, widow and mother
> Worry my mind.

Arinbjorn asked who this woman could be that he was writing a love-song about. 'The verse contains a clue to her name,' he said. Then Egil spoke again:

> I seldom conceal
> Her name in song,
> Gradually her grief
> Grows less:
> If your ear can interpret
> The art of verse,
> You'll soon make sense
> Of what I say.

'This is a case,' said Egil, 'as the saying goes, where a man can tell all to his friend. You want to know the name of the woman in my verse, so I'll tell you. It's your cousin Asgerd, and I hope you'll help me win her.'

Arinbjorn said he liked the idea very much. 'I'll gladly put in a good word for you,' he said, 'and help bring it about.'

So later Egil put the matter to Asgerd, but she referred it

to her father and her cousin Arinbjorn. She gave the same answer when Arinbjorn himself had a word with her about it. Arinbjorn was strongly in favour of this marriage, so he and Egil went to see Bjorn, and Egil made a proposal, asking for the hand of Asgerd, Bjorn's daughter. Bjorn's reply was favourable, but he said that the decision rested mainly with Arinbjorn, and as he urged the marriage so strongly the outcome was that Asgerd was promised to Egil, with the wedding feast to be held at Arinbjorn's. There was a great feast for Egil's marriage on the appointed day and for the rest of the winter he was in excellent spirits.

In the spring Egil got a merchant ship ready for a voyage to Iceland. Arinbjorn had advised him not to make his home in Norway while Queen Gunnhild's power there was so great.

'She hates you bitterly,' he said, 'and things have taken a turn for the worse since you met Eyvind off Jutland.'

When Egil was ready and the wind favourable, he put to sea. He had a good passage, making landfall in Iceland that autumn, and went straight up to Borgarfjord. He had been out of the country for twelve years. Skallagrim was getting old and Egil's homecoming was a happy time for him.

Egil went to stay at Borg along with Thorfinn the Strong and a good many others, all of them spending the winter with Skallagrim. Egil had an immense amount of money with him, though it's not said that he shared any of King Athelstan's silver with Skallagrim or anyone else. That winter Thorfinn married Sæunn, Skallagrim's daughter, and in the spring Skallagrim gave them a farm at Longriver Foss, including the land between Long River and Alft River, from Leiru Brook up into the mountains. Their daughter Thordis married Arngeir of Holm, son of Bersi the Godless. Their son was Bjorn the Hitardale-Champion.

Egil stayed with Skallagrim for several years and began to take charge of money matters and the running of the estate just as much as Skallagrim did himself. He was growing more and more bald.

By this time the district was widely settled. Hromund,

brother of Grim the Halogalander, made his home at Thverar-hlid, as did members of his crew. He was the father of Gunn-laug, father of Thurid Sowthistle, mother of Illugi the Black.

One summer, after Egil had been a good many years at Borg, some ships arrived in Iceland from Norway with the news that Bjorn the Yeoman was dead, and that all the money belonging to Bjorn had been taken over by his son-in-law, Berg-Onund. He had taken all the movable property, rented out the farmland, claiming all the rents for himself, and also got possession of all the estate-land there that had been held by Bjorn. When Egil heard about this, he began to question minutely, whether Berg-Onund had done all this on his own initiative, or with the backing of other powerful people. They told him that Onund had become King Eirik's close friend, and an even closer friend to Queen Gunnhild.

Egil did nothing about it that autumn, but as winter wore on and spring was coming he launched a ship that he owned which had been standing in a shed at Langriver Foss, got it ready for a voyage and hired a crew. His wife Asgerd decided to go with him but Thordis, Thorolf's daughter, was left behind.

As soon as everything was ready, Egil put out to sea, and reached Norway after an uneventful voyage. At the first opportunity he went to see Arinbjorn, who gave him a good welcome and invited him to stay. Egil accepted gladly, and went there with Asgerd and a number of his men. It wasn't long before he began to talk with Arinbjorn about the land claim it seemed to him he had there in Norway.

'It doesn't look too promising to me,' said Arinbjorn. 'Berg-Onund is a hard and difficult man. He's unjust and greedy, and now he's got the King and the Queen completely on his side. I don't need to tell you that Gunnhild's your worst enemy, and she's not going to encourage Berg-Onund to set the matter right.'

'The King will see that I get my lawful rights in this case,' said Egil, 'and with your backing I'm not afraid of taking Berg-Onund to law.'

So they decided that Egil should man a small ship, and off they went, twenty strong. They made south to Hordaland until they reached Ask, and there they went up to the house to see Onund. Egil had his say and demanded that Onund should divide up Bjorn's legacy, arguing that Bjorn's daughters had equal rights to the inheritance.

'In my opinion,' he went on, 'Asgerd is a great deal better born than your wife Gunnhild.'

'You're a very daring man, Egil,' answered Onund very sharply, 'an outlaw of King Eirik coming here to his kingdom and bullying his men. You can take it from me, Egil, that I've put down people like you before and for less reason than this. You claim an inheritance for your wife, when everyone knows that she's the daughter of a bondswoman.'

Onund ranted on like this for some time and Egil could see that he was never going to set matters right, so he summonsed him to a court, his case to be according to the laws of the Gula Assembly.

'I'll be there at the Gula Assembly,' said Onund, 'and if I have my way, you won't be in one piece when you leave there.'

Egil said that he would just have to risk it, and meant to go to the assembly in any event. 'Our case will go according to our luck,' he said.

Then Egil and his men left. When they got back home he told Arinbjorn about his trip and the reply that Onund had given. Arinbjorn was in an utter fury about his aunt Thora being called a slave-woman. He went to see King Eirik and put the case to him, but the King replied unfavourably and said that Arinbjorn had been supporting Egil too strongly for too long.

'It's thanks to you that I've let him stay here in Norway,' said the King, 'but I won't find it so easy if you keep backing him every time he walks all over my friends.'

'You'll have to let us win our rights in this case,' said Arinbjorn, 'in accordance with the law.'

The King didn't like this in the least, and Arinbjorn could

see that the Queen's attitude would be even worse, so he went back home saying that things looked far from hopeful.

The winter passed, and when it was time for people to go to the Gula Assembly, Arinbjorn gathered a large number of men to attend the assembly with him, including Egil. King Eirik was there with a large following, and Berg-Onund and his brothers joined the King's party with a good number of their own men. When proceedings began, both parties went to the place where the court had been established, to give their testimony. Onund was full of big talk.

The court was held on a level stretch of ground on which hazel poles had been arranged in a circle, with ropes called 'holy ropes' going all round. Inside the circle sat the judges, twelve from Fjord Province, twelve from Sogn and twelve from Hordaland. These were the thirty-six men who were to judge the cases. Arinbjorn had control over which judges were chosen from Fjord Province, and Thord of Aurland over the choice of judges from Sogn. All of these were on the same side.

Arinbjorn had brought a large body of men to the assembly. Besides a fast-sailing vessel, fully manned, he had a good many smaller ones, skiffs and ferries captained by farmers. King Eirik's following was also a large one, in six or seven longships, and there were many farmers with him, too. Egil opened his case by asking the judges to grant him his rights in law against Onund. He listed all the evidence for his claim to the money that had belonged to Bjorn Brynjolfsson, declaring that Asgerd, Bjorn's daughter and Egil's wife, was a rightful heiress, well-born and descended from land-holders in all branches of the family, with royal blood in the more remote past, and he asked the judges to award Asgerd half of Bjorn's legacy in both land and movable property. When he had finished his speech, it was the turn of Berg-Onund.

'My wife Gunnhild,' he began, 'is the daughter of Bjorn and of Alof, the woman he took as his lawful wife, so Gunnhild is the rightful heiress to Bjorn's property. That was the reason why I appropriated all that Bjorn had possessed: I knew that Bjorn's only other daughter was not his legal heiress. Her mother was taken as a concubine without her kinsmen's approval and carried to a foreign country. As for you, Egil, your behaviour's the same as it's been everywhere else, just as unreasonable and overbearing, but this time you won't get away with it. King Eirik and Queen Gunnhild have promised me my rights in every case that comes under their authority. I'll produce irrefutable evidence before the King and the judges to prove that Asgerd's mother, Thora Lace-Cuff, was carried captive from the home of her brother Thorir, and later from that of Brynjolf of Aurland, went overseas with vikings and the King's outlaws, and gave birth to Asgerd, this daughter of hers and Bjorn's during that exile. It's very odd that Egil should be trying to go against all that King Eirik himself has said: first of all, Egil, by remaining in this country after King Eirik had declared you an outlaw, and secondly, by claiming your wife to be a rightful heir when she's legally a bond-slave. I ask the judges to award me all the money left by Bjorn, and to declare Asgerd to be the King's slave as she was conceived when her father and mother had been outlawed by the King.'

Then Arinbjorn spoke. 'We shall bring witnesses, King Eirik, supported by sworn testimony, that it was stipulated in the agreement between my father Thorir and Bjorn the Yeoman that Asgerd, daughter of Bjorn and Thora, was to inherit from her father Bjorn: and secondly, you know very well, my lord, that you had Bjorn reinstated, and that the whole issue which once stood between the men's reconciliation has been completely settled.'

The King was slow to answer Arinbjorn's speech, so Egil spoke this verse:

> My bride was base born
> Declares this brooch-wearer:
> Only of his avarice
> Thinks this Onund.
> Spear-shaker, you can swear
> Asgerd serves no small beer:
> Trust this testimony,
> True-born King.

Then Arinbjorn had twelve carefully selected men give their testimony, each of them having heard the agreement between Thorir and Bjorn. After that the King and the judges were invited to take their oaths, but the King said he would have nothing to do with the matter, for or against.

Next Queen Gunnhild spoke up. 'It's very odd, my lord,' she said, 'that you let this big fellow Egil tangle up all your cases for you. I suppose you wouldn't even complain if he wanted to take the whole kingdom off your hands. But whether or not you're going to refuse Onund the verdict, I'm not going to put up with it. Egil isn't going to trample all over my friends, grabbing this money that doesn't belong to him. Where are you, Alf Askman? Take your people over to where the judges are and stop this miscarriage of justice.'

So Alf Askman ran with his people to the place of judgement, cut the holy rope, broke the poles and chased away the judges. The gathering turned into a brawl, but nobody there had any weapons. Then Egil spoke.

'Can Berg-Onund hear what I say?' he asked.

'I can hear you,' replied Onund.

'Then I'm challenging you to a duel to be fought here at the assembly. Whoever wins takes everything at stake, money, land and goods, but if you don't dare to risk it then everyone will know you for the coward you are.'

King Eirik gave the answer. 'If you're so keen to fight, Egil, we'll grant you that favour now,' he said.

'I don't want to fight you,' said Egil, 'or fight against the odds, but if I get the chance to fight on equal terms, I don't care who it is, I'll not run away.'

'Let's get out of here,' said Arinbjorn, 'there's nothing we can do to help our case.'

He started to leave with all his men, but Egil turned back.

'I refer this to you, Arinbjorn,' he announced, 'and to you Thord, and to all those who can hear my words, land-holders, lawmen, and every common man. I forbid anyone to settle or farm the land formerly belonging to Bjorn. I forbid you, Berg-Onund, and all other men, native or foreign, high or low, to do so, and whoever does will stand accused by me of breaking the laws of the land, of violating the peace, and of incurring the anger of the gods.'

After that Egil left with Arinbjorn. They went down to their ships which were on the far side of a certain hill so that they could not be seen from the assembly. When Arinbjorn got to the ships, this is what he said:

'Everyone knows how the assembly has turned out: we failed to get our rights and the King is in such a rage that if he gets the chance our people are likely to be much the worse for it. Now I want everybody to take his ship and sail home.'

Next he spoke to Egil. 'Board your ship with all your party,' he said, 'and get on your way quickly. Keep a sharp look-out, the King will be watching for another chance to arrange a meeting with you. But whatever happens between you and the King, come and see me.'

Egil did as he was asked, and with thirty other men he boarded a skiff and put out at speed, for the boat was a fast one. There were plenty more of Arinbjorn's boats pulling out of harbour, skiffs and ferries, but Arinbjorn's longship came last as it was the heaviest to row. As Egil's skiff raced ahead of the others he made this verse:

> The heir of Thorn-Foot,
> Thief of the inheritance,
> Has looted my legacy
> And threatens my life:
> Can I repay the pillage
> Of my ploughed fields?
> There's something to strive for,
> Money's at stake.

King Eirik had heard Egil's concluding words at the assembly and worked himself up into a great rage. As everyone there was unarmed he made no move to attack, but ordered all his men down to the ships, and they did as they were told. Then he held a meeting and explained to them what he planned to do.

'We'll take down the awnings on our ships,' he said. 'I'm

going to see Arinbjorn and Egil. I want you to know that if there's the least chance I'm going to have Egil put to death and I won't spare anyone who tries to stop us.'

At that they went aboard their ships, got them ready as fast as they could, put out to sea and rowed with all speed to the place where Arinbjorn's ships had been lying. Then the King told his men to row north through the channels, and when they reached Sognfjord they could see Arinbjorn's fleet. The longship changed course towards Sauesund and the King turned after it. He caught up with Arinbjorn's ship, sailed right up to it and exchanged words with Arinbjorn, asking if Egil was aboard.

'You can see easily enough for yourself that he isn't on my ship,' replied Arinbjorn. 'Everyone aboard here is known to you, and Egil isn't the man to skulk below deck when you two meet.'

The King asked Arinbjorn what was the last he knew of Egil, and Arinbjorn said that he had been in a skiff with thirty men. 'They were making their way out to Steinsund,' he said. The King and his men had noticed a large number of ships rowing in the direction of Steinsund, so he ordered his crew to row through the inner channels and then swing round to meet Egil. A man called Ketil, one of King Eirik's retainers, piloted the King's ship with Eirik at the helm. Ketil was a fine big man, good-looking and closely related to the King, and everyone agreed that he and the King were very much alike to look at.

Before he had gone to the assembly, Egil had floated his own ship by shifting its cargo. Now he rowed to the place where it lay and went aboard, but the skiff lay between the ship and the shore with its oars and rudder at the ready.

In the morning before it was fully light, the men on watch saw some big ships rowing towards them. As soon as Egil learned about this he got up, and saw very quickly that trouble was on the way. There were six longships making for them.

Egil told all his men to get into the skiff, then picked up

the two chests King Athelstan had given him, which he always kept close by him. The men jumped into the skiff and they all armed themselves fast, rowing on straight between the shore and King Eirik's ship, which was sailing closest to the land. It was all over in a minute. Before it was daylight the two ships had passed by each other. As the after-decks came into line Egil threw a spear, hitting the belly of the man sitting at the helm, Ketil the Hadalander. Then King Eirik called out orders for his men to row after Egil. As they went by the merchant-ship the King's men boarded it, and every single man of Egil's they could get at, all those who hadn't gone into the skiff, were slaughtered on the spot. Ten of Egil's men were killed there but some managed to scramble ashore. While some of the King's men went for the merchant-ship, and took everything of value before they set fire to it, others chased after Egil, working hard at the oars, two men to each, for there were plenty of hands aboard. Egil's ship was not well crewed, with only eighteen of them in the skiff, so the distance between the two soon started to narrow. To landward of the island there was a shallow channel that was fordable, separating it from the neighbouring island. There was an ebb tide, and Egil and his men ran their boat through the shallows, but the King's ship didn't have enough clearance and that was how they parted. Egil sailed north until he joined up with Arinbjorn, then he made this verse:

> Now the bitter bearer
> Of the blazing war-blade
> Has taken ten
> Of my trusted followers:
> But my salmon-like spear
> Settled the score
> When I cast it through
> The curved ribs of Ketil.

When Egil met Arinbjorn he told him about what had happened. Arinbjorn said that Egil could hardly have expected better from his dealings with King Eirik – 'but you won't be short of money, Egil,' he said, 'I'll compensate you for your ship and give you another one to go back to Iceland in.' While they'd been at the assembly, Egil's wife Asgerd had been staying with Arinbjorn, who gave Egil a fine ocean-going ship and had it loaded with a cargo of timber. Egil got it ready for the voyage, and still had about thirty men with him. He and Arinbjorn parted good friends, and he made this verse:

> May the Gods get rid
> Of this ruling robber,
> Let the heavens hang him
> For highway robbery!
> May Odin and the others,
> Frey and Njord, show their anger
> To this enemy of ease
> And order at assemblies.

57. Egil kills Berg-Onund

WHEN Harald Fine-Hair was getting on in years, he appointed King Eirik overlord of all his other sons, and when Harald had ruled for seventy years he handed over all his power to his son, King Eirik. It was about this time that Queen Gunnhild bore a son whom Harald gave his own name and sprinkled with water. Harald said that the boy should be king after his father when he was old enough, then settled down quietly, staying most of the time in Hordaland or Rogaland. Three years later he died in Rogaland and a burial mound was raised over him at Haugesund.

After he died there was bitter feuding between his sons, since the men of Oslofjord took Olaf as their king while the men of Trondlag chose Sigurd. But a year after King Harald died, Eirik killed these two brothers of his at Tonsberg. Everything happened the same summer: King Eirik led his troops from Hordaland east to Oslofjord to fight his brothers, and Egil and Berg-Onund faced each other at the Gula Assembly with the consequences that we've just described.

When the King set out on his expedition, Berg-Onund stayed at home on his farm since he thought it unsafe to leave while Egil was still in the vicinity. His brother Hadd was with him at the time.

There was a man called Frodi, King Eirik's foster-son and kinsman, still quite young but very handsome and fully grown to manhood. King Eirik left him behind, with the task of giving help to Berg-Onund. Frodi had a party of men with him at the King's estate in Aarstad. The son of Eirik and Gunnhild, called Rognvald, was staying with Frodi when all this happened. Rognvald was ten or eleven years old at the time, and a promising lad.

Before King Eirik set out on this expedition he declared Egil an outlaw throughout Norway. Any man could kill him. Arinbjorn went on this expedition with the King, but before he left home, Egil put out to sea towards an outlying fishing station called Vitar, beyond the isle of Alden and away from the normal sea-routes. It was a good place for getting news as there were fishermen there, and it was here that he heard the King had outlawed him, so he made this verse:

> Land-spirit, long the road
> The law-breaker makes me walk,
> Banished by the brother-killer
> And his bitter woman:
> Cunning and cruel
> The character of Gunnhild,
> But no beating about
> The bush for young Egil.

There were light winds blowing from the mountains by night and from the sea by day. One evening when Egil and his men put out to sea, the fishermen, who had been sent to spy on his movements, rowed to the mainland with the report that he had sailed away. The report came to the ears of Berg-Onund, and when he heard it he sent off all the men he had gathered there for self-protection, then rowed over to Aarstad to invite Frodi to a feast since he had plenty of ale at home. Frodi went with him, taking along a number of his men. They enjoyed a fine feast with plenty of fun and not a hint of anything to be afraid of. Rognvald, the King's son, had a boat with six oars a side and all painted above the sea-line. There were ten or twelve men who were his constant companions. After Frodi had gone, Rognvald took the boat and twelve of them rowed out to Herle Island, where there was a large royal estate. The man in charge was called Beard-Thorir, and it was here that Rognvald had been fostered as a child. Thorir gave the King's son a hearty welcome and there was no shortage of strong drink.

As we said, Egil sailed out to sea that night, and in the morning the wind dropped. The sea grew calm, so they set the boat on course and let it drift for a few days. When the sea breeze began to freshen Egil gave instructions to his crew.

'Now we'll sail up to the mainland,' he said. 'If there's a strong breeze from the sea, no one can tell where we might come to land, though there aren't many spots likely to bring us peace and quiet.'

The crew told Egil their journey was in his hands, so they hoisted sail and made for Herle Island where they found a good anchorage, set up the awnings and spent the night. They had a small boat aboard with them. Egil got into it with two of his men and that night they rowed up to Herle. He sent one of his men inland to get the news, and the man came back to say that the King's son Rognvald was there with his companions at the farm.

'They're sitting there drinking,' he said. 'I spoke to one of the servants and he was out of his mind with drink. He told me there wasn't going to be any less drinking there than at Berg-Onund's, where Frodi and four others were being feasted.' He added that with the exception of the people of the household, there was no one with Berg-Onund apart from Frodi and his companions.

Then Egil rowed back to the ship and told his men to get up and bring their weapons, which is what they did. They moved the ship farther out to sea and cast anchor. Egil left twelve men in charge, boarded the tow-boat with the rest, eighteen in all, and rowed up through the sounds. They timed it so that they reached the island in the evening and put in at a secret cove.

'Now I'm going alone up into the island,' said Egil, 'to find out what's going on there. Wait for me here.'

Egil had his usual weapons with him, helmet and shield, a sword at his waist and a halberd in his hand. He made his way up into the island, keeping to the edge of a certain wood. He had a long hood pulled down over his helmet. He came to a place where there were several young men with large sheep-dogs, and after they'd got talking together he asked where they came from and why they had such big dogs.

'You must be really stupid,' they said. 'Haven't you heard about the bear roaming the island? It's a proper menace, and it's killing men and cattle alike. There's a reward on its head. We keep nightly watch here at Ask guarding our livestock in their pens. What are you doing, carrying weapons at night?'

'I'm scared of the bear,' said Egil. 'I don't think you'll see many people going around unarmed just now. The bear's been after me all night – you can see him over there, just by the edge of the wood. Are all the people at the farm asleep now?'

One of the young men said that Berg-Onund and Frodi would still be up drinking. 'They're always sitting up at night,' he said.

'Then go and tell them where the bear is,' said Egil, 'I have to hurry back home.' At that he went away.

The lad ran up to the farmstead and into the hall where they were drinking. It so happened that everyone had gone to bed except three, Onund, Frodi and Hadd. The lad told them where the bear was, and they grabbed their weapons which were hanging beside them, and rushed outside into the wood. The edge of the wood was broken, with low bushes here and there, in which the lad told them the bear had been hiding. They saw that something was stirring the leaves so they assumed the bear must be there. Then Berg-Onund told Hadd and Frodi to run ahead between the copse and the main forest to prevent the bear from getting away into the wood.

Berg-Onund himself rushed straight into the bushes. He too had a helmet and shield, a sword at his waist and a halberd in his hand. But there was no bear in the thicket: only Egil was waiting there. As soon as he could make out where Berg-Onund was, he pulled out his sword: there was a loop attached to the grip and around his hand, from which the sword hung. He took his halberd in hand and ran forward to face Berg-Onund, who moved faster himself as soon as he saw this, holding his shield in front of him. Just before they met, each flung his halberd at the other. Egil let his shield take the halberd, holding it aslant so that a piece was sliced away. Then the halberd fell to the ground. But Egil's halberd struck Berg-Onund's shield right in the centre and passed through it some way up the blade so that it stuck firm in the shield. Berg-Onund began to find the shield heavy to carry, and tried to draw his sword, but before he could pull it half-way out of the scabbard, Egil had run him through. Onund staggered at the blow, and Egil tugged his sword out sharply, then struck at Onund, nearly slicing off his head. After that, Egil pulled the halberd from the shield.

Hadd and Frodi saw Berg-Onund fall and ran towards him. Egil turned to meet them and flung his halberd right through Frodi's shield and into his chest so that the point came out of his back. At once Frodi fell backwards, dead. Egil took his sword and turned to face Hadd. They hadn't exchanged many strokes before Hadd fell. Then the herdsmen came up and Egil spoke to them.

'Keep an eye on your master Onund and his companions,' said Egil, 'we don't want birds and beasts ripping up their corpses.'

At that Egil went on his way and it wasn't long before he was joined by eleven of his men. The other six had been guarding the ship. When they asked him what he'd been up to, he made this verse:

> Too much have I suffered
> The malice of this miser,
> More prudent in past days

Was I with my purse:
These warriors won't wake,
Not from wounds that I gave them,
A blood-coif I bestowed
On Earth, Odin's bed-mate.

'Let's go back to the farmstead and act the warrior's part,' said Egil, 'kill everyone we can get at, and grab all the loot we can carry.'

They walked over to the farmhouse, rushed inside and killed some fifteen or sixteen men there, though others took to their heels and got away. They looted everything of value there, and what they couldn't take with them they destroyed. The livestock they drove down to the shore and slaughtered, loading the boat with as much as it would carry, then went ahead, rowing out by way of the channels between the islands. Egil sat at the helm, and he was so worked up that no one could speak to him.

As they were making their way through the channel in the direction of Herle, the King's son Rognvald and his twelve companions came rowing towards them in the painted galley. They had learned that Egil's ship was anchored off Herle, and planned to warn Berg-Onund of Egil's travels. As soon as he saw it, Egil recognized the galley and steered straight for it. When they collided the prow of the skiff rammed the side of the galley so hard it keeled over and water came flooding in on the other side, filling the ship. Egil jumped to his feet and grabbed the halberd, calling on his men not to let anyone aboard the galley escape with his life. It wasn't a hard task since no one offered any resistence. Everyone aboard the galley died, not one got away. Rognvald and his companions, all thirteen of them, lost their lives there. After that, Egil and his men rowed up to the island and Egil made this verse:

We fought with no fear
Of future vengeance,
I dabbled my blade
In Bloodaxe's boy,
In one galley Gunnhild's son

With twelve gold-adorned men
Bleeding and broken:
Busy, these battle-hands.

When they got to Herle, Egil and his men wasted no time but ran fully armed up to the farmstead. When Thorir and his household saw this, every one of them who could shift for themselves, men and women alike, ran for their lives from the farm. Egil and his men looted everything they could get their hands on, then went back to their ship, and they didn't have long to wait before a good wind began to blow from the mainland. They prepared to sail, but when they were ready to set out Egil went ashore onto the island, picked up a branch of hazel and went to a certain cliff that faced the mainland. Then he took a horse head, set it up on the pole and spoke these formal words: 'Here I set up a pole of insult against King Eirik and Queen Gunnhild' – then, turning the horse head towards the mainland – 'and I direct this insult against the guardian spirits of this land, so that every one of them shall go astray, neither to figure nor find their dwelling places until they have driven King Eirik and Queen Gunnhild from this country.'

Next he jammed the pole into a cleft in the rock and left it standing there with the horse head facing towards the mainland, and cut runes on the pole declaiming the words of his formal speech. After that he went aboard, and they hoisted sail and made for the open sea. The wind increased steadily blowing fresh and favourable, and the ship made good progress. Then Egil made this verse:

The mast-beater blows,
The bow chisels
The smooth sea
Into spraystorms:
The wild willow-shaker
Whirls hard and cold,
Savaging the breast
Of my sailing swan.

They held on out towards the open sea and had a good passage with a landfall at Borgarfjord, where Egil brought his ship into harbour. They carried their baggage ashore, then Egil went home to Borg while his crew found other places to stay.

Skallagrim was getting on in years by now, and infirm with old age, so Egil took over the running of the estate and looked after the farm.

58. Skallagrim dies

THERE was a man called Thorgeir who married Thordis Yngvar's daughter, the sister of Egil's mother, Bera. He lived at Lambastead on Alftaness, and had come to Iceland with Yngvar. He was a wealthy man and people liked him. Thorgeir and Thordis had a son called Thord who took charge of Lambastead after his father's death just about the time Egil came back to Iceland.

It so happened that in the autumn, shortly before winter, Thord rode over to Borg to visit his kinsman Egil and invite him to a feast. He had had some ale brewed back at home. Egil promised to come and it was agreed that the feast would be held about a week later. When the time arrived, Egil got ready to go, along with his wife Asgerd and some eight or ten others.

As Egil was about to leave, Skallagrim came out with him. Before Egil mounted, Skallagrim gripped him tight.

'It seems to me, Egil,' he said, 'that you're in no great hurry to give me the money that King Athelstan sent me. What do you think should be done with it?'

'Are you really hard up, father?' asked Egil. 'I didn't know that! When I think you're short of silver I'll give it you, but it so happens that I know you've still got the odd chest-full.'

'It looks to me as if you've already decided about the division of our money,' said Skallagrim, 'so you'll be glad to see me do whatever I like with what I've got.'

'You won't want to ask my permission,' said Egil. 'No matter what I say, you'll do just as you want.'

At that he went on his way till he reached Lambastead, where he was given a warm and happy welcome. He was to stay there for three nights.

That same evening, when Egil had gone away, Skallagrim had a horse saddled and set out from home after the rest of the household had gone to bed, riding with a biggish chest on his knee and a brass cauldron under his arm. People say that he sank either one or both into Krum's Bog, with a great stone slab on top. He came back about midnight and went straight to bed without taking off his clothes. In the morning when it was light and people had got up and dressed, there was Skallagrim sitting on the edge of the bed, dead and so stiff they could neither lift him nor straighten him out, no matter how they tried. Then a man was put on horseback to ride fast over to Lambastead, and without wasting any time he found Egil and told him the news. Egil took his clothes and weapons and rode home to Borg that evening. As soon as he had dismounted he went inside across to an alcove off the main living-room, where there was a door leading to the inner benches. Egil went up to the bench, took hold of Skallagrim's shoulder and pulled him backwards, forcing him down onto the bench. Then he gave him the last rites. Next he asked for digging tools and broke a hole through the south wall. When that was done, he got hold of Skallagrim's head while others took his feet, and in this way they carried him from one side of the house to the other and through the hole that had been made in the wall. Without delay they next carried the body down to Naustaness, and pitched a tent over it for the night. The following morning, at high tide, Skallagrim was put into a boat and taken out to Digraness. Egil had a burial mound raised there on the tip of the headland, and inside it Skallagrim was laid with his horse, weapons and blacksmith's tools. There's no mention of any money being placed in the mound with him.

Egil took over his inheritance, the estate and all the movable goods, being already in charge of the farm. Thordis, the daughter of Thorolf and Asgerd, was there with him.

59. Egil comes to York

KING Eirik had been ruling in Norway for one year after the death of his father King Harald, when another of Harald's sons, Hakon, Athelstan's foster-son, came to Norway from England, the same summer that Egil Skallagrimsson had gone to Iceland. Hakon went north to Trondheim and there he was adopted as King, so both he and Eirik were rulers of Norway during the following winter. In the spring they both gathered armies, but since Hakon had by far the larger Eirik could see that his only choice was to leave the country; so he went away with his wife Gunnhild and their children.

Chieftain Arinbjorn was King Eirik's blood-brother and had been foster-father to one of his children. He was dearer to Eirik than any other of his landed men and the King had made him chieftain over the whole of Fjord Province. Arinbjorn shared the King's exile.

First they sailed west over the sea to Orkney where King Eirik gave his daughter Ragnhild in marriage to Earl Arnfinn, then he went south with his troops, raiding in Scotland, and from there to England where he continued to raid. When King Athelstan heard about this he gathered an army and marched against Eirik, and when they met, after appeals for peace had been made to both sides, it was agreed that King Athelstan should give Eirik charge of Northumberland, and that Eirik would defend the country for King Athelstan against the Scots and Irish. King Athelstan had made Scotland tributary to him after the death of King Olaf but the people there had never been loyal to him. King Eirik took up permanent residence in York.

The story goes that Gunnhild had it brought about by witchcraft that Egil Skallagrimsson would never find peace in Iceland until she had seen him again. But during the summer that Hakon and Eirik were in conflict over Norway there was an embargo on all ships leaving Norway, so no ships sailed to Iceland that summer, and no news reached there.

Egil Skallagrimsson stayed on his farm, but the second winter that he farmed at Borg after the death of Skallagrim he began to grow moody, and the more winter wore on the more miserable he became. When it was summer again, Egil let it be known that he was planning to get his ship ready for a voyage that summer. He hired a crew and sailed for England with thirty men aboard, while Asgerd stayed behind to look after their farm.

Egil had meant to go and see King Athelstan about the offers the King had made him when they parted, but his preparations were late and on putting out he had to wait around for a favourable wind. It was getting near autumn and they ran into strong gales. They sailed north of Orkney, but Egil chose not to land there since he bore in mind that King Eirik's rule extended right through the islands. So they sailed southwards along the Scottish coast in heavy weather and with contrary winds, but managed to tack south beyond Scotland as far as the north of England. Late one day, with darkness falling and a strong gale blowing, they suddenly found themselves with breakers both to seaward and ahead, so there was nothing for it but to make straight for the shore, which is what they did, deliberately wrecking the ship when they made land in the Humber estuary. Everyone aboard was saved along with most of the cargo, but the ship was broken to matchwood.

When they met some people and talked to them, they heard news which sounded ominous to Egil, that King Eirik Blood-Axe and Gunnhild were ruling that part of the country and that the King was in residence near by, at the town of York. Egil also heard that Chieftain Arinbjorn was staying with the King, and was a great favourite with him.

When Egil learned this he made his decision. He realized there was little chance of escape even if he were to risk travelling secretly and in disguise during the long journey out of Eirik's kingdom, since all who saw him would find him easy to recognize. It also seemed cowardly to be caught trying to run away, so he plucked up his courage, got himself a horse, and set out for the town.

Egil reached it in the evening and rode straight in, wearing a long hood down over the helm and carrying a full set of weapons. He asked whereabouts in town he could find Arinbjorn's house and someone told him, so he rode there. When he reached the door he got down from his horse and spoke to a man there, who told him that Arinbjorn was still at table.

'My good fellow,' said Egil, 'I want you to go into the hall and ask Arinbjorn whether he'd prefer to talk to Egil Skallagrimsson inside or outside.'

'It's no great labour to perform that little task,' said the man, and went into the hall shouting out, 'there's a man as tall as a troll at the door who's told me to come in and ask whether you'll talk to Egil Skallagrimsson inside or outside.'

'Ask him to wait outside,' said Arinbjorn, 'he won't have to wait long.'

The man did as Arinbjorn had told him and gave Egil the message. Arinbjorn ordered the tables to be cleared from the hall, then went outside with his retainers. He greeted Egil when they met and asked what brought him there. Egil told him the reason for his travels in a few plain words.

'If there's any help you're ready to give,' he said, 'now's the time to speak up.'

'Did you meet anyone in town before you came to the house who might have recognized you?' asked Arinbjorn.

'Nobody,' said Egil.

'Then let the men arm themselves,' said Arinbjorn, and so they did.

When everyone, servants and all, had his weapons, Arinbjorn set out for the King's residence, knocked on the door upon his arrival, announced who he was and asked for it to be opened. At once the doorkeepers opened up. The King was sitting at table, and Arinbjorn asked Egil and ten other men to go inside with him.

'Now, Egil,' said Arinbjorn, 'you'll have to offer your head to the King and take his foot in your hand while I plead your case for you.'

At that they went in. Arinbjorn went up to the King and greeted him. The King made him welcome and asked what he wanted.

'There's a man in my company who's come a long way to pay you a visit and seek a settlement with you,' said Arinbjorn. 'It's a mark of profound respect, my lord, when your enemies travel of their own free will from far-distant lands, and all because, no matter what the distance, they can't bear the thought of your anger. Show your great heart to this man, settle generously with him for, as all can see, he pays you great honour by journeying so far from his farmstead, crossing oceans and obstacles. Nothing drove him forth on this journey but his goodwill towards you.'

The King looked around, saw Egil standing head and shoulders above the others, and gave him a hard look.

'Why so bold as to come visiting me, Egil?' he asked. 'After our last meeting you could hardly have expected me to spare you.'

Then Egil went up to the table, took the King's foot in his hands and spoke this verse:

> Headlong I came, hard-tacking
> My ocean-horse
> Eagerly to King Eirik
> On England's isle:
> Scion of the great king,
> The sword-scarer greets you,
> The high-couraged one,
> Confronts Harald's kin.

'There's no need for me to list all the charges against you,' said the King, 'they're so many and so serious that any one of them is reason enough why you're not getting away from here alive. There's no chance of your finding anything here but death. You must have realized before this that you'd get no reconciliation from me.'

'Why not kill Egil here and now,' said Gunnhild, 'or have

you forgotten what he's done? Killed your friends and your kinsmen, even your own son, and slandered you! Can anyone say where royalty has ever been treated like that?'

'If Egil has slandered the King, he can make up for it with words of praise that will be remembered for all time,' said Arinbjorn.

'We don't want to hear his words of praise,' said Gunnhild. 'Have him taken out and killed, Eirik. I don't want to hear him or see him.'

'The King isn't going to let you talk him into doing all your dirty work,' said Arinbjorn, 'and he won't let Egil be killed at night because a night killing would be murder.'

'Let it be as you wish, Arinbjorn,' said the King. 'Egil can have his life for tonight. Take him home with you and bring him back to me in the morning.'

Arinbjorn thanked the King for what he'd said.

'I'm hoping Egil's problems will soon take a turn for the better,' said Arinbjorn. 'It's true that Egil has caused you serious offence, but bear in mind how much he's suffered himself at your hands and those of your kinsmen. Your father, King Harald, had Egil's uncle, that fine man Thorolf, put to death for no more reason than the slanderous talk of villains. You yourself, my lord, twisted the law to help Berg-Onund against Egil. On top of that you wanted him put to death, you had some of his men killed, you took all his money from him, and made him an outlaw and drove him out of the country – but Egil's not a man to play games with. Every case has to be judged on its merits. I'm taking Egil home with me now to my house for the night.' And that's what he did.

When they got to Arinbjorn's house, he and Egil went into a small loft-room to talk matters over.

'The King was in a fury just now,' said Arinbjorn, 'though towards the end his mood seemed to me to soften a little. But it's luck that will decide what's to come. I'm sure of one thing, that Gunnhild will do all she can to ruin your case. Now I'd like to give you this advice: stay awake all night and compose a poem in Eirik's praise. I'd like it to be a *drápa*[1] of twenty stanzas that you could recite when we see the King tomorrow morning. That's what my kinsman Bragi the Old did when he had to face the anger of King Bjorn of Sweden. He made a *drápa* of twenty stanzas overnight and that's what saved his head. Maybe we'll be able to use the same method with the King and get you reconciled with him.'

'I'll give it a try if you like,' said Egil, 'but I never expected to make a praise-song for King Eirik.'

Arinbjorn told him to have a try, then went back and sat drinking with his men till midnight. After that they went to their sleeping quarters, but before Arinbjorn undressed he went upstairs to Egil in the loft and asked him how the poem was getting on. Egil said he hadn't composed a line.

'There's a swallow been sitting at the window twittering all night long and I haven't been able to get a moment's peace,' he said.

Then Arinbjorn went off out through the door leading up to the roof, and settled down by the window where the bird had been sitting. He saw a shape changer of some kind going in the opposite direction, away from the house. Arinbjorn sat at the window all night till daybreak, and after his arrival, Egil managed to complete the whole poem and memorize it so well that when he saw Arinbjorn again in the morning he was able to recite it. They waited till it was time to see the King.

60. Egil escapes with his head

KING Eirik went to table as usual along with a large number of people. When Arinbjorn saw this, he set out with all his men, fully armed, and came to the royal residence where the King sat at table. Arinbjorn asked permission to enter the

1. *Drápa*: a poem, normally a eulogy of a king or great man, and having a regular refrain: for this reason it is considered superior to the *flokkr*, which has no refrain.

hall and this was granted. He and Egil walked inside, taking half of Arinbjorn's men with them and leaving the rest outside the door. Arinbjorn greeted the King and the King received him well.

'Now, sir,' said Arinbjorn, 'Egil is here and has not tried to get away during the night, so I'd like to know what's to become of him. I shall expect you to be fair. For my part, I've done all that I can to add to your reputation, as it was fitting that I should. I've given up all my possessions, friends and kinsmen in Norway to go with you, even though all your landed men abandoned you. But what I did was only decent and proper in view of the exceptional generosity you've shown to me.'

'Stop that, Arinbjorn,' said Gunnhild, 'don't go on about it. You've often done well by King Eirik and he's repaid you well, so you've a greater obligation to him than to Egil. You're in no position to ask King Eirik to let Egil leave here scot-free. Look at the offences he's committed.'

'If you, my lord, and Gunnhild have decided between you,' said Arinbjorn, 'that Egil is not going to get a settlement here, then it's only a matter of decency to allow him a week to travel freely where he likes, and the chance to save his own life, since he's come to you of his own free will expecting peace from you. After that, let your dealings go as they will.'

'Arinbjorn,' said Gunnhild, 'I can see from this that you're more loyal to Egil than to the King. If Egil is given a week to ride away from here unhindered, he'll have time to reach King Athelstan. And there's no need for Eirik to fool himself, every king is proving to be a better man than he is, though time was when nobody would have thought he lacked either the will or the way to take revenge on a man like Egil.'

'No one,' said Arinbjorn, 'is going to think Eirik any the greater for killing a foreign farmer's son who'd already given himself up into Eirik's hands. But if he really wants to make himself a reputation, I can help him to it in a way that people will talk about. Egil and I will stand by each other, so any man who attacks one of us will have to face the other as well, and by the time you've laid us all low you'll have paid quite a price for Egil's life. I hoped for better things from you than to be cut to the ground rather than granted a man's life when I ask for it.'

'You're being very impertinent, Arinbjorn,' said the King, 'over the help you're giving Egil. I'd be very reluctant to cause you any injury, should things come to that, and should you choose to sacrifice your own life rather than see him killed. But whatever I decide to have done to him, I've plenty to charge him with.'

When the King said this, Egil stepped forward to face him, began to declaim his poem, and was given an immediate hearing:

> *By sun and moon*
> *I journeyed west,*
> *My sea-borne tune*
> *From Odin's breast,*
> *My song-ship packed*
> *With poet's art:*
> *It's word-keel cracked*
> *The frozen heart.*

> *And now I feed*
> *With an English king:*
> *So to English mead*
> *I'll word-mead bring,*
> *Your praise my task,*
> *My song your fame,*
> *If you but ask*
> *I'll sound your name.*

> *These praises, King,*
> *Won't cost you dear*
> *That I shall sing*
> *If you will hear:*
> *Who beat and blazed*
> *Your trail of red,*
> *Till Odin gazed*
> *Upon the dead.*

The scream of swords,
The clash of shields,
These are true words
On battlefields:
Man sees his death
Frozen in dreams,
But Eirik's breath
Frees battle-streams.

The war-lord weaves
His web of fear,
Each man receives
His fated share:
A blood-red sun's
The warrior's shield,
The eagle scans
The battlefield.

As edges swing,
Blades cut men down.
Eirik the King
Earns his renown.

Break not the spell
But silent be:
To you I'll tell
Their bravery:
At clash of kings
On carrion-field
The red blade swings
At blue-stained shield.

When swords anoint
What man is saved?
Who gets this point
Is deep engraved:
And men like oak
From Odin's tree,
Few words they spoke
At that iron-play.

The edges swing,
Blades cut men down.
Eirik the King
Earns his renown.

The ravens dinned
At this red fare,
Blood on the wind,
Death in the air;
The Scotsmen's foes
Fed wolves their meat,
Death ends their woes
As eagles eat.

Carrion birds fly thick
To the body stack,
For eyes to pick
And flesh to hack:
The raven's beak
Is crimson-red,
The wolf goes seek
His daily bread.

The sea-wolves lie
And take their ease,
But feast the sly
Wolf overseas.

Valkyries keep
The troops awake,
There's little sleep
When shield-walls shake,
When arrows fly
The taut bow-string,
To bite or lie
With broken wing.

The peace is torn
By flying spears,
When bows are drawn
Wolves prick their ears,

The yew-bow shrills,
The edges bite,
The warrior wills
His men to fight

His arrows fly
Like swarms of bees
To feast the sly
Wolf overseas.

I praise the King
Throughout his land,
And keenly sing
His open hand,
His hand so free
With golden spoil:
But vice-like, he
Grips his own soil.

Bracelets of gold
He breaks in two
And, uncontrolled,
Pours gifts on you:
The lavish King
Loads you with treasure,
And everything
Is for your pleasure.

On his gold arm
The bright shield swings:
To his foes, harm:
To his friends, rings;
His fame's a feast
Of glorious war,
His name sounds east,
From shore to shore.

And now my lord,
You've listened long
As word on word
I built this song:

Your source is war,
Your streams are blood,
But my springs pour
Great Odin's flood.

To praise my lord
This tight mouth broke,
The word-floods poured,
The still tongue spoke,
From my poet's-breast
These words took wing:
Now all the rest
May learn to sing.

61. Egil's reward

KING Eirik sat bolt upright, his eyes fixed on Egil while he recited his poem. When it was finished the King spoke.

'The poem was finely delivered,' he said. 'Now, Arinbjorn, I've made up my mind how to settle the case between me and Egil. You've pleaded Egil's case with so much determination you've even reached the point of risking trouble from me, and it's for your sake that I'm going to do now what you ask, to let Egil leave here safe and unharmed. As for you, Egil, make your travel arrangements, from the moment you leave this room and my sight, in such a way that neither I nor my sons set eyes on you again. Never get in the way of me or my men. You can have your head as a present this time, because you put yourself in my hands and I'm not going to be hard on you, but there's something I want you to know. This is no settlement with me, or my sons, or any of my kin who want revenge.'

Then Egil made this verse:

Ugly as I, Egil, am
I'm not in the way
Of refusing from a ruler

My rock-helm of a head:
Was there ever an enemy
Won such an elegant
Gift from a great-hearted
Gallant like Eirik?

Arinbjorn thanked the King with all the words at his command for the honour and friendship he had shown. Then he and Egil went back to his house where he had horses ready for the men of his household. With a hundred and twenty of them, fully armed, he rode off to see Egil on his way. Arinbjorn and his men rode all the way to King Athelstan where they got a good welcome. The King invited Egil to stay and asked about how he'd been getting on with King Eirik. Then Egil said:

That juggler of justice,
That gift-lord of jackals,
Let the black-brow boast
Of his boon to Egil:
My wife's kinsman's courage
Came to my aid,
In spite of that sword-king
I keep my old skull.

On parting, Egil gave Arinbjorn the two gold bracelets he'd been given by Athelstan, each weighing a full mark. And in return Arinbjorn gave Egil a sword called Dragvendil given him by Thorolf Skallagrimsson, who had it from Skallagrim, and he from his brother Thorolf Kveldulfsson, who in turn had been given the sword by Grim Hairy-Cheek, the son of Ketil Trout. Once the sword had belonged to Ketil Trout who used it in single-combat, and there wasn't a sharper edge. So they parted the best of friends.

Arinbjorn went back to his home at York and King Eirik. Egil's companions and ship-mates took things easy and with the aid of Arinbjorn they were able to sell their cargo. Late in the winter they travelled south to England and joined Egil.

62. Egil goes to Norway

THERE was a land-holder in Norway called Eirik All-Wise, married to Thora the daughter of Chieftain Thorir, Arinbjorn's sister. Eirik All-Wise owned estates east of Oslofjord and was very wealthy, well thought of and a man of good judgement. He and his wife had a son called Thorstein who had been brought up with Arinbjorn and was by this time full grown, though still young. He had gone west with Arinbjorn to England.

The same autumn that Egil travelled to England, news came from Norway that Eirik All-Wise was dead and that the King's stewards had declared everything he left royal property and had confiscated it. When Arinbjorn and Thorstein heard about this they decided that Thorstein should go east and claim his inheritance.

Late that spring, when people planning to sail overseas were getting their ships ready, Thorstein went south to London and saw King Athelstan. He showed his credentials and a message from Arinbjorn to both the King and Egil asking for Athelstan to plead with his foster-son Hakon in Norway for Thorstein's property and inheritance there. King Athelstan agreed gladly, knowing Arinbjorn for the man he was.

Then Egil had a word with King Athelstan and told him his own plans.

'I want to go to Norway in the summer,' he said, 'and lay claim to the money King Eirik and Berg-Onund robbed me of. The man who's sitting on it now is Berg-Onund's brother, Atli the Short, but I know that when your words are given a hearing I'll get my rights in this case.'

The King said that where he went was for Egil himself to decide.

'But I'd prefer you to stay here,' he said, 'and defend my

country and take charge of my army. The revenues I'd grant you would be large.'

'It looks a very tempting offer to me,' said Egil, 'and I'd rather take it than leave it. But first of all I must go to Iceland for my wife and the money I have there.'

So King Athelstan gave Egil a fine trading ship and loaded it with a cargo of flour, honey, and plenty of other valuable things. Egil prepared the ship for the voyage and Thorstein Eiriksson, whom we mentioned before, or Thoruson as he was now called, decided to go with him. As soon as they were ready they put out to sea, Egil and King Athelstan parting the best of friends. Egil and Thorstein had a good journey to Oslofjord, east in Norway, then sailed right up into the fjord, where Thorstein owned estates along with others inland at Romerike.

As soon as Thorstein reached land he made claim to his inheritance before the stewards who had taken over his estates, and plenty of people gave him backing in this. Meetings were arranged to deal with the matter. Thorstein had a good many well-born kinsmen there, and as it turned out, the whole issue was handed over to the King for his decision, but in the meantime, Thorstein took over the property that his father had owned.

Egil and eleven of his men spent the winter with Thorstein. Honey and flour were brought over to Thorstein's place and there was ample entertainment over winter. Thorstein was a man who lived in style and had more than enough in the way of resources.

63. King Hakon's verdict

As we have already said, King Hakon, Athelstan's foster-son, was ruling in Norway at the time, and that winter he was in residence at Trondheim. Late in the winter Thorstein and Egil got themselves ready for a journey together with almost thirty men. When everything was set, they travelled first to the Uplands, then north over Dovrefjell to Trondheim where they went to see King Hakon and told him their business. Thorstein stated his case, and supported it with the testimony of witnesses, that he was entitled to all the inheritance he laid claim to. The King reacted in a friendly way to his plea and let him keep his property, and at the same time Thorstein became one of the King's men just like his father.

Egil went before the King and told him his business, giving him Athelstan's message and tokens of proof. Egil claimed as his right the property which had once belonged to Bjorn the Yeoman, both the estate and the movable goods, demanded half of everything for himself and his wife Asgerd, and supported his claim with sworn witnesses. He added that he had failed to get his rights because of King Eirik's power and Queen Gunnhild's influence, describing the whole case in detail as it had happened at the Gula Assembly. Then he asked the King to grant him his rights in the case.

'I've been told, Egil,' said Hakon, 'that my brother Eirik and Queen Gunnhild are of one mind, and think you've overstepped the mark in your dealings with them. As I see it, Egil, you ought to be pleased if I steer clear of the matter, though as it happens Eirik and myself don't see eye to eye.'

'You can't keep silent about an important case like this, sir,' said Egil. 'Everyone in this land, native or foreign, has to obey your word. I've heard that you're making new laws in the country to secure everybody's rights, and I know you'll let me have mine along with everyone else. As I see it, I've both the family background and the goodwill here in Norway to hold my own against Atli the Short, but as to my disagreement with King Eirik I can tell you this, that I went to see him, and when we parted he told me I could go in peace wherever I liked. My lord, I want to offer you my service and support, and I know there are men here who are thought less warlike than me. I don't think much time will pass, assuming that you and Eirik live long enough, before you two meet again. I'd not be surprised if the time comes when you think Gunnhild has too many ambitious sons.'

'You'll never be a retainer of mine, Egil,' said the King. 'You and your kin have done too much harm to my family to be able to settle down in this country. If you go back to Iceland and stay on your father's farm, you'll not suffer harm at the hands of our kin. But here in Norway no matter how long you live, you'll have to put up with the fact that my family is the stronger. However, for the sake of my foster-father, King Athelstan, you'll be granted peace in this land and get your rights according to the law, for I know how fond of you he is.'

Egil thanked the King for what he'd said, and asked for tokens of proof to take to Thord of Aurland and the other land-holders of Sogn and Hordaland. The King agreed to that.

64. Egil kills Ljot

THORSTEIN and Egil got ready for their journey as soon as they had completed their business. They set off home, but when they got south of Dovrefjell, Egil said he wanted to go down to Romsdale and then take the sea-route south between the islands.

'First of all I want to finish my business here in Sogn and Hordaland,' he said, 'then get my ship ready in the summer and sail back to Iceland.'

Thorstein told Egil he was free to go wherever he wanted, so they parted company, Thorstein travelling south through the Dales without a break till he got home to his farmstead, where he showed the King's stewards the tokens of proof and gave them the King's message telling them to surrender all the property they had taken and that he laid claim to.

Egil went on his way with his eleven companions. When they came to Romsdale they got transport south to More, and there's nothing to tell of their travels until they reached an island called Hod and took lodgings for the night at a farm-stead called Blindheim. It was a fine farm owned by a land-

holder named Fridgeir, a young man who had just taken over
his inheritance from his father. Fridgeir's mother Gyda was a
strong-minded woman and a great lady, and the sister of
Chieftain Arinbjorn. She helped her son with the manage-
ment of the estate and they ran a good farm there.

Egil and his men were given the friendliest of welcomes.
In the evening he was given a place next to Fridgeir, with his
men below him. There was plenty to drink and the feast was
a lavish one.

The housewife Gyda came to have a word with Egil that
evening, to ask about her brother Arinbjorn and the friends
and relatives who had gone to England with him. Egil told
her all she wanted to know. Then she asked him what had
happened on his own travels. He gave her a full account and
spoke this verse:

> The look of the land-grabber
> Was loathsome to me:
> Cuckoos won't perch
> To be killer-birds' carrion.
> I had Arinbjorn to aid me,
> As so often before;
> No man's lost when led
> By a loyal guide.

Egil was in high spirits all evening but Fridgeir and his
household were fairly subdued. Egil noticed a beautiful and
well-dressed young girl there and people told him she was
Fridgeir's sister. The girl was unhappy and kept crying all
evening, which Egil and his men thought very strange.

They spent the night there, but in the morning there was a
gale blowing, with heavy seas, and they had no boat to carry
them from the island. Then Fridgeir and Gyda went to see
Egil and invited him to stay there, with his companions, until
the weather was good enough for travelling. They also
offered him any transport he might need. Egil accepted the
invitation and they were weatherbound there for three nights,
though the entertainment was excellent. Then the weather
began to grow calmer, so Egil and his men got up early in the

morning and prepared to set out. They sat down to eat and were served with ale, then after they'd been sitting there for a while, they collected their clothes. Egil stood up and thanked the farmer and his mother for their hospitality, and they all went outside, the farmer and his mother, Gyda, seeing them on their way. Gyda started talking to her son, Fridgeir, in a whisper, so at this Egil stopped and waited for them, then spoke to the young woman.

'What are you crying for, girl?' he asked. 'I've never seen you look cheerful.'

She couldn't answer him and only cried more than ever.

Then Fridgeir spoke out loud to his mother. 'I'm not going to ask for that now they're ready and on their way,' he said. So Gyda came up to Egil.

'I'll tell you what's the matter with us here, Egil,' she said. 'There's a man called Ljot, a berserk and duel-fighter, hated by everyone. He came here and asked to marry my daughter, but we gave him a short answer and said no to his offer. After that, Ljot challenged my son Fridgeir to single combat, so he has to go and fight the duel tomorrow on the island of Valdero. What I'd like, Egil, is for you to go to the duel with Fridgeir. I know that if Arinbjorn were in Norway we wouldn't have to endure the brute-force of men like Ljot.'

'Lady,' said Egil, 'for your brother Arinbjorn's sake it's my duty to go with your son if he thinks I can be any help.'

'You're doing us a good turn,' said Gyda, 'let's go back to the hall, then, and spend the rest of the day together.'

Egil went back to the hall with his men, and started drinking. They sat there all day and in the evening some of Fridgeir's friends who had agreed to accompany him turned up, so there was quite a gathering there that night, and quite a feast.

Next day Fridgeir and a number of men, Egil among them, got ready for the journey. The weather was fine for travelling and they went on their way till they came to the island of Valdero. A short distance from the sea there was a pleasant field, and it was here that the duel was to be fought. The

combat area was laid out and marked with stones all around.
Then Ljot came up with his party and got himself ready for
the duel. He was a very big man, strong-looking, and carried
a shield and a sword. As he approached the combat area his
berserk fit came on and he began howling horribly and biting
his shield. Fridgeir wasn't very big. He was handsome-looking
but slenderly built and far from strong, and had never fought
a battle in his life.

When Egil saw Ljot, he made this verse:

> Fridgeir's sure to fail,
> So, friends, let's fight
> And guard the young girl
> Against this maniac,
> This violent valkyrie-maddened
> Shield-swallowing villain;
> The glaring god-feaster
> Goes to his own death.

Ljot saw where Egil was standing, and heard his verse.

'You, big man,' he said, 'come over here to the field and
fight me, if you're all that keen. We'll try each other out. It
would be more of a match than fighting Fridgeir. I wouldn't
think more highly of myself just for laying him out.'

Then Egil made this verse:

> It's not fair to refuse
> Ljot this little favour.
> I'll play swinging-the-sword
> With this sallow-faced man,
> He hasn't a hope,
> I'll hack him down when I'm ready;
> At this massacre on More
> No mercy from the poet.

After that Egil got himself ready for the duel with Ljot.
He was carrying his usual shield with him, the sword Adder
was at his waist and the sword Dragvendil in his hand. When
Egil entered the combat-area Ljot was not yet ready, so Egil
brandished the sword and spoke this verse:

Let's strike with a sword-flash
To shatter the shield;
To batter the blade
Till the enemy bleeds;
Play with the pale man,
Then pitch him to earth;
Stop his mouth with steel,
And serve him up as carrion.

Then Ljot entered the field of battle and the two men rushed at one another. Ljot warded off Egil's blow with his shield, but Egil kept pressing him with stroke after stroke so hard that Ljot couldn't hit back and had to give ground in order to find room to strike. But Egil stayed close to him pounding away so that Ljot was chased all over the field and outside the stone markers, and that was how the first bout ended. Ljot asked for a break, which Egil agreed to, and they sat down for a rest. Then Egil made this verse:

I feel this flashing swordsman
Falls back when I force him:
He's afraid, this unfortunate
Over-fed fighter.
The blood-sucking battler
Backs away from my blows,
And beats a retreat
From the bald-headed bard.

It was a rule at that time for duelling that when the challenger won, he was to get everything at stake, but if he lost he had to redeem himself by paying the previously-agreed sum; and if he were to be killed in the duel, he forfeited all his property, which was inherited by the one who killed him in combat. It was also the law then that if a foreigner died without an heir in the country, all the money he left was to go to the King's treasure.

Egil told Ljot to get ready. 'I want us to settle this duel,' he said. Then he ran up and struck Ljot, pressing him so close that Ljot was forced to back away, and his shield was no use to him any more. Then Egil caught Ljot just above the knee,

slicing off his leg, and Ljot dropped down dead on the spot.
Egil went over to Fridgeir and the others and they thanked
him warmly for what he had done. Then Egil made this verse:

> *The foul wolf-feeder*
> *Fell flat on the ground,*
> *The leg of Ljot*
> *Lanced off by the bard.*
> *This poet gave Fridgeir peace*
> *But seeks no payment,*
> *This play with the pale-face*
> *Was a pleasure to me.*

There were few people to grieve over the death of Ljot, as
he had been a great trouble-maker. He was of Swedish descent
and had no family in Norway: he had come there to make
money by duelling, and had killed a number of good farmers
by challenging them to single combat for their estates and
farms, so that he had become very rich in both land and
movable goods. After the duel, Egil went home with Fridgeir
and stayed there a short time before travelling south to More.
Egil parted from Fridgeir the best of friends, and asked
Fridgeir to lay claim on his behalf to the property which had
belonged to Ljot.

After that Egil went on his way till he came to Fjord Province, and from there he travelled to Sogn to see Thord of
Aurland, who gave him a good welcome. Egil told Thord
his business and gave him the message from King Hakon.
Thord responded well to what Egil had said and promised to
help him in the matter. Egil spent most of the spring with
Thord.

65. Egil kills Atli the Short

EGIL set out on a journey south to Hordaland, travelling in
a ferry with thirty men aboard, and came one day to Ask on
Fenhring Island. Egil went with twenty men, leaving the
other ten to guard the boat. Atli the Short was at home with

a number of followers, and Egil had him called outside with the message that Egil Skallagrimsson had some business with him. Atli and all the able-bodied men there picked up their weapons and went outside.

'I've been told, Atli,' said Egil, 'that you're looking after the property which rightly belongs to me and my wife Asgerd. You'll have heard already that I've laid claim to the legacy of Bjorn the Yeoman which your brother Berg-Onund withheld from me. Now I've come to claim this property, both estates and movable goods, and I'm ordering you to surrender it and hand it over to me.'

'We've long heard about what a bully you are, Egil,' said Atli, 'and now that you're asking me for the property King Eirik awarded to my brother Onund, I can see what you are for myself. In those days King Eirik's word was law in the land, and I thought you might have come here to offer me compensation for killing my brother and pay me back for the plunder you took here at Ask. If that had been your business I'd have given the matter some thought, but as it is I've nothing to say.'

'What I want to do,' said Egil, 'is to make you the same offer as I made Onund, let the law of the Gula Assembly decide between us. As I see it, what your brothers did justified their being killed, since they denied me my legal rights and took my property by force, and I've royal approval to take up my rights against you in this matter: so I'm summonsing you to the Gula Assembly and seek its decision on the case.'

'I'll come to the Gula Assembly,' said Atli, 'and we'll argue about the case there.'

Egil went off with his men and travelled north to Sogn till he reached Aurland, where he went to his wife's uncle, Thord, and stayed with him till the Gula Assembly. Egil came with the other people to the assembly and found Atli already there. They began to talk over their case and put it before the men who were to act as judges, Egil stating his claim to the money, and Atli defending himself with the sworn testimony of twelve men that he had no money belonging to Egil in his keeping.

When Atli went before the judges with his testimonials, Egil stood up against him and said he wanted his money, not Atli's oaths.

'I'm offering you another law,' he said, 'that the two of us fight a duel here at the assembly, winner take all.'

What Egil had said was law and ancient custom. Every man who went to law had the right to challenge his opponent to a duel, whether he was the plaintiff or the defendant.

Atli said that he wouldn't refuse to fight a duel with Egil. 'I should have spoken those words of yours myself,' he said. 'I've good reason to seek vengeance on the man who killed my two brothers. If I've either to give up my property to you despite the law, or take up your offer of a fight, then I prefer to hold on to what's rightly mine.'

At that, Atli and Egil shook hands in firm agreement to fight a duel, with the winner to get all the property they had been quarrelling about. So they made themselves ready for the duel.

When Egil stepped forward, he was wearing a helmet and holding a shield before him, a halberd in his hand and the sword Dragvendil hanging from his right arm. It was the custom for duellers to keep the sword ready at hand to use whenever they wanted rather than to have to draw it. Atli had the same outfit as Egil. He was a strong man, a seasoned dueller and very brave.

Then a big old bull was led forward. It was called the sacrificial bull and the winner was supposed to kill it: sometimes there was only one bull, sometimes each of the duellers brought his own.

As soon as they were ready to fight, they each ran at the other flinging their spears. Neither spear struck the shield but hit the ground, so each of the fighters took his sword and began hewing away at close range. Atli refused to give an inch. They struck at each other hard and fast and soon their shields were useless. When Atli's was shattered he threw it away, took his sword in both hands and laid on furiously. Egil struck him on the shoulder but the sword didn't bite. He swung again, then a third time, and it was easier now for him to find a weak spot on Atli, who had nothing to protect himself with, but though Egil swung with all his might, no matter where he tried to hit Atli the sword didn't bite.

Egil saw that things couldn't go on like this. His own shield was useless by this time so he threw away both shield and sword, made a rush at Atli and grappled with him. He was the stronger and Atli fell backwards. Then Egil leaned over and bit right through his throat, and that was how Atli died. Egil jumped quickly to his feet, walked over to the sacrificial bull, took it by the mouth with one hand and the horn with the other and kept twisting until the bull's feet were in the air and its neck broken. Then Egil went back to his companions and made this verse:

> My blade, blue Dragvendil,
> Was a blunt shield-biter,
> Short-Atli's arts
> Enfeebled its edges.
> On the prating sword-pusher
> I used my true power,
> My teeth solved my troubles
> And tore out his throat.

Egil now got possession of all the property he had been claiming on behalf of his wife Asgerd as her father's lawful heir. Nothing else that might have happened at the assembly is mentioned.

First of all Egil went over to Sogn to make arrangements about the property that was now his, and stayed there most of the spring. After that he travelled east to Oslofjord with his companions to visit Thorstein, and stayed with him for a while.

66. Egil goes to Iceland

IN the summer Egil got his ship ready and set out for Iceland. He had a good passage to Borgarfjord and put in near to his farm. He had his cargo taken to his home and berthed his ship, then stayed at the farm over winter. Egil had brought plenty of money and was now a very wealthy man, running his farm in fine style.

Egil was not a man to interfere in other people's affairs, and while he was here in Iceland he left most men in peace: nor were there many who wanted to set themselves against him. This time, Egil spent a number of years at home.

These are the children of Egil and Asgerd whose names are known: one son called Bodvarr and another called Gunnar; their daughters Thorgerd and Bera; and Thorstein their youngest son. Thorgerd was the eldest, and after her, Bera. All Egil's children were able and intelligent.

67. Egil goes back to Norway

EGIL received news from Norway that Eirik Blood-Axe had been killed on a viking expedition in the British Isles, that Gunnhild and her sons had travelled to Denmark and that all the troops that had been with Eirik in England had gone away. Arinbjorn had returned to Norway. He had been given back the estates and revenues that had formerly been his, and was now on friendly terms with the King, and for this reason Egil was tempted to go back again to Norway. It was also said that King Athelstan had died and that his brother Edmund was ruling England.

Egil got his ship ready and hired a crew. Onund Sjoni, the son of Ani of Anabrekkur, decided to travel with him. Onund was a tall man and stronger than anyone in the district. People were of two minds about whether or not he was a shape-changer. Onund had often travelled abroad. Egil was slightly younger than him, and the two men were old friends.

When Egil was ready he put out to sea and had a good passage, making landfall half way along the Norwegian coast. As soon as they sighted land they set course for Fjord Province. The news they got from the mainland was that Arinbjorn was at home on his farm. Egil brought the ship into harbour as close as possible to Arinbjorn's farmstead, then went up to see him, and there was a happy reunion between them. Arinbjorn invited Egil to stay there, along with any of his men that he chose. Egil accepted the offer and had his ship hauled ashore. He went to stay at Arinbjorn's with eleven companions while the rest of his men found places elsewhere.

Egil had had a fine longship-sail made which he gave to Arinbjorn along with other very desirable gifts. Egil stayed there over winter enjoying excellent entertainment, though during the winter he made a trip south to Sogn to see about his estates, and stayed there some considerable time before returning north to Fjord Province.

Arinbjorn held a great feast at Christmas, to which he invited his friends and the leading farmers of the district. It was a magnificent occasion and a great number of people attended. At Christmas he gave Egil a long silk gown, heavily embroidered with gold and ornamented with gold buttons all the way down the front. Arinbjorn had had this gown made specially to fit Egil. He also gave Egil a full set of clothes for Christmas, newly tailored, and made of English cloth in several colours. Arinbjorn gave all sorts of friendly Christmas gifts to those who were visiting him, for he was unparalleled in his generosity and in every way a remarkable man. Egil made this verse:

> *The great man gave me*
> *The gold-spun silk gown,*
> *Freely he conferred it,*
> *No finer friend than he.*

Arinbjorn has power
That compares with princes';
Long the wait
Till his like lives again.

68. Egil and the berserk's money

AFTER Christmas Egil grew very gloomy and said not a word to anyone. When Arinbjorn noticed this, he went to have a talk with Egil and asked why he was so unhappy.

'I want you to tell me whether you're ill,' he said, 'or if something else is the matter. Then we might be able to find the remedy.'

'I'm not sick,' said Egil, 'but I'm very concerned about how to get the money I earned by killing Ljot the Pale north in More. I've heard that the King's stewards have taken everything and claimed it as royal property. I'd like your help to get it for myself.'

'I don't think it would go against the law of the land if you were to get the money,' said Arinbjorn, 'but I don't think it would be easy to lay hands on it now: kings' halls have wide entrances and narrow exits. I've had many a hard time trying to get money out of bullies, even when I enjoyed more royal support than I have now. The friendship between me and the King is a shallow one, though I have to go by the old saying, "Take care of the oak, and live under its cloak."'

'Still, I'd very much like us to have a try,' said Egil, 'since we have the law on our side. Maybe the King will let me have my rights in this. I'm told that he's a just man and observes himself the laws he makes for the land. What I'd like to do most of all is go to see the King and try to put my case.'

Arinbjorn said that he was none too keen on the idea.

'You're sharp and daring, Egil,' he said, 'and to my way of thinking that's going to be hard to reconcile with the King's authority and personality. I don't think he's any friend of yours and no doubt he has his own reasons for that. I'd prefer to forget about the idea and not raise the matter, but if you insist, Egil, then I'll go to the King and put your case for you.'

Egil said it would make him happy and grateful, since that was exactly what he did want.

King Hakon was in residence at the time in Rogaland, but staying for a while in Hordaland, so it was easy to pay him a visit. Shortly after this conversation, Arinbjorn set out to see him. He made himself ready for the journey and told his men that he planned to visit the King. He manned a twenty-oared boat with his household servants, but he didn't want Egil along, so Egil was left behind.

Arinbjorn put out to sea as soon as he was ready and had a good passage. King Hakon gave him a friendly welcome, and after he had spent a while there he told the King his business, that Egil Skallagrimsson had arrived in the country and was claiming all the money that had belonged to Ljot the Pale.

'I understand that Egil has the law on his side, my lord,' said Arinbjorn, 'but your stewards have seized the money on your behalf. I'd like to ask you to give Egil his rights, sir.'

The King took some time before replying. Then he spoke.

'I don't see why you come to me on Egil's behalf with such a case,' he said. 'The one time he came himself, I told him I didn't want him in this country. You know the reasons for that already. There's no point in Egil raising the same sort of claim against me as he made against my brother Eirik, and I tell you this, Arinbjorn, that you yourself will only stay in the country as long as you don't go setting foreigners above me and my words. I happen to know how devoted you are to your foster-son, Harald Eiriksson, and it might be better for you to go and join Harald and his brothers, and stay with them. I've a strong suspicion that men like you aren't to be trusted in a crisis, should matters come to a head between me and the sons of Eirik.'

Since the King came out so strongly against the case, Arinbjorn could see no point in trying to argue with him, and

got ready for his journey home. The King was harsh and un-
friendly towards Arinbjorn once he knew the reason for his
visit, and it wasn't in Arinbjorn's nature to crawl before the
King over this affair, so that was how they parted. Arinbjorn
went back home and told Egil how his mission had ended.

'I'm not going to the King again over a matter like that,'
he said.

When he heard about this, Egil turned very sullen, for it
seemed to him that he was losing a lot of money rightfully his.

Early one morning a few days later, it happened that Arinbjorn, who was in his room with one or two other people,
sent for Egil. When he came, Arinbjorn had a chest opened
and from it he weighed out forty marks of silver.

'Egil,' he said, 'I'm paying you this money for the estates
that belonged to Ljot the Pale. It seems only fair to me that
you should have it as a reward from my kinsman Fridgeir
and myself for defending his life against Ljot. I know you
did it for my sake, and for that reason I'm only too pleased to
see that you're not cheated out of your lawful rights in this
matter.'

Egil took the money, thanked Arinbjorn for it, and cheered
up again.

69. A viking expedition to Friesland

ARINBJORN stayed at home through the winter, looking
after his estates, but in the spring he let it be known that he
was planning a viking expedition. He owned some good
vessels, and in the spring he fitted out three big longships.
He took three hundred and sixty men with him, and the ship
he commanded himself was well manned with his own farmhands and a number of farmers' sons. Egil decided to join
him on the expedition and took charge of another ship, which
he manned with most of the men who had come with him from
Iceland. Egil had the merchant-ship that he had brought from

Iceland taken east to Oslofjord, and hired people there to see to the cargo.

Arinbjorn and Egil sailed their longships south along the coast, then made for Saxony, where they raided and collected loot all summer. At the beginning of autumn they sailed north again and dropped anchor off Friesland. One night in calm weather they put into a large estuary, as there were few harbours and a long ebb-tide. Inland there were wide marshes and a forest near by. The ground was sodden as it had been raining heavily. They decided to go ashore there and left a third of their men behind to guard the ships. They made their way along the river bank, between the river and the forest, and soon came to a settlement where a number of peasants were living. All the people in the settlement who could do so ran inland as soon as they realized there were raiders, and the vikings started chasing after them. Soon they came to another settlement, then a third, and all the inhabitants who could ran off. The land was very flat, with great marshes. Ditches had been dug everywhere and were full of water. The people used the ditches to mark off their fields and meadows, and in some places big logs had been laid over them so that people could cross. These bridges were floored with planks.

The local people fled into the forest and gathered together there as the vikings penetrated deep into the settlements. When the Frisians were about three hundred and sixty strong, they faced up to the vikings and began to fight them. The battle was a fierce one, but the outcome was that the Frisians were routed by the vikings and fled, scattering in all directions. The pursuers did the same until they had split up into small groups. The Frisians kept on running till they came to a ditch and after they had crossed it they took away the bridge, with Egil hard at their heels on the other side. He jumped across, but since it was beyond the powers of the rest, no one followed him. When the Frisians saw that, they turned to attack him, and he had to defend himself. Eleven of them went for him but he killed them all, then replaced the bridge and walked back across the ditch. Then he realized that all his men had gone back to the ships. He stayed as close to the edge of the forest as possible on his way down to the ships, so that he could take cover in it if necessary.

The vikings took a great deal of plunder down with them and also raided the coast. When they reached the ships, some of them started slaughtering the cattle they had taken, while others loaded the plunder aboard. The Frisians had followed with a large force and kept shooting missiles at them, so a number of the vikings made a protective wall with their shields. By now the Frisians had formed yet another column.

When Egil came down and saw what was going on, he raced ahead as fast as he could right up to the thickest part of the column. He was gripping his halberd in front of him in both hands, and his shield was thrown onto his back. He lunged about him with the halberd and everyone in his way fell back, so that he cleared a path through the crowd and managed to get right down to his men, who had given him up for dead.

Now they boarded their ships, put out to sea and sailed to Denmark. When they had reached Limfjord and were lying at anchor off Hals, Arinbjorn called his men together and told them his plans.

'I'm going to see the Eirikssons now,' he said, 'and anyone who wants to can come with me. I've heard that the brothers are in Denmark in command of a large army, staying here over winter and out raiding during the summer. All those who want to go back to Norway rather than stay here with me have my leave to go. It seems wise to me, Egil, for you to go back to Norway as soon as we part company, and then try to get to Iceland as quickly as possible.'

At that, the men split up and went to different ships. Those who wanted to go back to Norway joined Egil, but most preferred to stay on with Arinbjorn. So Egil and Arinbjorn parted in friendship and goodwill. Arinbjorn went to the Eirikssons and joined his foster-son Harald Grey-Cloak, with whom he remained as long as they both lived.

Egil went north to Oslofjord and sailed up to the place where he kept his merchant ship, the one he had had taken south in the spring. The cargo was aboard, as well as the men who had been sailing the ship. Thorstein Thoruson came and invited Egil to stay with him over winter with as many men as he liked. Egil accepted the offer and had the ship hauled ashore and the cargo taken to market. Those men who had come with him split up, some settling there, others going to their homes in the north of the country. Egil went to Thorstein's with ten or twelve men and spent the winter there enjoying good hospitality.

70. Trouble in Vermaland

KING Harald Fine-Hair had brought all the regions east as far as Vermaland under his rule. The first king to conquer Vermaland was Olaf the Wood-Cutter, father of Halfdan White-Leg, who was the first of his line to become king in Norway. King Harald was his direct descendant, and all the royal line down to him had ruled Vermaland and collected tribute from it, leaving men there to govern. When King Harald was an old man the ruler of Vermaland was an earl called Arnvid, but now it was true of Vermaland as of many other places, that tribute was much less readily paid than when King Harald was in his prime. One reason was that his sons were quarrelling over who was to rule Norway, so that little attention was being paid to the more remote tributary regions. After Hakon had established peace, he tried to extend his authority over all the lands his father Harald had controlled. Once he sent twelve men east to Vermaland to collect tribute from the earl, but on their way back through Eida Wood they were attacked by robbers, who killed them all. The same thing happened to the next envoys that King Hakon sent east to Vermaland: some were killed and none of the tribute ever reached him. Some people put it about that Earl Arnvid must have sent his men to kill the King's envoys and bring the tribute back to him.

So the King sent off a third group of men. At that time he

was in residence at Trondheim. They were to travel east to Oslofjord and give Thorstein Thoruson instructions to go east to Vermaland to claim the royal tribute. If he refused, he was to leave the country, for the King had been told that Thorstein's uncle Arinbjorn had gone south to Denmark and joined the Eirikssons, who, people added, had a large body of troops and spent the summers raiding. King Hakon saw this as a dangerous combination, for he expected the Eirikssons to start attacking him as soon as they had built up enough strength. So he sent word to all the friends and kinsmen of Arinbjorn, banishing many of them from the country and giving an ultimatum to others. This is what happened in Thorstein's case when, for the reason given, the King offered him an ultimatum.

The man who delivered the message was widely travelled. He had spent long periods in Denmark and Sweden so that he was very familiar with the routes and the people of these countries, as well as Norway, where he had also travelled extensively. After the messenger had carried the King's words to Thorstein Thoruson, Thorstein told Egil what message the envoys had brought and asked how he should answer it.

'The message is clear enough to me,' said Egil. 'The King wants you out of the country, just like Arinbjorn's other kinsmen. I'd call it a dangerous mission for a man of your standing. I'd advise you to summon the King's envoys, and I want to be there when you talk. Then we'll see what happens.'

Thorstein followed his suggestion and had a talk with them. The envoys gave a clear and full account of their mission and repeated the King's message that Thorstein should either fulfil his charge or be banished from the country.

'I understand your mission very well,' said Egil. 'If Thorstein refuses to go, you'll go and claim the tribute yourselves.'

The envoys said that he was right.

'Thorstein won't be going on this mission,' said Egil. 'A man of his distinction isn't duty bound to run such petty errands. On the other hand, Thorstein is ready to carry out his duty to accompany the King at home and abroad, if that's

what the King wants. Also, if you need any men from here
to travel with you on your journey you're welcome to them,
besides any kind of transport you might want from Thorstein.'

The messengers talked it over among themselves and all
agreed to accept the offer provided Egil would go with them
on their journey.

'The King doesn't care for him at all,' they said, 'and if we
can arrange things so that he's killed, the King will think our
trip well worth the taking. After that he can drive Thorstein
out of the country if he chooses.'

So they told Thorstein that they would be glad to take
Egil with them and let Thorstein stay behind.

'Then that's how it will be,' said Egil. 'I'll take Thorstein's
place on the journey. How many men do you want from here?'

'There are eight of us,' they said, 'and we'd like to have
four more men to make us up to twelve.'

Egil said that was how it would be.

Onund Sjoni and a number of other men from Egil's party
had gone down to the shore to see about Egil's ship and the
cargo they had put into storage in the autumn. They hadn't
come back, and Egil was very put out by this as the King's
envoys were keen to get away and refused to wait for them.

71. Drinking at Armod's

EGIL and three of his men got ready for the journey, taking
horses and sledges with them, as did the King's envoys. There
was a lot of snow about and they had to alter their route. As
soon as they were ready they all set off, driving inland and
making their way east to Eidar. Then one night there was
such a heavy fall of snow that they could barely make out the
road. They made little progress next day, as whenever they
strayed off the road they sank deep into the snow. Late in the
afternoon they stopped to rest their horses near a wooded
ridge.

'Here's where our ways part,' said the envoys to Egil. 'There's a farmer called Arnald living just below the ridge ahead of us. He's a friend of ours and we're going there to spend the night with him. But you go over the ridge and soon you'll come to a big farmstead where you'll be welcome to stay the night. The farmer there is a rich man called Armod Beard. We'll all meet first thing tomorrow morning and travel till the evening. Then we'll be at Eida Wood, where a good farmer called Thorfinn lives.' At that they parted.

Egil and his companions travelled up the ridge, but as for the King's men, no sooner were they out of Egil's sight than they took the skis they had with them, put them on and started back as fast as they could. They kept on the move night and day, first turning towards the Uplands, then north from there to Dovrafjell, and didn't let up until they were at King Hakon's court, where they told him what had happened on their travels.

Egil and his companions carried on that evening across the ridge, and to cut a long story short, they soon lost their way. The snow was so deep that the horses sank right down time and again, and had to be hauled out. There were steep slopes and at times low brush which made it very hard going. The horses held them back badly and it was very difficult for a man to walk, so they were growing very tired when they saw a big farmstead ahead of them and made their way to it. When they reached the home field they saw some people standing outside the farm, Armod and his men. They exchanged a few words and asked each other the news, and when Armod learned that they were the King's messengers he invited them to stay for the night. They accepted the invitation and while Armod's servants took care of the horses and gear, he asked Egil into the living-room. When they went in, Armod placed Egil on the bench opposite the high seat and his companions down from him. They had a long talk about the difficulties they'd experienced that evening trying to make headway, and the people of the household thought it amazing that they should have been able to manage it, saying that nobody could travel that route even when there was no snow on the ground.

'Can you imagine a better sight,' said Armod, 'than the table laid and supper served? After that you can go to bed and have a good rest.'

'We'd like that very much,' said Egil.

Armod had the table laid for them, then they were served with great bowls full of sour curds. Armod said he was sorry he had no ale to offer them. Egil and his men were tired and thirsty, so they picked up the bowls and began to drink very fast, though none as fast as Egil. No other food was served than this. There were a good many people about, with the housewife sitting on her dais, her womenfolk beside her, and the farmer's daughter, ten or eleven years old, playing on the floor. The housewife called her over, and whispered something in her ear. Then the girl went down the table to where Egil was sitting, and made this verse:

> Mother asks you, Egil,
> To lend an ear;
> She gives you guidance,
> Stay on your guard.
> Spare your stomach
> Was what she said:
> Appetites can ask for
> Better to eat.

Armod slapped the girl and told her to be quiet.

'Whenever you open your mouth it's the worse for us,' he said.

The girl went away, and Egil flung down the bowl of curds, now almost empty. Then the bowls were cleared away, tables were set up all over the room, the people of the household took their seats and the food was laid out, choice dishes being served to Egil and all the others. After that a very strong brew of ale was served, and it wasn't long before each man was drinking at will from his own individual horn. Most attention was paid to Egil and his companions. The drinking was meant to go ahead at full speed, and for a long time Egil kept at it without cheating. When his companions had drunk all they could take, Egil tossed back whatever they couldn't manage. So it went on until the tables were taken down, and by that time everyone there was getting very drunk. Every toast Armod drank, he said, 'I drink to you, Egil,' and the servants toasted Egil's companions using the same formula.

One man was given the job of serving each toast to Egil and his men, and kept egging them on to drink up quickly, but Egil told his men not to have any more, and he drank their share, that being the only way out of it. When Egil realized that he couldn't keep going any longer, he stood up, walked across the floor to Armod, put both hands on his shoulders and pressed him up against the pillar, then heaved up a vomit of massive proportions that gushed all over Armod's face, into his eyes, nostrils and mouth, and flooded down his chest so that he was almost suffocated. When he recovered his breath he spewed up and all of his servants there began to swear at Egil. What he'd just done, they said, made him the lowest of the low, and if he'd wanted to vomit he should have gone outside, not made a fool of himself inside the drinking hall.

'I shouldn't be blamed by anyone for this,' said Egil, 'I'm only doing the same as the farmer. He's spewing with all his might, just like me.'

Then Egil went back to his seat, sat down and asked for a drink. After that he recited this verse at the top of his voice:

> With my spew I swear
> Thanks for your sociability!
> We have witnesses that
> I could walk the floor:
> Many a guest's gift
> Is even more gushing;
> Now the ale has ended up
> All over Armod.

Armod jumped to his feet and ran out, but Egil asked for something more to drink. The housewife told the man who had been serving all evening to carry on as long as they wanted to drink, and make sure they had enough. The man took a great ox-horn, filled it and gave it to Egil, who swilled it down in one draught. Then he said:

> *Let's swallow each swig*
> *This sailor keeps serving;*
> *The bard is kept busy*
> *With barely a break:*
> *Not a lick shall I leave*
> *Of this malted liquor,*
> *Though the fellow keep filling*
> *Fresh horns till day break.*

Egil kept on drinking for some time, tossing down each horn he was given, but there was little fun to be had in the room as not many were still drinking. Then Egil and his companions got up, took down their weapons from the wall where they had hung them, and went over to the granary where their horses were kept. There they lay down on the straw and slept through the night.

72. Egil visits Thorfinn

EARLY next morning as soon as it was daylight Egil got up. He and his men made themselves ready and went straight to the farmhouse looking for Armod. They came to the room where he was sleeping with his wife and daughter, and pushed open the door. Egil went over to Armod's bed, drew his sword, and taking Armod's beard in his other hand dragged him to the edge of the bed. Armod's wife and daughter leaped to their feet and started begging Egil not to kill him. Egil said he would do as they asked, for their sake. 'That's only decent,' he said, 'but he fully deserves that I should kill him.' Then he made this verse:

> *The gold-bangled blabber-mouth*
> *Gets this plea-benefit:*
> *He may stir up strife*

But he doesn't scare me.
You perhaps hoped the poet
Would praise you more highly?
Well, it's time to trudge off
And take to our travels.

Then Egil cut off his beard close to the chin, and gouged out an eye with his finger so that it hung out over his cheek. After that Egil went back to his companions and they went on their way.

They got to Thorfinn's farm about breakfast-time, close to Eida Wood. Egil asked if he and his men could be given breakfast, and hay for the horses. Thorfinn said they were welcome to it, and then Egil and his men went into the living-room. Egil asked if Thorfinn had heard anything about his former companions – 'we'd arranged to meet here,' he said.

'Some time just before dawn six heavily armed men went by,' said Thorfinn.

Then one of Thorfinn's farmhands spoke up.

'I was driving out by night for timber,' he said, 'and I came on six men, Armod's farmhands. That was a long time before dawn, and I can't say now whether or not they were the six men you were talking about.'

Thorfinn said that the men he had spoken of had been there after the servant had come home with the load of timber.

While Egil and his men were sitting at table he noticed a sick woman lying on the dais. He asked Thorfinn who was the woman over there in so much pain, and he said she was his daughter, Helga. 'She's been weak for a long time,' he added. He said it was a bad wasting sickness and she could never sleep at night because of what seemed like delirium.

'Have you tried anything to help her get better?' asked Egil.

'I've had runes carved,' answered Thorfinn. 'A farmer's son from near by did it, but since then she's been even worse. Do you know anything about curing diseases like this, Egil?'

'If I give it a try,' he said, 'maybe it won't do her any harm.'

When Egil had finished his meal, he went over and spoke

to her. Then he asked for her to be lifted out of bed, and clean sheets to be placed under her. This was done. Egil searched the bed where she had been lying and found a whale-bone there with runes carved on it. After he had read them, he scraped them off and burnt them in the fire. He burnt the whole bone and had the bedclothes she had been using thrown to the winds. Then he made this verse:

> *None should write runes*
> *Who can't read what he carves:*
> *A mystery mistaken*
> *Can bring men to misery.*
> *I saw cut on the curved bone*
> *Ten secret characters,*
> *These gave the young girl*
> *Her grinding pain.*

Egil carved some runes and placed them under the pillow of the bed where she was resting, and it seemed to her as if she had woken from sleep. She said she was well again though still a little weak. Her mother and father were overjoyed, and Thorfinn offered Egil all the help he thought he might need.

73. Egil visits Alf

EGIL told his companions that he wanted to be on his way and not wait any longer. Thorfinn had a bold-looking son called Helgi, and father and son offered to escort him through the forest. They told him they knew for sure that Armod Beard had sent six men there to waylay them, and that even if they escaped the first ambush there would probably be others elsewhere in the wood. There were four who offered to go with them, including Thorfinn. Then Egil made this verse:

> *No six enemies on earth*
> *Dare use their arms on me*
> *If I've four good fellows*

To aid me in fight.
And if I have eight men
No twelve could ever
Scare me, the black-browed
Bard of the battle-storm.

So Thorfinn and his men got what they wanted and went with Egil into the forest, eight of them all told. When they came to the ambush they could see the men waiting for them. These were Armod's farmhands sitting there, but when they saw the eight coming they didn't think they had much of a chance and so they slunk away into the forest. When Egil's party came to the place where the men had been lying in wait, they could see that things weren't going to be all sweetness and light, and Egil said that Thorfinn and his men ought to go back, but they wanted to go further. Egil would have none of it and ordered them to go home, so that's what they did. They turned back, while Egil and his men went on their way, now only four of them. Late in the afternoon they came upon six men in the wood and drew the conclusion that these must be Armod's servants. The men lying in ambush jumped to their feet and set on them, so they swung round to face them. As things turned out, Egil killed two and those that were left ran off into the wood.

Egil and his men went on their way and nothing more happened until they got out of the forest. A farmer called Alf, nicknamed Alf the Wealthy, gave them lodgings for the night. He was an old man and very rich, but so unsociable that he couldn't stand servants except for one or two. Egil was given a good welcome there, however, and Alf talked freely with him. Egil asked a great many questions, and Alf replied to everything he asked. They talked most of all about the earl and the envoys from the King of Norway who had gone east for the tribute, and to judge by his words, Alf was no friend of the earl's.

74. Egil visits the earl

EARLY in the morning Egil got himself ready to set out with his party, and as they left he gave Alf a fur coat, a gift which Alf cheerfully accepted. 'I can have a fur cloak made out of this,' he said, and asked Egil to call in and see him on his way back. They parted friends, and Egil went on his way. In the evening he arrived at the court of Earl Arnvid, where he was given a good reception, he and his companions being placed next to the seat of honour.

After Egil and his men had spent the night there, they told the Earl their mission, giving him the message from the King of Norway that he wanted payment of all the tribute still outstanding since Arnvid had been put in charge. The Earl said that he had turned over all the tribute into the hands of the King's envoys.

'I've no idea what they did with it afterwards,' he said, 'whether they took it to the King or ran off with it abroad. But since you carry genuine evidence that the King sent you, I'll pay out all the tribute that he has the right to, and place it in your hands, though I won't be held responsible for whatever happens to you afterwards.'

Egil and his men stayed there for some time and before they set off the Earl gave them the tribute, partly in silver and partly in furs. When they were ready they went on their way, Egil saying these parting words to the Earl: 'Now, this tribute we've received we'll take to the King; but I want you to know, Earl, that it's a lot less than the King thinks you owe him, even leaving out the compensation he considers you should pay for the messengers you're said to have had killed.'

The Earl said that this was not true, and with that they parted. After Egil had gone, the Earl had two brothers summoned to him, both named Ulf, and spoke to them.

'That big Egil who's been staying here a while is going to

prove a great nuisance to us, I think, if he gets to the King,'
he said. 'We can judge how he'll put our case to the King by
the way he threw the killing of the King's men in our faces.
Now, you're to go after them, and kill them all so that they
don't go carrying this slander to the King. I think it's best
for you to ambush them in Eida Wood. Take as many men
with you as you need to make sure none of them get away,
and none of you lose your lives at their hands.'

The brothers got ready to set out, taking thirty men with
them. They travelled into the forest, where they were familiar
with every track, and began to spy on Egil's movements.
There are two routes through the forest, one across a certain
ridge where the slope is steep and the path narrow. That's the
shorter way. The other passes round the ridge, with wide
marshes and a lot of fallen timber. This is a narrow path too.
Fifteen of them sat in ambush on either route.

75. A skirmish in the wood

EGIL travelled on until he came to Alf, and spent the night
with him being entertained well. In the morning before dawn
he got ready to set out, and as they were sitting down to
breakfast, Alf came up and spoke to them.

'You're up and ready early, Egil,' he said, 'but I'd advise
you not to be in too much of a hurry. Better take a good look
first. I think some people are lying in wait for you in the
wood. I don't have the men to send with you, not enough of
them to make any difference to your strength, but I'll offer
you a place here until I can assure you the wood's safe to
travel in.'

'That's nothing but a load of nonsense,' said Egil. 'I'm
going on my way just as I planned.'

Egil and his men got ready to set out on their journey,
while Alf tried to dissuade them, asking them to turn back if
the path was trodden. He said that no one had travelled west

through the forest since Egil came east – 'except,' he added, 'for the men I think will be expecting to meet you.'

'If what you say is right,' said Egil, 'how many of them do you think there will be? We won't be exactly helpless even though we face some difference in numbers.'

'I went into the forest with my servants,' said Alf, 'and we came on some footprints. The men's tracks went into the wood and there must have been a good many of them. If you don't believe what I tell you, you can go there and look at the tracks for yourself. And if you see what I've told you, turn back.'

Egil went on his way, and when they came to the path in the forest they could see the tracks of men and horses. Egil's companions said they wanted to turn back.

'We're going ahead,' said Egil. 'It's no great surprise to me that people have travelled through Eida Wood; it's the usual route.'

So they carried on with their journey, and there were clear tracks, with a lot of footprints. When they got to the place where the road divided, the footprints separated too, with equal numbers on each path.

'It seems likely to me now,' said Egil, 'that Alf was telling the truth. Best get ourselves ready. The chances are that we're due for a confrontation.'

Egil and his men took off their cloaks and other outer clothing, and put them on the sledge, where there was a big thick bast rope: it was usual for people driving long distances to carry ropes with them in case they needed to fix the harness. Egil picked up a great slab of stone, held it in front of his chest and belly, then tied the bast rope round it and wound the rope all the way up to his shoulders. After that they started off again.

Eida Wood is a vast forest, spreading out with settlements on either side; but in the middle there is a great deal of copse-wood and undergrowth, and in some places no trees at all. Egil and his men took the shorter route, across the ridge. They all bore shields and helmets, and weapons for hacking and lunging, with Egil taking the lead. As they approached the ridge, the lower ground was wooded but there were no trees up on the slopes. While they were making their way up the slope, seven men came running out of the wooded part and up the steep rise after them, shooting. Egil turned and they took their stand on the path. Then other men attacked them from the bluff above, pelting them from there with stones, which was a great deal more dangerous.

'Get into the lee of the bluff, now,' said Egil, 'do what you can to protect yourselves while I try to scale it.'

They did that, and when Egil got beyond the rise there were eight men there waiting for him. They all set on him together and tried to overpower him, but there's no need to tell any more about the exchange of blows than the outcome, that Egil killed them all. Then he went himself to the edge of the bluff and started hurling stones so that there was no withstanding him. Three of the Vermalanders were struck down and the other four got away into the wood, bruised and battered.

After that Egil and his men took their horses and went on their way till they had the ridge behind them; but the men who had escaped warned their fellows who were waiting in the marshes, so they took the lower route to cut Egil off. Then Ulf spoke to his men.

'We must be clever now in dealing with them,' he said, 'and make sure they don't get a chance to run. Here's how the land lies. The path is at the base of the ridge. At the point where the marshes stretch up to the ridge there's a bluff above them. The path lies between the marsh and the bluff and it's no more than a narrow track. Some of us will go beyond the bluff and be ready to take them when they try to go forward. The rest are to wait here in the wood and attack from behind when they reach the others. We must see to it that none of them gets away.' They did as Ulf had told them, and he went with ten men to the far side of the bluff.

Egil and his men carried on with no suspicion of this plan until they came to the narrow track, when some men attacked them from behind, lunging at them with weapons. Egil and his men turned to face them and defended themselves. Then other men came at them, the ones who had been on the far side of the bluff, and when Egil saw this he faced them himself. Before many blows had been struck, some had been killed by Egil on the path and others had withdrawn to the level ground, with Egil chasing after them. Ulf was killed there, and before it was all over Egil had cut down eleven men. After that he went over to the place where his companions were defending the path against eight attackers, with damage to both sides. When Egil came up, the Vermalanders ran for their lives, and as the forest was very close at hand five of them managed to get away, all wounded, but the other three were killed. Egil had a number of wounds himself, but none of them were serious, so now they continued their journey. Egil saw to the wounds of his companions, none of which were fatal, then they settled onto their sledges and drove on for the rest of the day.

The Vermalanders who got away took their horses and struggled back east through the forest till they reached the settlements, where their wounds were seen to. They got their things together and travelled back to the Earl with the story of their trip and how badly it had turned out. They said that the two Ulfs had been killed and that, altogether, twenty-five men were dead. 'Only five escaped alive,' they said, 'all of them bruised and battered.'

The Earl asked what had happened to Egil and his companions.

'We can't say how badly they were wounded,' said the men, 'but they went for us hard enough. When there were eight of us to four of them, we had to run for it. Five of us got into the wood but we lost three, and from what we could tell, Egil and his men were as bright as new pennies.'

The Earl said their trip had been a total disaster.

'I could have stood heavy losses,' he said, 'if you'd killed these Norwegians, but now, once they get west of the forest and give the news to the King of Norway, the only terms we can expect from him will be the worst.'

76. Egil goes back to Iceland

EGIL kept on until he came out west of the forest. He went with his men to Thorfinn that evening and they were all given a good welcome. Their wounds were treated and they stayed there for several days. The farmer's daughter Helga was up and about, completely recovered from her illness; she and all the others gave Egil the credit for her recovery. He and his men rested themselves and their horses.

The man who had carved the runes for Helga lived not far away from there, and it turned out that he had proposed to her, but Thorfinn had refused to give her to him in marriage. The man had tried to seduce her, and when she'd have none of it he'd tried to carve love-runes for her, but didn't have the skill; so the runes he carved had caused her illness.

When Egil was ready to leave, Thorfinn and his son saw him on his way. Altogether there were ten or twelve of them and they stayed with Egil all day as a precaution against Armod and his household. When the news got around that Egil and his men had fought and won against such over-whelming odds, Armod decided that it would be hopeless to set himself up against Egil, so he and all his men stayed at home. Egil and Thorfinn exchanged gifts on parting and sealed their friendship with the words they spoke.

Egil and his men went on their way, and there's no mention of anything happening on their journey until they reached Thorstein, by which time their wounds had healed, and there they stayed till spring. Thorstein hired messengers to bring King Hakon the tribute Egil had taken from Vermaland, and when they saw the King they handed it over, telling him all that had happened on Egil's journey. Then the King realized that his earlier suspicions had been well founded, that Earl Arnvid had caused the deaths of the two parties he had sent out east. He said that Thorstein was welcome to stay on in his kingdom, and declared themselves reconciled. When the messengers went back home and saw Thorstein again, they told him how pleased the King was with the expedition, and that he and Thorstein were now on peaceful and friendly terms.

In the summer King Hakon travelled east to Oslofjord, then east from there to Vermaland with a large army. Earl Arnvid fled, and the King imposed heavy payments on all the farmers who, in view of what he had been told by the tribute collectors, he thought had offended against him. He appointed another earl there and took hostages from him and the farmers.

On that expedition, King Hakon travelled widely through West Gotaland and laid it under his rule as is reported in his saga, and described as well in the poems written about him. It is also said that he went to Denmark and raided there far and wide. With only two ships of his own, he swept clear the decks of twelve Danish ships, and it was then that he conferred the title of king on his nephew Tryggvi Olafsson, and let him rule over Oslofjord.

In the summer, Egil got his merchant ship ready and hired a crew for it. The longship he brought from Denmark he gave to Thorstein as a parting gift, and Thorstein gave him splendid presents in return, each declaring the strength of his friendship for the other. Egil sent messengers to his wife's kinsman, Thord of Aurland, making him his agent and placing in his charge the estates which Egil owned in Sogn and Hordaland. Egil asked him to sell them if he could find any buyers.

When Egil was ready to set out and the wind was favourable, they sailed down Oslofjord, north along the Norwegian coast and then out into the open sea. The winds were very reliable and they made land at Borgarfjord. Egil sailed up the fjord, put in near to his farm, and had his cargo taken home and his ship hauled ashore. People were very happy to see him when he came home, and there he spent the following winter.

77. Trouble with Irish slaves

By the time that Egil had come back from this trip, the district was fully settled. Though all the original settlers were dead, their sons and grandsons were living and farming there.

Ketil Gufa came to Iceland when the country was almost fully settled, and spent the first winter at Gufuskalar in Rosmhvalaness. Ketil had come from Iceland and brought a good number of Irish slaves with him. All the land in Rosmhvalaness had been claimed by then, so Ketil crossed over from there to the Nesses and spent the next winter at Gufuness, though he found no place to live there either. After that he travelled up to Borgarfjord and spent the third winter there at a place since known as Gufuskalar. The river that runs into the sea where he kept his ship over winter is called the Gufu River.

At that time, Thord Lambason was living at Lambastead. He was married with a fully-grown son called Lambi, a tall lad, strong for his years. In the summer when people went to the assembly, Lambi decided to ride there too.

By this time Ketil Gufu had gone west to Breidafjord in search of a place to live. Then his slaves ran away, and one night they came to Thord's house at Lambastead, set fire to it, and burned Thord to death there with all his household. Then they broke open his store-house and carried goods and valuables outside, drove in some horses, loaded them with packs and went over to Alftaness.

That morning about sunrise Lambi came back home. He had seen the fire during the night. He had several men with him and rode off at once in search of the slaves, while people from the other farms came to join him. When the slaves saw they were being followed, they dropped their loot and tried to get away. Some ran west through Myrar, others down to the sea till they came to a fjord. Then Lambi and his men came up and killed the one named Kori there, and the place has been called Koraness ever since, but the slaves named Skorri, Thormod and Svart dived into the sea and started swimming away from the shore. Lambi and his men began searching among the boats, then rowed after the slaves. At Skorra Isle they came on Skorri and killed him there, then rowed out to Thormod's Skerry where they killed Thormod, after whom the skerry takes its name, and so caught up with the other slaves at the places named after them.

After that, Lambi farmed at Lambastead. He was a good farmer, physically very powerful but no trouble-maker. Ketil Gufa travelled west across Breidafjord and made his home at Thorskafjord. Gufu Dale and Gufufjord are named after him. He married Yri, the daughter of Geirmund Hell-Skin and their son was Vali.

There was a man called Grim Svertingsson living at Mosfell below the Moor. He was a wealthy man and came from a good family. His half-sister, Rannveig, was married to Thorodd the Priest in Olfus and their son was Skapti the Law-Speaker. After the events described, Grim became Law-Speaker. He asked for the hand of Thordis, daughter of Thorolf and Egil's niece and step-daughter. Thordis was a very beautiful woman and Egil was as fond of her as he was of his own children. He knew that Grim came from a good family and that this would be an excellent match, so it was decided that the offer should be accepted, and Thordis married Grim. Egil paid out her father's legacy, she went home to Grim, and they lived at Mosfell for a long time.

78. Egil's poetry

THERE was a man called Olaf, the son of Hoskuld Dala-Kollsson and of Melkorka, the daughter of King Myrkjartan[1] of Ireland. Olaf lived west at Hjardarholt in Laxriverdale, in the Dales of Breidafjord. He was very rich and the most hand-

1. *Myrkjartan*: Irish *Muirchaertach*: see *Laxdæla Saga* (Penguin, 1969), Chapter 21.

some man in Iceland at the time, a man of great distinction. Olaf asked for the hand of Thorgerd, Egil's daughter, a fine-looking woman, very tall, intelligent and proud, but usually rather quiet. Egil knew all about Olaf and realized that it was a fine match, so Thorgerd was married to Olaf and went to live with him at Hjardarholt. Their children were Kjartan, Thorberg, Halldor, Steindor, Thurid, Thorbjorg, and Bergthora who married Thorhall Oddason the Priest. Thorbjorg married first Asgeir Knattarson, and later Vermund Thorgrimsson. Thurid married Godmund Solmundarson and their sons were Hall and Killer-Bardi.

Ozur Eyvindarson, the brother of Thorodd of Olfus, married Bera, Egil's daughter.

It was then that Bodvar Egilsson was reaching his prime, an exceptionally promising man, fine-looking, tall and strong, just as Egil and Thorolf had been at his age. Egil loved him deeply, and Bodvar was very fond of his father.

One summer it so happened that a ship was lying at Hvit River where there was an important market. Egil had bought a great deal of timber there and was having it brought home by ship. His servants used an eight-oared boat of his to fetch it, and one day Bodvar asked them to let him come with them. They said he could, so he went with the servants to Vellir, six of them altogether in the eight-oared boat.

When they were due to set out, high tide was late in the day and they had to wait for it, so that it was evening before they left. Then a sharp south-westerly gale sprung up and they found themselves going against an ebb tide. As often happens, it grew very rough on the fjord. The end of it all was that their boat foundered and all of them were drowned. The following day their bodies were washed ashore, Bodvar's at Einarsness and the others south of the fjord, where the boat drifted.

Egil heard the news that same day and rode off at once to search for the bodies. He found Bodvar washed ashore, lifted the body up onto his knee and rode with it out to Digraness, to Skallagrim's burial mound. He had the mound opened, and laid Bodvar there beside Skallagrim, after which the mound was closed up again. This all took until about sunset. After that Egil rode back home to Borg. When he got there he went straight to the bed-closet where he usually slept, lay down and locked himself in. No one dared speak to him.

People say that when Bodvar was laid under the mound, Egil was dressed in this way. He wore his hose tight upon the leg, and a red fustian tunic tight in the upper part and laced together at the side. People say that he grew so swollen that both tunic and hose burst apart on his body. Next day Egil neither opened the bed-closet nor took food and drink, but lay there all day and all the following night. No one dared speak to him.

On the third day at first light, Asgerd had a man ride on horseback west to Hjardarholt as fast as he could go, to tell Thorgerd all that had happened. The man arrived about noon, and added that Asgerd wanted her to come south to Borg as quickly as she could. Thorgerd had a horse saddled at once and rode off in the evening with two companions, travelling through the night until they reached Borg. Thorgerd went straight into the hall. Asgerd welcomed her and asked if they had had any supper. Thorgerd spoke in a loud voice.

'I've had no supper,' she said, 'and I'll not take any until I come to Freyja. I know no better choice than my father's, and I don't want to live on after he and my brother are dead.'

She went up to the bed-closet and called out.

'Open up, father,' she cried. 'I want us to go one road together.'

Egil unbolted the shutter and after Thorgerd had gone inside he bolted it again. She lay down on the other bed there. Then Egil spoke.

'My daughter,' he said, 'it's good that you want to join company with your father. You've shown how very much you love me. Can there be any reason to go on living with such sorrow?'

After that they said nothing for a while, and then Egil spoke. 'What's going on here, daughter, are you chewing something?' he asked.

'I'm chewing sea-weed,' she replied, 'I expect it will make me feel worse than ever. Even so, I don't think I'll live long.'

'Is it bad for you?' asked Egil.

'Terrible,' she replied. 'Would you like to try some?'

'What would be the use?' asked Egil.

A little later she called out and asked for something to drink and she was offered some water. Then Egil said, 'That's what happens when you eat sea-weed, it makes you all the more thirsty.'

'Would you like something to drink, father?' she asked.

He took hold of the horn she had, and drank great draughts. Then she said, 'We've been tricked, it's milk.' He bit off a part of the horn as big as his teeth could take, then threw the horn down.

'What are we going to do,' asked Thorgerd, 'now this plan of ours has failed? My own choice, father, would be for us to keep going a little longer. Then you can compose a dirge for Bodvar, and I'll carve the poem in runes on a log. After that we can die if we want to. I think it will be a long time before your son Thorstein makes a poem in memory of Bodvar. Nor will it do if Bodvar isn't honoured with a funeral feast, though I don't expect that we'll sit drinking at it.'

Egil said there was little hope of his composing a poem even if he made the effort.

'But I can try,' said Egil.

Egil had had another son called Gunnar who had died a little earlier, and this is how the poem begins:

> *My mouth strains*
> *To move the tongue,*
> *To weigh and wing*
> *The choice word:*
> *Not easy to breathe*
> *Odin's inspiration*
> *In my heart's hinterland,*
> *Little hope there.*

My sorrow the source
Of the sluggard stream
Mind-meandering,
This heavy word-mead,
Poet's power
Gold-praised, that
Odin from ogres tore
In ancient time.

Purest of possessions,
Poetic craft, power
That dwarf-devised
Drew first breath:
Now I feel it surge, swell
Like a sea, old giant's blood,
About the cragged cliff face
Of the dwarf-caves.

A storm-bowed maple,
I sorrow for my son,
My boy, who has bent
His body to earth:
Unhappy, he
Whose kin is hewn down
And must bear away the bones
From the bed.

I muse how my mother
Met her end,
First that, then my father's
Fall I sing
In a poem of praise
From my palace of words,
From my temple the word-tree
Tells its growth-tale.

Cruel crashed
The curled sea
Wave on the once well-formed
Family shield-wall,

Now broached and battered
Like the beaten boat
Of my son, smashed
By the sea-storm.

Could my sword stroke take
Vengeance on the sea-surge,
Bitter ale brewer
None can bend or break,
Could my hand kill
The crushing wave,
With god and goddess
I should grapple.

But I've no strength to subdue
The slayer of my son
Nor the boldness to beat
Down my boy's killer:
Obvious to all,
An old man, unaided,
Helpless, unhappy,
Can hold out no hope.

The rough storm has robbed me
Of my best riches,
It's cruel to recall
The loss of that kinsman,
The safeguard, the shield
Of the house has sailed
Out in death's darkness
To a dearer place.

I know it now!
Never a trace
Of sour spirit
Was shown by my son:
What a fighter, fearless
He'd have been, fulfilled,
The eager one, if only
His end had not come early.

The warrior would warm
To his father's words
Even when every
Man was my enemy:
My comrade in combat,
A column of strength,
My prop and my pillar,
His power was mine.

Now the bard has no brother,
Bitter the mind-surge
Beating and battering
About the brain-cliff,
These thoughts throng
In the war-thunder,
In the bellow of battle
Thus I brood.

Will no comrade of courage
Cleave to me,
To be at my back
In bitter peril?
No help can I hope for
Against the hard hero,
Few are my friends,
Yet I cannot fly battle.

A helping hand
Is hard to come by,
True and trusty
In time of need:
Now befoulers of family,
Faithless kin,
Will sell their souls
And their brothers for silver.[1]

*

No purse can pay
The fair price
Due him who endures

1. The text of the next stanza is too defective for translation to be possible.

The death of a son,
Till a boy is born
In his brother's place
To be fostered and fill
The family void.

No person pleases me,
Not even the peacemakers,
Not even when all men
Act in friendship:
My own one haunts Odin's
Under-kingdom,
He has wandered away,
My wife's child.

The bitter old ale-brewer
Beats in my brain,
The shock of the sea-wave
Shatters my sense,
The cracked rock-face crumbles,
How can I keep
My misery masked?
My mind is in my face.

My boy was borne off
By a burning sea-fever,
The searing storm
Was his sea-sickness:
My son, who shunned
All spite and slander –
I must weep. But why
For one so all-worthy?

Forgive his fate
And forget I will not,
Odin not Egil
Enjoys him for ever,
He has stolen my son,
The sapling growth
From my wife's womb,
The warrior-seed.

The spear-god shared
Spoil with me,
My oath was to Odin,
He gave me aid:
Now that maker of mystic
Runes only mocks me,
Voids all my victories,
That breaker of vows.

I'll make offerings to Odin,
Though not in eagerness,
I'll make my soul's sacrifice,
Not suffer silently:
Though this friend has failed me,
Fellow of gods,
To his credit he comforts me
With compensation.

That wolf-killer, that warrior
God, well seasoned in war
Bestowed a bounty
Not to be bettered:
To my art he added
One other gift,
A heart that held
Not craft only: hatred!

The end is all.
Even now
High on the headland
Hel stands and waits,
Life fades, I must fall
And face my own end
Not in misery and mourning,
But with a man's heart.

As the poem progressed, Egil began to get back his spirits and when it was completed he tried the poem out before Asgerd, Thorgerd and his household. Then he got up out of bed and took his place on the high-seat. He called the poem 'Lament for My Sons'. After that, according to custom, Egil held a funeral feast for his sons. When Thorgerd set out for home Egil saw her off and gave her parting gifts.

Egil farmed at Borg for a long time and grew to be a very old man. There is no mention of his having quarrels with the people here in Iceland, nor are there any reports of fighting and duelling after he settled down. People say that Egil did not leave Iceland after the events which have been recorded here, the main reason being that he could not stay in Norway owing to the offences already described which the Kings of Norway could charge him with. Egil ran his farm in fine style, having ample means and a temperament well-suited to the life.

King Hakon, Athelstan's foster-son, ruled Norway for a long time and when he was getting on in years the sons of Eirik came over to Norway and quarrelled with him about the throne. They fought several battles which Hakon always won. The last battle was fought at Fitjar in Stord, Hordaland. King Hakon won, but also received a mortal wound, and after that the Eirikssons ruled in Norway.

Chieftain Arinbjorn was with Harald Eiriksson, became his counsellor and received large sums of money from him, besides being commander of his troops and having charge of the country's defences. He was a great warrior and very successful in war. It was he who took the revenues of Fjord Province.

Egil Skallagrimsson heard the news that there had been a change of rulers in Norway, and that Arinbjorn had gone back to his estates there in high esteem, so he composed a poem in honour of Arinbjorn. This is how it begins:

> I'm quick to commend
> A king in verse,
> But slow of speech
> About stinginess:
> I'm eager to honour
> The acts of princes,
> But my tongue stays tied
> At treachery.

I make free fun
Of anything false,
But for my friends
I'm full of praise:
Many a monarch
I've made the object
Of my innocent
Open eye.

On one occasion
I stirred the anger,
The choler of a king,
Kinsman of Yngvi:
With a hardy hat
On my black head
I marched to meet
The mighty monarch.

The cross-grained King
Kept house at York,
Where the barren beaches
Are beaten by rain,
The sodden coastline
Soaked and stormy;
There in helmet of horror
Sat the heroic one.

Not safe to stand
And stare at him;
I saw his eye shine
Like a serpent's by moonlight,
I saw the broad brow
Beam like the moonlight,
On the fearsome forehead
A radiant frown.

Still I kept constant
In my courage,
Presented the prince
With my poem:

In each man's ear
Odin's horn sounded,
His word-mead melted
Every man's heart.

People thought my poem
Poorly paid for,
Rudely rated
In the royal hall,
When I won as reward
My own wolf-grey head
With the King's consent,
A kindly gift.

I accepted this offer
With darkened eyes,
And beetling above them
The steep brow;
My lips paid the legacy,
Laid out my head-ransom,
Carried my case
Before the King's knee.

My teeth and my tongue
Displayed their talents,
As did my ears also,
Ably equipped.
As good as gold
Was this gift to me,
Nay, better, this boon
From the bounteous Eirik.

Stood there by my side,
The friend of my soul,
None more just or generous,
The gentle Arinbjorn:
True to his trust
In all my troubles,
He added to his honour
With every deed.

Admired by all,
The Chieftain Arinbjorn
Exalted me over
The anger of Eirik;
The King's comrade
Who kept away
From the hall and homestead
Of the warrior-hero.[1]

*

Unless I offer
The praise I owe,
A fraud and a failure
I'll seem to my friend;
Unfit for honour,
Breaker of oaths,
Traitor and turncoat,
Will be terms for the poet.

Easy to understand
My eagerness
To perform in praise
Of the princely leader;
Hard to hew out
A hymn in his honour,
Lines that the living
Might listen to.

Easy to outline
With the axe of my tongue,
To fashion the form
Of my friend's achievements;
Hard to handle
His whole nature,
From the tip of my tongue
So much tumbles.

What most men know
I mention first,
Everyday words

1. The text of the next stanza is too defective for translation to be possible.

To all men's ears;
How generous and gentle
The just Arinbjorn;
He has found friends
Far and wide.

All men admire
The magnanimous Arinbjorn,
Who freely feasts
his fellows with riches;
The gods have granted
Gold to Arinbjorn,
Blessed him with abundance
And the bounty of wealth.

Great Arinbjorn's gold
Glides like a stream,
Like a flood it flows
To his fellow men;
On all Arinbjorn
Empties his treasure,
And pours his plenty
Upon the people.

His ears are attentive
To every answer,
No king is more curious
To listen and question;
He prizes and protects
The holy places,
And gains the goodwill
Of the gods themselves.

His attainments exceed
The aims of all others,
So powerful his purse
Rich men seem penniless;
Such givers of gold
Have grown rare;
Few souls supply shafts
For all men's spears.

No man is mocked
In Arinbjorn's mansion
For lack of luxury
Or for late rising;
He persecutes his purse,
This man from Fjord Province,
He beats the earth with bracelets
And bruises his gold.

A fertile field
Is his free-sown life,
He has reaped his reward
In the riches of battle;
Sadly I'll have served him
If the seed he has given me
Should be wasted, not winnowed,
And blow in the wind.

So I rise up early
To erect my rhyme,
My tongue toils,
A servant at his task;
I pile the praise-stones,
The poem rises,
My labour is not lost,
Long may my words live.

There was a man called Einar, the son of Helgi, son of Ottar, son of Bjorn the Easterner who settled at Breidafjord. Einar was the brother of Osvif the Wise, and even as a young man he was tall, strong and very capable. He began composing poetry at an early age and was very eager to learn.

One summer at the Althing, it so happened that Einar went to Egil Skallagrimsson's booth and they started talking. Before very long they were discussing poetry, for that was the subject they both found most enjoyable. After that, Einar made a habit of going to talk with Egil and this led to a close friendship between them. Shortly before, Einar had returned from a trip abroad, and Egil kept asking him the news from Norway, not only about his friends but about people Einar knew to be Egil's enemies. He also asked a great deal about people of importance. In return, Einar questioned Egil about all that had happened on his travels, and the outstanding deeds he had performed. That was the sort of talk Egil liked, so they got on well together. Einar asked Egil to tell him where it was that he'd undergone his worst ordeal, and Egil made this verse:

> *Alone I fought eight men,*
> *Twice took on eleven,*
> *I carved the wolf's carrion*
> *And killed them all:*
> *Blows battered the shield,*
> *Blades clashed,*
> *My hard hand*
> *Hurled the steel-flash.*

Egil and Einar agreed on parting to stay friends. Einar spent most of his time abroad with men of high rank, and he was usually short of money, though a generous man, enterprising and good-hearted. He became the retainer of Earl Hakon Sigurdarson.

At that time there was a great deal of fighting and unrest in Norway because of King Hakon and the Eirikssons, the leaders of first one side then the other fleeing the country. King Harald Eiriksson was killed by treachery, fighting south in Denmark, at Hals in Limfjord. He first fought Harald Knutsson, who was known as Gold-Harald, then he fought Earl Hakon. Chieftain Arinbjorn, whom we've described above, fell with King Harald Eiriksson, and when Egil got news of his death, he made this verse:

> *One fewer, the famous sea-kings*
> *Who fed us with gold;*
> *Where to look now for leaders,*
> *Lavish-fisted ones?*
> *Who from oversea showered*
> *Silver like snowflakes*
> *Into this hand, old hawk-perch,*
> *Like hailstones, for my poems.*

The poet Einar Helgason used to be called the Scale-Clatterer. He composed a praise-poem in honour of Earl Hakon. It was called 'The Gold-Dearth' and for a long time the Earl refused to give it a hearing as he was angry with Einar, so Einar wrote this:

> *Eagerly Einar*
> *Exalted the King's honour:*
> *While others slept, I spun*
> *Words, to my sorrow.*
> *I was greedy to go*
> *To the wise gold-scatterer,*
> *Protector of the people;*
> *No poet praised him better.*

Then he made another verse:

> *Let's follow a friendlier*
> *Feeder of wolves:*
> *Let's beat the oar-blades*
> *Of our shield-adorned boat.*
> *That sword-bender won't shun*
> *Me, seeking his company:*
> *Let's sling our shields*
> *Aboard, let's make sail.*

Since the Earl did not want Einar to leave him, he listened to the poem and afterwards gave Einar a most precious gift, a shield painted with illustrations of heroic legends, inlaid between the pictures with spangles of gold and set with jewels.

Einar went back to Iceland to stay with his brother Osvif, then in the autumn set off westwards and came to Borg, where he spent the night. Egil was away up north but expected back, so Einar waited there for three nights – it was not the custom to spend more than three nights when visiting. After that he got ready to leave, but before he set out, he hung up the precious shield and told the people of the household that it was a gift to Egil. Then he rode off.

That same day Egil returned home and when he went to his seat, he caught sight of the shield. He asked who owned such a treasure, and someone told him that Einar the Scale-

Clatterer had been visiting, and given him the shield as a present.

'Damn the man!' exclaimed Egil. 'Does he really expect me to stay up all night making up a poem about his shield? Get my horse, I'm going to ride after him and murder him.'

They told Egil that Einar had left early in the morning. 'He'll have arrived west in the Dales by now,' they said. So Egil composed a *drápa* and here is the beginning:

> *Time now to tell*
> *Of the radiant targe,*
> *The gleaming guardian*
> *Given me by*
> *My free-handed friend,*
> *A fond farewell;*
> *My powers will repay him;*
> *Now, hear my poem.*

Egil and Einar stayed friends for the rest of their lives, and here is what people say happened to the shield: Egil took it with him when he went north to Vidimyri along with Thorkel Gunnvaldsson and Trefil of Helgi, the sons of Ore-Bjorn, to attend a marriage feast. The shield got damaged there and thrown into a whey-vat, so Egil had all the ornaments stripped off. The gold-spangles alone weighed twelve ounces.

79. Egil's family

THORSTEIN Egilsson grew up to be an exceptionally handsome man. He was fair-haired and fair-complexioned, and tall and strong though not quite in his father's way. He was a man of peace, intelligent, modest and very easy-going. Egil had no great affection for him, and as far as Thorstein was concerned this was mutual, though he and his mother Asgerd were very close. By this time, Egil was getting to be a very old man.

One summer it so happened that Thorstein rode to the

Althing while Egil stayed at home. Before Thorstein set out, he and Asgerd got together. From one of Egil's coffers they took the silk gown that Arinbjorn had given him, and Thorstein carried it off with him to wear at the assembly, but it was far too long, and when he took part in the procession to the Law Rock the hem got dirty. When he went home, Asgerd took the gown and put it back where it used to be. Much later Egil happened to open up his coffers. When he saw how his gown had been soiled he asked Asgerd how this had happened, and she told him the truth. Then Egil made this verse:

> No use to Egil,
> His son and heir.
> My child cheated me
> Before death chose me:
> That waterman could have waited
> Until the warriors
> Had built up the burial stones
> Upon my old body.

Thorstein married Jofrid, the daughter of Gunnar Hlifarson. Her mother was Helga, Olaf Feilan's daughter and sister of Thord Gellir. Jofrid had been married before to Thorodd Tongue-Oddsson.

A little after this Asgerd died, and Egil gave up farming, handing the estate over to Thorstein. He moved house south to stay with his son-in-law Grim of Mosfell, because he loved no living soul apart from his step-daughter, Thordis.

One summer it so happened that a ship put in at Leira Creek, captained by one of Thorstein Thoruson's men, a Norwegian called Thormod. He brought with him a valuable shield that Thorstein had sent to Egil Skallagrimsson, and Egil received it with gratitude. The following winter Egil composed a poem, called 'Bera's Drápa', on the shield he'd been given and this is how it begins:

> Listen, land-owner,
> And let your folk hear
> The grave sea-growl

Of my god-granted verse:
The measured mead-brew
Mulled in your honour
Will be held high in Hordaland
As long as men harvest.

Thorstein Egilsson lived at Borg. He had two natural sons, Hrifla and Hrafn, and after he married Jofrid they had ten children. Their daughter was Helga the Fair about whom Poet-Hrafn and Gunnlaug Adder-Tongue quarrelled. Their eldest son was Grim, the second Skuli, the third Thorgeir, the fourth Kollsvein, the fifth Hjorleif, the sixth Halli, the seventh Egil, the eighth Thord, and they also had a daughter Thora, who married Thormod Kleppjarnsson.

The line of descent from Thorstein's children was a great one, and included many people of distinction. All the descendants of Skallagrim are known as the Men of Myrar.

80. Thorstein's feud with Steinar

WHILE Egil was living at Borg, Anabrekka was farmed by Onund Sjoni and he was married to Thorgerd, the daughter of Bjorn the Stout of Snæfjalla Strand. Their children were Steinar, and Dalla who married Ogmund Galtason, whose sons where Thorgils and Kormak. When Onund was old and half-blind, he gave up farming and his son Steinar took over. Both father and son were very wealthy men.

Steinar was exceptionally big and powerful, but an ugly-looking man, stooping, lanky and short-waisted. He was very overbearing and hot-tempered, a rough, ruthless man who hated to lose. After Thorstein Egilsson started farming at Borg, he and Steinar got on badly together.

To the south of the Hafs Brook there is a marsh called Stakksmyri. In winter it lies under water, but in spring, once the ice has thawed, the pasture there is so good that people judge it equal to a stack of hay. According to old tradition, the Hafs Brook marked the boundary between the two farms. Every spring, Steinar's cattle used to graze on the marsh when driven east across the brook, and Thorstein's farmhands kept making complaints, but Steinar paid no attention to them. Nothing happened over the first summer, but when Steinar started using the pasture there the following spring, Thorstein went to have a word with him. He spoke reasonably and asked Steinar to graze his cattle according to custom. Steinar answered that the cattle would go wherever they liked. He was totally inflexible, and before they parted there were words between the two of them. After that, Thorstein had the cattle driven back across the brook to the marsh on the other side. When Steinar learned about this, he got his slave Grani to herd the cattle at Stakksmyri, and there Grani spent every day. This was late in the summer, and all the grazing to the east of the Hafs Brook had been completely used up.

One day when Thorstein had climbed a hill to get a view of his property, he saw Steinar's cattle and set out across the marshes. It was late in the afternoon. He saw that the cattle had made their way up a lane that ran between thickets. Thorstein began to run across the marshland, and when Grani saw him he started to goad the cattle furiously till he got them to the milking-pen, with Thorstein chasing after him. Thorstein caught up with him at the gate and killed him, and this has been called Grani's Gate ever since – it's in the fence round the home-meadow. Thorstein pushed over the fencing wall to cover the body and then went home. The women who came to the milking-pen found Grani lying there and went back to tell Steinar what had happened. He buried Grani there among the thickets and then got another slave, whose name isn't known, to herd the cattle. For the rest of the summer Thorstein took no notice of what was done to the pasture.

Early in winter it so happened that Steinar travelled west to Snæfjalla Strand and stayed there for a time. He saw a slave there called Thrand, a very big, strong man, and tried to buy him, offering a high price. The slave's owner valued him at three marks of silver, twice the normal cost of a slave, but the terms were agreed. Steinar took the slave away with him, and when they got home he spoke to Thrand.

'Here's how matters stand,' he said. 'I want to get some work out of you, but all the work on the farm has been divided up among the others. Now I'll give you a job that you won't find too strenuous. You can herd my cattle. It's a matter of great importance to me that they're grazed on the very best pasture, so take no notice of other people and graze the herd wherever in the marshes you think the pasture is best. If you don't have the strength and courage to stand up to any of Thorstein's farmhands, I'm no judge of men.'

Then Steinar gave Thrand a great axe, very sharp, its edge almost an ell long.

'You don't look like the kind of man to be impressed very much by Thorstein's rank of chieftain, Thrand,' he said, 'should the two of you happen to meet.'

'I don't think I owe anything to Thorstein,' answered Thrand, 'but I understand well enough what sort of job it is you're giving me. You'll be thinking you're not taking any great risk with me. Whatever happens, I daresay I'd have a good chance if Thorstein and I are to have a go at one another.'

Thrand started herding the cattle. Though he hadn't been around long, he realized where Steinar had been grazing them, and drove the herd to Stakksmyri. When Thorstein discovered this, he sent one of his servants to tell Thrand where the boundary lay between his farm and Steinar's. The servant saw Thrand and gave him the message, telling him to herd the cattle elsewhere as they were grazing on Thorstein Egilsson's land.

'I don't care who owns the land,' Thrand answered. 'I'm herding the cattle where I think there's the best pasture.'

At that they parted, the servant going home to tell Thorstein what the slave had said. Thorstein did nothing about it, but Thrand sat watching the herd day and night.

81. Thorstein kills Thrand

ONE morning Thorstein got up at sunrise and climbed a hill. From there he could see Steinar's cattle, and set out across the marshes till he reached the herd. Beside the Hafs Brook is a wooded bluff and Thrand was sleeping on top with his shoes off. Thorstein climbed up onto the bluff carrying a small axe, the only weapon he had, prodded him with the handle and told him to wake up. Thrand jumped quickly to his feet, grabbed his axe with both hands, raised it in the air, and asked Thorstein what he wanted.

'What I want,' said Thorstein, 'is to let you know I'm the owner of this land and that the pastures belonging to your people are on the other side of the stream. But it's no great surprise that you're not clear about the boundaries hereabouts.'

'I don't care who the land belongs to,' said Thrand. 'I'm letting the cattle graze wherever they like.'

'Most likely I'll have the last word over my own land,' said Thorstein, 'not one of Steinar's slaves.'

'You're a much more stupid sort of man than I'd expected, Thorstein,' said Thrand, 'if you're ready to risk your credit and take lodgings under my axe. It seems a fair guess to me that I'm twice your strength. I'm not short on courage and I'm better armed than you are, too.'

'If you don't do something about the grazing,' said Thorstein, 'I'll have to take the risk. I trust our luck will differ as much as the justice of our causes.'

'Now you'll see how scared I am of your threats,' said Thrand.

He sat down and started to tie up his shoe-thongs, but Thorstein swung his axe hard and brought it down on Thrand's neck, so that his head was left hanging down on his chest. After that, Thorstein gathered stones, covered Thrand's body and then went back home to Borg.

In the evening Steinar's cattle were late coming in, and when people had given up hope of seeing them, Steinar took his horse, saddled it, and armed himself with a full set of weapons. He rode south to Borg, and when he got there he spoke to some people, asking where Thorstein was. They told him that Thorstein was inside, so he asked for Thorstein to come out as he had business to discuss. When Thorstein heard this, he took his own weapons, went to the door and asked Steinar what his business was.

'Did you kill my slave Thrand?' asked Steinar.

'I did,' answered Thorstein. 'You won't need to blame it on anyone else.'

'I can see you must be very proud of yourself,' said Steinar, 'putting up such a mighty defence of your land by killing a couple of my slaves, but I don't think it all that much of a triumph. So now I'll offer you the chance of something much better, since you're so keen to defend your land: I'm not asking others to herd my cattle any more, and I want you to know that my herd will be grazing on your land day and night.'

'It's true that I killed your slave last summer,' said Thorstein, 'the one you'd told to graze your cattle on my land. Since then I've let you have all the grazing you wanted till winter came. And now I've killed another slave for you, for the same reason I killed the first. Now, if you want, you can use my pastures as much as you like for the rest of this summer; but when next summer comes, if you try to graze my land and send men to drive your cattle over to this side, I'll kill every single man herding them, you included, and I'll carry on doing that every summer as long as you make a habit of using my pasture.'

Steinar rode off back home to Anabrekka, and a little later he rode over to Stafaholt, where the Chieftain Einar was living. Steinar asked for his support and offered him money in return.

'My support won't make much difference to you,' said Einar, 'not unless you get other men of substance to back you up.'

So Steinar rode up to Reykjardale to see Tongue-Odd,

where again he asked for support and offered money. Odd took the money and promised his support to help Steinar get his rights in his case against Thorstein.

In the spring, Odd and Einar joined Steinar and went with him to issue the summonses accompanied by a large force of men. Steinar charged Thorstein with the killing of the slaves, on penalty of the three-year outlawry for either killing. This was the law at the time for the killing of anyone's slave, unless compensation for the slave had been paid before the third sunrise. Two three-year sentences were regarded as equivalent to outlawry for life. Thorstein did not raise any counter-action, but a little later he sent some men south to the Nesses, where they called on Grim at Mosfell and told him the news. Egil had little to say about it, but quietly asked for full details of Thorstein's dealings with Steinar, and also about who had given Steinar support in the case. After that the messengers returned home. Thorstein was very satisfied with their trip.

Thorstein Egilsson went to the spring assembly with a large body of men. They arrived there a night before the other people. They pitched their tents, as did the farmers supporting Thorstein who had their own booths there, and when they had made themselves comfortable, Thorstein told his supporters to erect the walls for a large booth. Next he covered it with canvas, making it by far the largest booth there, though no one stayed in it.

Steinar rode to the assembly with a large force, of which Tongue-Odd had charge. He had a good following of his own, as did Einar of Stafaholt. They put up their booths.

A great many people attended the assembly and litigants started to plead their cases. Thorstein offered no settlement for himself, and to those who tried to mediate he gave the reply that he intended to wait for the judgement. He said that the lawsuit Steinar had brought over the killing of his slaves was a trivial one, since the slaves themselves had already done enough wrong. Steinar was full of his lawsuit and very aggressive about it, as he thought he had a lawful case and enough men to press it to extremes.

That day people gathered at the Assembly Slope to discuss

their lawsuits, the courts being due to convene in the evening to try the cases. Thorstein was there with his following and had the most say about how the assembly was to be conducted, just like Egil before him when he was in authority, and responsible for the chieftaincy. Both sides were fully armed.

Then the people at the assembly saw a group of men come riding up by Gljufur River, their shields glinting in the sun, and as they rode into the assembly the man who led them was seen to be wearing a blue cloak. On his head was a gilded helmet, a gold-adorned shield was at his side, a barbed spear in his hand, its socket incised with gold, and about his waist a sword. This was Egil Skallagrimsson who had come with eighty men all fully armed as if ready for battle, a choice company, for Egil had taken with him all the best farmers' sons in the Nesses, those whom he thought most warrior-like. Egil rode with his men to the booth which Thorstein had erected and which was still empty. There they dismounted, and when Thorstein learned that his father had come he went to meet him with all his men and give him a welcome. Egil and his companions had their gear carried into the booth and their horses driven to pasture, and when that had been done Egil and Thorstein went with all their following up to the Assembly Slope and sat down in their customary place. Then Egil stood up and spoke in a loud voice.

'Is Onund Sjoni here on the Assembly Slope?' he asked.

Onund said he was there.

'And I'm very happy that you've come, Egil,' he added. 'That will set right all the disagreements between the people here.'

'Is it your doing,' said Egil, 'that your son Steinar is prosecuting my son Thorstein and has got together a great army to make him an outlaw?'

'It's no fault of mine that they're at loggerheads,' said Onund. 'Time and again I've urged Steinar to make a settlement with Thorstein, for it seems to me that in every way your son Thorstein is a man who least deserves to be dishonoured. My reason for saying this, Egil, is the old affection we've felt for one another ever since we grew up together as close neighbours.'

'We'll soon see whether you're speaking honestly or telling lies,' said Egil, 'though I don't think the latter is very likely. I remember the days when neither of us would have considered taking the other to court, or been unable to curb our sons and stop them making such fools of themselves, as I gather they're doing. It seems to me that the best we could do, while we live to witness their quarrel, would be to take charge of the case ourselves and settle the matter, not let Tongue-Odd and Einar set our sons against each other like a pair of fighting horses. There must be another way for them to make money than to meddle in this.'

Then Onund stood up and spoke.

'You're right, Egil,' he said, 'and it's not fitting that we should have to attend an assembly where our sons are quarrelling: we mustn't allow such a scandal, we shall look like utter fools if we don't reconcile them. Now, Steinar, I want you to hand over this case to me and let me deal with it in my own way.'

'I don't know that I'm so keen to throw away my lawsuit, now that I've got so many important people behind me,' said Steinar. 'I want Odd and Einar to be content with the way my case ends up.'

Odd and Steinar talked the matter over together, and here is what Odd said:

'I'll keep my promise to you, Steinar, to back you up and see your case through to your satisfaction; but if Egil is going to arbitrate, then the outcome must be on your own head.'

Then Onund had his say.

'I've no need to depend on the tongue-twisters of Odd,' he said, 'for I've neither good nor ill to say to him, but Egil has done me many a great favour. I trust him much more than I do the others, and I'm going to have my way in this. It will suit you better not to have all of us against you. I've taken decisions for the two of us before now, and that's how it's going to be this time.'

'You're very keen to have your own way, father,' said Steinar, 'but I think we'll live to regret it.'

At that, Steinar handed over the lawsuit to Onund, who was to prosecute or get a settlement in accordance with the law. As soon as he had charge of the case he went to see Thorstein and his father Egil.

'Now, Egil,' he said, 'I want you alone to shape and settle this case in any way you choose, for I trust you above anyone to sort out this or any other case.'

Onund and Thorstein shook hands and named witnesses to testify to their agreement, that Egil Skallagrimsson alone was to arbitrate in this case, as he wished and without reservation, there at the assembly: and that was the end of the court-case. After that people went back to their booths, and Thorstein had three oxen taken to Egil's booth to be slaughtered for his table at the assembly.

When Tongue-Odd and Steinar came back to their booth, Tongue-Odd said this: 'Now, Steinar, you and your father have settled the outcome of your lawsuit, and so I reckon myself free of obligation to you over the support I promised, for our agreement was that I'd help you bring your case to a satisfactory conclusion. But as for Egil's arbitration, it remains to be seen what you think of that.'

Steinar said that the backing Odd had given him had been manly and generous, and that their friendship was going to be much firmer than before.

'I concede that you're free of all the obligations you undertook on my behalf,' he said.

In the evening the courts convened, but there's no mention of anything that happened there.

82. Egil's verdict

NEXT day Egil Skallagrimsson went up the Assembly Slope along with Thorstein and all their followers. Onund and Steinar were there too, as well as Tongue-Odd and Einar. After people had completed their legal business there, Egil stood up and spoke.

'Are Steinar and his father Onund here and able to follow what I say?' he asked.

They said that they were.

'Then I'd like to announce the terms of my settlement between Steinar and Thorstein,' he said, 'and I'll start by saying that when my father, Grim, came to this country he claimed possession of all the lands in Myrar, as well as wide areas beyond, making his home at Borg. He assigned so much land to his own estate, but apart from that he gave land to his friends, and there they made their homes. He gave Ani the homestead at Anabrekka where Onund and Steinar have farmed to this day. We all of us know, Steinar, where the boundary runs between Borg and Anabrekka, along the course of Hafs Brook. Now, Steinar, it wasn't out of ignorance that you used Thorstein's land for your grazing. You laid hands on his property in the hope that he'd so disgrace his family as to let you rob him. You must know, Steinar, and you too, Onund, that Ani received his land from Grim, my father. So Thorstein killed two of your slaves. Now it must be obvious to everyone that they were killed as a result of their own actions, and that there need be no atonement for their deaths: even if they'd been free-men, as criminals they would not get atonement, and so because you, Steinar, tried to rob my son Thorstein of his land, which he took over with my approval and which I inherited from my father, you forfeit your farm at Anabrekka and won't get a penny for it. And there's yet another condition attached to this, that you will be allowed neither homestead nor hospitality in this district south of the Lang River, and unless you're out of Anabrekka before Removal Days, any man who wants to help Thorstein can kill you with impunity if you refuse to leave or to abide by any injunction that I've placed on you.'

And the moment Egil sat down, Thorstein called witnesses to his verdict.

'People are bound to say, Egil,' said Onund, 'that the arbitration you've determined and declared is utterly unjust. For my part, I can say that I did everything I could to prevent trouble between them, but from now on I'll spare no effort to make things awkward for Thorstein.'

'What I think,' said Egil, 'is that the longer we quarrel the worse things will be for you and your sons. I'd have thought you'd realize, Onund, that I've held my own before against people like your son Steinar and you, and as for Odd and Einar, who found this case so appealing, they'll reap from it the kind of honour they deserve.'

83. Thorstein gets a warning

EGIL's nephew, Thorgeir Blund, had been at the assembly and had given strong support to Thorstein in this lawsuit. He asked Thorstein and his father for some farmland there to the west in Myrar. Previously he had been farming below Blundsvatn, south of the Hvit River. Egil gave a favourable answer and urged Thorstein to let Thorgeir come, so when Steinar moved house across the Lang River and went to live at Leira Brook, they settled Thorgeir at Anabrekka. Egil rode back to the Nesses and he and his son parted the best of friends.

There was a man called Iri staying with Thorstein, a great runner and very keen sighted. He was a foreigner and Thorstein's freed-man, and was in charge of Thorstein's sheep. One of his main duties was to round up the barren sheep in the spring and drive them to summer pastures; then in the autumn he would muster them for sorting.

After Removal Days, Thorstein had all the barren sheep left behind in the spring rounded up, and planned to have them driven up to the mountains. Iri was there at the round-up, while Thorstein and his farmhands, eight of them in all, rode up to the mountains. Thorstein had a fence built right across Grisar Tongue from Langavatn to Gljufur River, and employed a number of men at this task throughout the spring. When Thorstein had looked over the work of his farmhands he rode off home, and just as he was passing the place of the assembly, Iri came running up and said that he wanted a word with Thorstein in private. Thorstein told his companions to ride on while they talked.

Iri told Thorstein that he had gone up to Einkunnir that day looking for sheep.

'And then,' he said, 'in the wood just above the winter path I saw the gleam of a dozen spears and some shields.'

Thorstein spoke out in a loud voice, so that his companions could hear him distinctly.

'Why is he so keen to see me,' he said, 'and won't let me ride on my way? But of course, Olvald must know it's not likely that I'd refuse to see him when he's ill.'

Iri ran off as fast as his feet would carry him up into the mountains. Then Thorstein spoke to his companions.

'I'm making a detour,' he said, 'we've first got to ride south to Olvaldsstead. Olvald sent me word to come and see him. He'll be thinking it's not much to pay for the ox he gave me last autumn if I go and visit him when he thinks the matter's so important.'

So Thorstein and his men rode south through the marshes above Stangarholt all the way to the Gufu River, then down the bridle-path on the river bank. When they got down below Vatn they could see a number of cattle south of the river and Olvald's servants herding them. Thorstein asked if everyone there was well, and the servants said yes, everyone was very well and Olvald was in the wood cutting timber.

'Then tell him that if he has urgent business with me he must come to Borg,' said Thorstein. 'I'm riding back home now.'

And so he did, but it came out later that Steinar Sjonason had been lying in ambush that same day with eleven men near Einkunnir. Thorstein pretended to have heard nothing about it, and all was quiet after that.

84. Thorstein and Steinar

THERE was a man called Thorgeir, a kinsman and good friend of Thorstein's living on Alftaness at the time. He was in the habit of holding an autumn feast every year, and went to see Thorstein to invite him to the feast. After Thorstein gave his promise to come, Thorgeir went back home. On the appointed day, four weeks before the start of winter, Thorstein got ready to go. A Norwegian trader went with him, as well as two of his servants. Thorstein had a ten-year-old son called Grim who travelled with his father, so that there were five of them altogether. They rode west to the waterfall, across the Lang River, and then by the usual route over to the Aurrida River, where Steinar, Onund and their farmhands were working on the opposite side.

As soon as they recognized Thorstein they ran for their weapons and set out after him and his companions, who were just beyond Langaholt when Thorstein saw Steinar in pursuit. A hillock rises there, high but not very broad, and Thorstein's men dismounted and began to climb up. Thorstein told the boy Grim to go into the wood and keep away from the fighting. Once Steinar and his men reached the hill they made for Thorstein's party and the fight began. Steinar had five full-grown men with him and his ten-year-old son, so there were seven of them in all. People from other farms who were at work in the meadows saw the clash and ran to separate them, but by the time the two sides had been parted both

Thorstein's servants were dead and one of Steinar's, who also had some men wounded. After they had been separated Thorstein set out to look for Grim, and they found him badly wounded with Steinar's son lying beside him, dead. When Thorstein mounted his horse, Steinar called after him.

'Are you running away now,' he shouted, 'Thorstein whey-face?'

'You'll be running a lot further yourself before the week's out,' Thorstein replied.

Thorstein and his men rode on across the marshes carrying young Grim with them. When they came to a small hill over there, the boy died, so they buried him at the hill, called Grimsholt. The place where they fought is called Orrustuhvall. As he had intended, Thorstein rode across in the evening to Alftaness and spent three nights at the feast before preparing to go back home. There were people ready to go with him, but he wouldn't let them, and rode back with only one companion. On the day Steinar expected Thorstein to ride home, he set out on horseback west along the shore, and when he came to the sand-dune below Lambastead he got down onto the dune. He was carrying a very fine weapon, the sword Skrymir, and stood there on the sand-dune with drawn sword, gazing in the direction he had seen Thorstein set out across the sands.

Lambi was living at Lambastead and saw what Steinar was up to, so he set off walking down to the sand-dune, and when he got there he took hold of Steinar from behind, seizing him under the arms. Steinar tried to shake him off but Lambi held on tight. Just as they were rolling down from the dune to the level ground Thorstein and his companion came riding up along the lower path. Steinar had been on his stallion and the horse ran off along the shore. Thorstein and his companion saw this and were very surprised, since they hadn't known about Steinar's movements. Steinar hadn't noticed Thorstein going past, which was why he stayed struggling on the dune, but when they came to the edge, Lambi pushed Steinar down over it, which took him by surprise. Lambi ran home, and when Steinar managed to get to his feet he started chasing after him. When Lambi reached the door of his house, he ran inside and bolted it. Steinar made a lunge at him but the sword stuck fast in the weather-boards, and that's how they parted. Steinar walked back home.

The day after Thorstein got home he sent a servant out to Leirabrook to tell Steinar to move house to the other side of Borgarhraun, otherwise he'd show him which of them had the most power.

'And then you'd not even have the choice of leaving,' he added.

Steinar got ready to move house to Snæfells Strand and made his home at a place called Ellidi. After that he had no more dealings with Thorstein Egilsson.

Thorgeir Blund, who had gone to live at Anabrekka, caused untold trouble to Thorstein and his neighbour. One day Egil and Thorstein got together and had plenty to say about their kinsman Thorgeir Blund. They were in complete agreement about everything, and then Egil made this verse:

> *Time was when I tricked*
> *The troublesome Steinar,*
> *I thought to help Thorgeir*
> *And earn his thanks:*
> *But the fellow failed me*
> *For all his fine promises;*
> *Why he sought to cause suffering*
> *I'll never understand.*

Thorgeir Blund left Anabrekka and went south to Floka-dale, for Thorstein didn't think he could stand any more of him even though Thorgeir was ready to give way. Thorstein was a just and honest man who never imposed on others, though he looked after his own rights when people attacked him and most men found him hard to beat.

At that time, Tongue-Odd was the leading chieftain to the south of Hvit River. He was a priest and in charge of the temple to which all the farmers south of Skards Moor paid their dues.

85. The death of Egil

EGIL Skallagrimsson grew to be an old man. In old age his movements became heavy and his sight and hearing began to fail him badly. At that time he was living with Grim and Thordis at Mosfell. One day Egil was walking outside beyond the wall when he stumbled and fell. Some of the women saw this and laughed at him.

'You're really finished now, Egil,' they said, 'when you fall without being pushed.'

'The women didn't laugh so much when we were younger,' said Grim. Then Egil made this verse:

> My bald pate bobs and blunders,
> I bang it when I fall;
> My cock's gone soft and clammy
> And I can't hear when they call.

Egil became totally blind. One day in winter when the weather was cold, he went up to the fire to warm himself. The cook started saying it was a funny thing when a man like Egil started lying around under their feet and hindering the women at their chores.

'Go easy with me when I want to bake myself by the fire,' said Egil. 'Let's try not to get in each other's way.'

'On your feet!' said the woman. 'Get back to your place and let us do our work.'

Egil stood up, walked over to his seat and made this verse:

> I flounder by the fireside,
> Ask females for mercy,
> Bitter the battle
> On my brow-plains;
> The prince has praised me
> With precious gold,
> The wild king once
> Was tamed by my words.

Another day when Egil came to warm himself somebody asked him if his feet were cold and told him not to stretch them right up to the fire.

'I'll do as you say,' answered Egil, 'but I find it hard to control my feet now that I can't see. It's a bore to be blind.' Then he made this verse:

> Time passes tediously,
> I tarry here alone,
> An old, senile elder
> With no king to aid me.
> I walk on two widows,
> Once true women,
> Now frosted and feeble,
> Needing the old flame.

In the early years of Hakon the Powerful, Egil Skallagrimsson was in his eighties but still an active man apart from his blindness. People were getting ready to go to the Althing and Egil asked Grim to let him go to the assembly with him. Grim wasn't too keen on the idea, and when he talked it over with Thordis he told her what Egil was asking for.

'I'd like you to find out what's behind it,' he said.

Thordis went to her kinsman Egil, whose greatest pleasure was to talk with her.

'Is it true, kinsman,' she asked, 'that you want to ride to the Althing? I'd like to know what you have in mind.'

'I'll tell you what's in my mind,' he said. 'I want to take my two coffers with me, the ones I got from King Athelstan, both full of English silver. I want them carried up to the Law Rock when the crowd gathered there is at its biggest, and I'm going to throw the silver about, and it will be a big surprise to me if people agree to divide the silver evenly. I'll bet there'll be a bit of pushing and punching. Maybe in the end the whole assembly will start fighting.'

'That's a great idea,' said Thordis, 'and as long as people live here in the land, they'll remember it.'

Then she went to have a word with Grim and told him what Egil was planning to do.

'It's an absolutely crazy idea,' she said, 'he mustn't be allowed to do it.'

So when Egil came to talk with Grim about going to the assembly, Grim did all he could to dissuade him, and Egil had to stay at home as long as the assembly lasted. He didn't like it in the least and there was an ugly look about him.

The people at Mosfell had a sheiling and that was where Thordis was staying during the assembly. One evening as the people of Mosfell were getting ready for bed, Egil called over two of Grim's slaves and told them to fetch him a horse.

'I want to go over to the bath-house,' he said.

When he was ready, he went outside carrying his chests of silver, mounted on horseback and rode down the home-field beyond the slope there. That was the last they saw of him till next morning. When they got up, they saw Egil stumbling about on the low hill east of the fence leading his horse along behind him.

They went to Egil and brought him home, but neither the slaves nor the two coffers were ever seen again, and there have been plenty of guesses about where Egil hid his money. East of the fence at Mosfell there is a ravine that plunges down from the top of the hill. People have thought it significant that following a sudden thaw with heavy flooding, English silver coins have been found in the ravine after the water has subsided, and some of them have speculated that Egil may have hidden his money there. But below the homefield at Mosfell there are widespread bogs with deep pits in them, and other people think Egil must have thrown his money into these pits. There are deep pits south of the river where the hot springs are, and since fires have often been seen coming from the burial-mounds there, it has been suggested that this may be where Egil hid his money. Egil admitted that he had killed Grim's slaves and also that he had hidden the money, but he never told anyone where.

Later on that autumn Egil fell sick, and died from that illness. When Egil was dead, Grim had him dressed in fine clothes and carried down to Tjaldness, where he built a mound and laid Egil inside it with his clothes and weapons.

86. Egil's bones

WHEN Christianity was adopted by law in Iceland, Grim of Mosfell was baptized and built a church there. People say that Thordis had Egil's bones moved to the church, and this is the evidence. When a church was built at Mosfell, the one Grim had built at Hrisbru was demolished and a new graveyard was laid out. Under the altar some human bones were found, much bigger than ordinary human bones, and people are confident that these were Egil's because of the stories told by old men. Skapti Thorarinsson the Priest, a man of great intelligence, was there at the time. He picked up Egil's skull and placed it on the fence of the churchyard. The skull was an exceptionally large one and its weight was even more remarkable. It was ridged all over like a scallop shell, and Skapti wanted to find out just how thick it was, so he picked up a heavy axe, swung it in one hand and struck as hard as he was able with the reverse side of the axe, trying to break the skull. But the skull neither broke nor dented on impact, it simply turned white, and from that anybody could guess that the skull wouldn't be easily cracked by small fry while it still had skin and flesh on it. Egil's bones were re-interred on the edge of the graveyard at Mosfell.

87. The end of the saga

WHEN Christianity came to Iceland, Thorstein Egilsson received baptism and had a church built at Borg. He was a firm believer and kept well to his faith. He lived to be an old man and died in his bed, to be buried at the church he himself had built at Borg.

A great family line descends from Thorstein, including a

large number of prominent men and poets, all called the Men of Myrar and including those descended from Skallagrim. For long it was a characteristic of the family that the men were strong and great fighters, and some of them very intelligent. It was a very mixed family, in that some were the most handsome people ever to be born in Iceland – such as Thorstein Egilsson, his nephew Kjartan Olafsson, Hall Gudmundarson, and Thorstein's daughter Helgi the Fair over whom Gunnlaug Adder-Tongue and Poet-Hrafn quarrelled – but most of the Men of Myrar were outstandingly ugly.

Of all the sons of Thorstein Egilsson, Thorgeir was the strongest, but the greatest of them was Skuli who lived at Borg after his father died, and spent much of his time on viking expeditions. Skuli fought seven battles during his viking career, and was forecastleman for Earl Eirik on the *Iron-Prow* when King Olaf Tryggvason fell.

Glossary of Proper Names

This Glossary is not a complete index of all the names in the saga: it is intended as a guide to the roles played by the major characters, to show the place of certain minor characters in the pattern of the tale, and to place characters of historical significance in a context. The numbers are those of the chapters in which the characters play a part or are mentioned.

Adils, an earl in Wales: tributary to King Athelstan, 51; joins forces with Olaf, King of the Scots, 52; fights in the Battle of Vin Moor, 53; killed, 54.

Aki, a wealthy farmer in Denmark: rescued by Egil from captivity in Courland, 46; takes part in a raid on Lund, 47; goes back to Denmark, 48; warns Egil, 49.

Alf Askmann, a nephew of Queen Gunnhild: kills Thorolf's forecastleman, disturbs the court at the Gula assembly, 56.

Alfgeir, an earl in Northumberland: 51; defeated in battle by Olaf, King of the Scots, 52; flees from the Battle of Vin Moor, 53.

Arinbjorn Thorisson, a chieftain in Norway, King Eirik's blood-brother, and cousin to Asgerd: becomes Egil's friend, 41; urges his father to plead with King Eirik on Egil's behalf, 45; gives Egil hospitality, 48; goes to a temple to offer sacrifices, 49; is made a land-holder, invites Egil to stay with him, 55; supports Egil's proposal of marriage and backs his inheritance claim, 56; goes on expedition with King Eirik, 57; goes to England with King Eirik, receives Egil at York, 59; pleads for Egil's life, 60; escorts Egil to King Athelstan, 61; 62; 64; goes back to Norway, feasts Egil, 67; pleads Egil's case before King Hakon, 68; goes on a viking expedition and joins Harald Grey-Cloak in Denmark, 69; 70; returns to Norway as King Harald's counsellor, is praised in a poem by Egil, killed, 78.

Armod Beard, a farmer at Eida Wood, near the boundary between Norway and Sweden: gives Egil hospitality and insults him, 71; his eye is gouged out by Egil, 72; lays an ambush for Egil, 73; 76.

Arnfinn, Earl of Halland: entertains Egil and Thorolf, 48.

Arnvid, Earl of Vermaland: tributary to the King of Norway, 70; forced by Egil to pay the King's tribute, 74; flees from Vermaland, 76.

Arnvid, King of South More in Norway: persuaded to take a stand against King Harald, 3; killed, 10.

Asgerd, daughter of Bjorn the Yeoman and Thora Lace-Cuff: born and brought up at Borg, 35; goes with Thorolf to Norway, 38; 41; betrothed and married to Thorolf, 42; 55; married to Egil, 56; in charge of their estate during his absence, 59; her inheritance in Norway claimed by Egil, 63; 65; their children, 66; death of their sons Gunnar and Bodvar, 78; dies, 79.

Athelstan, King of England 924–39: takes Egil and Thorolf into service, 50; his tributary earls, 51; prepares for battle against Olaf, King of the Scots, 52; arrives at the camp, 53; victory on Vin Moor, 54; compensates Egil for the death of Thorolf, 55; appoints King Eirik ruler of Northumbria, 59; 60; receives Egil, 61; offers Egil a position in England, 62; 63; dies, 67; Egil hides his gift, 85.

Atli the Short, of Ask in Norway: brother of Berg-Onund, 37; in charge of Asgerd's inheritance, 62–3; killed by Egil, 65.

Bard, of Atley Isle in Norway: King Eirik's steward, 43; fills Egil with ale and is killed by him, 44; 45; 48.

Bard the White, of Torg Island in Norway: asks for the hand of Sigrid, 7; joins King Harald, marries Sigrid and becomes a land-holder, 8; killed in battle, 9.

Bera, daughter of Yngvar: married to Skallagrim, 19; foster-mother to Asgerd, predicts her son Egil will become a viking, 40; 58.

Berle-Kari, Egil's great-grand-father: on a viking expedition, 1; joins King Harald, 4; 8; 9; 22.

Berg-Onund, of Ask in Norway: marries Gunnhild, Asgerd's half-sister and prevents Egil from claiming Asgerd's share of her father's patrimony, 56; killed by Egil, 57; 59; 62; 65.

Bjorgolf, a land-holder at Torgar in Norway; father of Brynjolf: makes Hildirid his wife and has two sons by her, 7; dies, 8; 9.

Bjorn Brynjolfsson, 'the Yeoman', a chieftain's son in Norway: abducts Thora Lace-Cuff and spends a winter in Shetland, 32; sails to Iceland with his bride and joins Skallagrim's household, 35; Skallagrim discovers his secret, 34; his daughter Asgerd born, sails back to Norway and is reconciled with Thora's

Eirik Bloodaxe, son of King Harald Fine-Hair: is given a ship by Thorolf, 36; marries Gunnhild, 37; sends Skallagrim a gift which is rejected, 38; accepts a gift, 41; feasted by Bard, 44; accepts payment for the killing of Bard, 45; grants Thorir leave to shelter Egil, 48; sends Eyvind Shabby to Denmark, 49; chases Egil, 56; succeeds his father to the throne, kills his own brothers, 57; flees from Norway, is given charge of Northumbria, 59; listens to Egil's poem, 60; spares Egil's life, 61; 62; 63; 65; killed on a viking expedition, 67; his sons, 68; 78.

Eyvind Lambi, of Berle in Norway: goes on a viking expedition with his brothers and Thorolf Kveldulfsson, 1; comes back to Norway, 6; joins King Harald, 8; in the Battle of Hafsfjord, 9; marries Thorolf's widow, 22.

Eyvind Shabby, brother to Queen Gunnhild: kills Thorolf's fore-castleman and is outlawed, clashes with Egil, 49; 56.

Fridgeir, a land-holder at Blindheim in Norway, nephew to Arinbjorn: acts as host to Egil, 64; 68.

Frodi, King Eirik's kinsman and foster son: killed by Egil, 57.

Godrek, earl in Northumbria, 51; killed in battle, 52.

Grim, eldest son of Thorstein Egilsson, 79; kills a boy and is killed himself at the age of ten, 84.

Grim Svertingsson, of Mosfell, law-speaker 1002-3: marries Thordis, Egil's niece and step-daughter, 77; takes Egil in, 79; 81; dissuades Egil from attending the Althing, 85; builds a church, 86.

Gunnhild, daughter of Bjorn the Yeoman: half-sister to Asgerd, 37; married to Berg-Onund, 56.

Gunnhild, Ozur's daughter: married to King Eirik, 37; friend of Bard of Atley Isle, 43; attends a feast at Bard's, 44; 45; urges his brothers to kill Thorolf Skallagrimsson, 49; supports Berg-Onund, 56; gives birth to Harald Grey-Cloak, cursed by Egil, 57; flees Norway with her husband, is hostile to Egil at York, 59–60; 63; goes to Denmark after her husband's death, 67.

Gyda, of Blindheim in Norway, sister to Arinbjorn: persuades Egil to fight the berserk Ljot, 64.

Hadd, of Fenhring in Norway: brother of Berg-Onund, 37; killed by Egil, 57.

Hakon the Good, son of King Harald Fine-Hair: foster-son to King Athelstan, 50; becomes King of Norway, 59; 62; rejects Egil's offer to serve him, 63; 64; refuses Egil the berserk's money, 68; sends messengers to Thorstein Thoruson telling him to collect the tribute from Earl Arnvid, 70; 71; leads a campaign to Vermaland, 76; killed in battle fighting his nephews, 78.

Hallvard the Hard-Sailer and *Sigtrygg the Fast-Sailer*, of Hising in Norway, King Harald's envoys: seize Thorolf's ship and cargo, 18; their farm destroyed by Thorolf, 19; granted leave by King Harald to kill Thorolf, 21; pre-empted by the king, 22; sent on a mission by the king, 26; killed by Kveldulf and Skallagrim, 27.

Harald Fine-Hair, son of Halfdan the Black: fights his way to power in Norway, 3–4; Kveldulf refuses to become his man, 5; Thorolf Kveldulfsson decides to join him, 6; his poets, 8; wins the decisive Battle of Hafursfjord, makes Thorolf a land-holder, 9; gives an ear to the Hildiridarsons' slander of Thorolf, 12 and 15; 14; receives the Lapp tribute from Thorolf, 16; sends Sigtrygg and Hallvard to seize Thorolf's ship, 18; gives them leave to put Thorolf to death, 21; kills Thorolf, 22; 24; Skallagrim refuses to become his man, 25; sends Hallvard and Sigtrygg on a mission, 26; his cousins killed by Skallagrim in revenge for Thorolf's death, 27; appropriates the estates of Kveldulf and Skallagrim, 30; sends a message to the earl of Orkney to put Bjorn the Yeoman to death, 33; refuses to receive Thorolf Skallagrimsson, 36; 50; abdicates in favour of his son Eirik, 57; his death, 57; 59; 70.

Harald Grey-Cloak, son of Eirik Bloodaxe and Queen Gunnhild: born, 57; fostered by Arinbjorn, 68; joined by Arinbjorn in Denmark, 69; becomes king of Norway, 78; killed in battle, 78.

Harek and *Hrærek*, 'the Hildiridarsons', of Leka in Norway: cast out by their half-brother Brynjolf, 7; unsuccessfully claim their inheritance from Thorolf, feast King Harald and slander Thorolf; 14; given charge of Halogaland, 17; 18; killed by Ketil Trout, 23.

Hrærek, see *Harek* and *Hrærek*.

Hring, an earl in Wales: tributary to King Athelstan, 51; joins forces with Olaf King of the Scots, 52; killed in the Battle of Vin Moor, 53.

Ketil Trout, son of Earl Thorkel in Namdalen in Norway: kills the Hildiridarsons, settles in Iceland, 23.

Kveldulf, a farmer in Norway: goes on viking expeditions, 1; refuses to fight King Harald, 3; refuses to become King Harald's man, 5; warns Thorolf against the king, 6; 8; concerned about Thorolf's fate, 18; sees Thorolf for the last time, 19; 20; learns of Thorolf's death, 24; decides to emigrate to Iceland, 25; kills Hallvard, dies at sea on his way to Iceland, 27; 28; 30; 36.

Lambi, of Lambastead, Egil's cousin: avenges his father, 77; grapples with Steinar, 84.

Ljot the Pale, a berserk in Norway: killed by Egil in single combat, 64; 68.

Olaf the Red, king of the Scots: his family background, 51; on a campaign in England, 52–3; killed in the Battle of Vin Moor, 54; 55; 58.

Olvir, one of Thorir's servants: takes Egil with him on a trip collecting land-dues, 43; gets drunk at Bard's, 44; his life spared by King Eirik, 45.

Olvir Hnufa, son of Berle-Kari: on a viking expedition, 1; falls in love with Solveig, 2; joins King Harald, 4; warns Kveldulf of King Harald's anger, 5; his position at court, 8; in the Battle of Hafursfjord, 9; pleads with King Harald on behalf of Thorolf Kveldulfsson, 13; warns Thorolf of slander, 16; with King Harald in the attack on Thorolf, 22; tries to bring about a settlement after Thorolf's death, 24–5.

Onund Sjoni, of Anabrekka: travels abroad with Egil, 67; 70; 80; tries to bring about a settlement between his son Steinar and Thorstein Egilsson, 81–2, 84.

Sigrid Sigurd's daughter, of Sandness in Norway: married to Bard Brynjolfsson, 7; married a second time, to Thorolf Kveldulfsson, 9; pleads unsuccessfully for her husband's life, widowed again, married a third time, to Eyvind Lambi, 56.

Sigtrygg the Fast-Sailer, see *Hallvard* and *Sigtrygg*.

Sigurd, a land-holder at Sandness in Norway: promises his daughter Sigrid in marriage to Bard Brynjolfsson, 7; her wedding, 8; accepts Thorolf's proposal to marry the widowed Sigrid, dies, 9.

Skallagrim, son of Kveldulf: description, 1; refuses to become King Harald's man, 5; marries Bera, 20; tells his father to keep his spirits up after the death of Thorolf, 24; insults King Harald, decides to go to Iceland with his father, 25; kills Sigtrygg in revenge for his brother Thorolf, sails to Iceland, 27; makes his home at Borg, 28; his farming and other activities, 29–30; his children, 31; gives hospitality to Bjorn the Yeoman and Thora Lace-Cuff, 33; criticizes Bjorn for abducting Thora, 34; sends messengers to Norway to plead for Bjorn, 35; 36; destroys the axe sent as a gift by King Eirik, 38; his daughter Thorunn marries Geir, 98; tries to kill his son Egil, 40; 41; 48; 49; 56; dies, 58; 59; 61; 78; 79; 82; 87.

Steinar, son of Onund Sjoni: quarrels with Thorstein Egilsson, 80–84.

Chronological Note

The author of *Egil's Saga* was not a historian in the modern sense and evidently had little interest in absolute chronology. It would be hard to fault him for inconsistency in his treatment of time within the framework of the narrative, but it has proved difficult to reconcile the timing of these narrative-events with historical dating. However, several attempts have been made to set up an absolute chronology for the saga in relation to English and Norwegian history, and following the Swedish scholar, Per Wieselgren, Sigurður Nordal has proposed this tentative scheme (*Íslenzk fornrit*, vol. 2):

c. 858	Thorolf Kveldulfsson born
c. 863	Skallagrim Kveldulfsson born
c. 885	The battle at Hafursfjord
c. 890	Thorolf killed. Ketil Trout emigrates to Iceland
c. 891	Skallagrim emigrates to Iceland
c. 900	Thorolf Skallagrimsson born
c. 910	Egil Skallagrimsson born
c. 910	Bjorn Brynjolfsson goes to Iceland. Asgerd born
c. 915–26	Thorolf Skallagrimsson's first journey abroad
c. 927	Egil goes abroad with Thorolf
935	Thorolf marries Asgerd
936	Thordis Thorolf's daughter born
937[1]	The battle at Vin Moor
938	Egil travels from England to Norway
939	Egil marries Asgerd and goes back to Iceland
945	Egil's second journey abroad
946	Egil's case considered at the Gula Assembly. He returns to Iceland
946	Skallagrim dies
947	Eirik Bloodaxe forfeits the throne of Norway
948	Egil composes the 'Head-Ransom' at York
949	Egil goes to Norway

1. This battle has been identified with the one fought at Brunnanburh (see the poem in the *Anglo-Saxon Chronicle* for the year 937).

CHRONOLOGICAL NOTE

950	Egil visits King Hakon, fights Atli and returns to Iceland
954	Eirik Bloodaxe killed
955	Egil's fourth journey abroad
956	Egil joins Arinbjorn on a viking expedition
956–7	Egil travels to Vermaland
957	Egil returns to Iceland
c. 959	Grim Svertingsson marries Thordis
c. 960	Olaf the Peacock marries Thorgerd
c. 961	Egil composes the 'Lament for my Sons'
962	Egil composes the 'Lay of Arinbjorn'
c. 972	Thorstein Egilsson marries Jofrid
c. 974	Asgerd dies. Egil moves over to Mosfell
c. 975–8	Thorstein's quarrel with Steinar
990	Egil dies

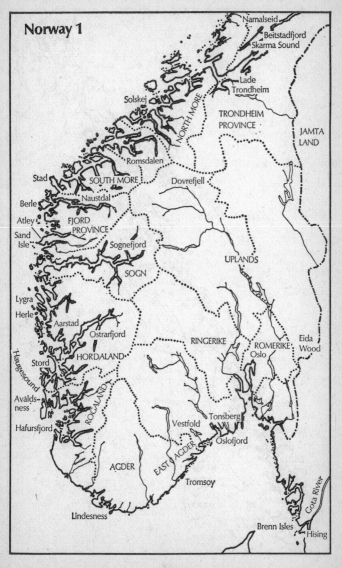

Norway 1

Namalseid
Beitstadfjord
Skarma Sound
Lade
Trondheim
Solskej
TRONDHEIM
PROVINCE
NORTH MORE
JAMTA
LAND
Romsdalen
Stad
SOUTH MORE
Dovrefjell
Berle
Naustdal
Atley
FJORD
PROVINCE
Sand
Isle
Sognefjord
UPLANDS
SOGN
Lygra
Herle
Aarstad
Ostrarfjord
RINGERIKE
ROMERIKE
Eida
Wood
Oslo
HORDALAND
Haugesound
Stord
ROGALAND
Avaldsness
Hafursfjord
Vestfold
Tonsberg
Oslofjord
AGDER
EAST AGDER
Tromsoy
Gota River
Lindesness
Brenn Isles
Hising

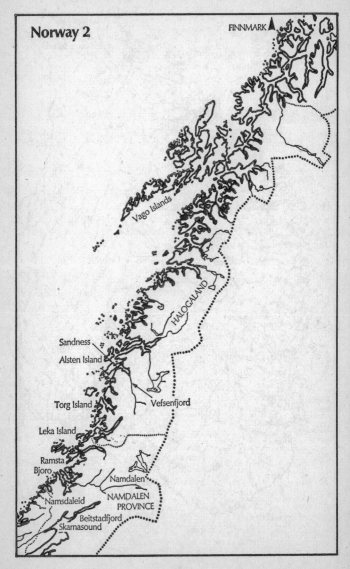

Norway 2

FINNMARK

Vago Islands

HALOGALAND

Sandness

Alsten Island

Torg Island

Vefsenfjord

Leka Island

Ramsta
Bjoro

Namdalen

Namsdaleid

NAMDALEN
PROVINCE

Beitstadfjord

Skarnasound

West Iceland

West Fjords

Thorska Fjord

Breida Fjord

Laxriverdale

Snæfells Strand

Nord River

Hvals Isle

Myrar

Borg

Hvit River

Lang River

Borgarfjord

Thingvellir

Rosmhvalsness

Mosfell

Olfus

Reykjaness

Thjors River

Outer Rang River

Eastern Rang River

Fljotshlid

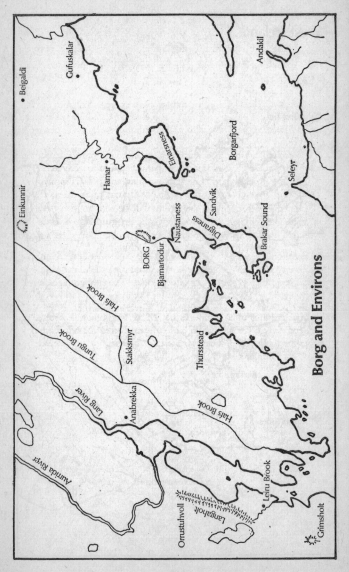

Borg and Environs

MORE ABOUT PENGUINS
AND PELICANS

Penguinews, which appears every month, contains details of all the new books issued by Penguins as they are published. From time to time it is supplemented by *Penguins in Print*, which is our complete list of almost 5,000 titles.

A specimen copy of *Penguinews* will be sent to you free on request. Please write to Dept EP, Penguin Books Ltd, Harmondsworth, Middlesex, for your copy.

In the U.S.A.: For a complete list of books available from Penguins in the United States write to Dept CS, Penguin Books, 625 Madison Avenue, New York, New York 10022.

In Canada: For a complete list of books available from Penguins in Canada write to Penguin Books Canada Ltd, 41 Steelcase Road West, Markham, Ontario.

THE PENGUIN CLASSICS

Some Recent and Forthcoming Volumes

LIVY

Rome and the Mediterranean
*Translated by Henry Bettenson with an
introduction by A. H. MacDonald*

FLAUBERT

Bouvard and Pécuchet
Translated by A. J. Krailsheimer

Lives of the Later Caesars
Translated by Anthony Birley

ARETINO

Selected Letters
Translated by George Bull

The Mabinogion
Translated by Jeffrey Gantz

BALZAC

Ursule Mirouët
Translated by Donald Adamson

The Psalms
Translated by Peter Levi